At one end of the stretcher, almost hidden amongst the blackest of the animal hides, a pair of eyes glinted open.

At first Joe couldn't make out anything else. It was as if the mountain of furs itself had grown eyes. Then he realized the shadows around the eyes were made not of animal hide but human hair. Thick, black, greasy locks, shot with grey, hung low over the brow and a heavy growth of coarser hair completely obliterated the lower half of what must be a face. Only the eyes were visible – dark, shining, blank.

With a shiver of surprise Joe realized he was looking at a man.

Also by Mark Barratt:

JOE RAT

THE WILD MAN

MARK BARRATT

RED FOX

THE WILD MAN
A RED FOX BOOK 978 1 862 30219 8

First published in Great Britain by Red Fox,
an imprint of Random House Children's Books,
in association with The Bodley Head
A Random House Group Company

This edition published 2009

1 3 5 7 9 10 8 6 4 2

The Random House Group Limited supports the Forest Stewardship Council (FSC), the
leading international forest certification organization. All our titles that are printed on
Greenpeace-approved FSC-certified paper carry the FSC logo. Our paper procurement
policy can be found at www.rbooks.co.uk/environment.

Set in 11.5/14pt Adobe Garamond
by Falcon Oast Graphic Art Ltd.

Red Fox Books are published by Random House Children's Books,
61–63 Uxbridge Road, London W5 5SA

www.**kids**at**randomhouse**.co.uk
www.**rbooks**.co.uk

Addresses for companies within The Random House Group Limited can be found at:
www.randomhouse.co.uk/offices.htm

THE RANDOM HOUSE GROUP Limited Reg. No. 954009

A CIP catalogue record for this book is available from the British Library.

Printed in the UK by CPI Bookmarque, Croydon, CR0 4TD

For Luke, Adam and Jessica

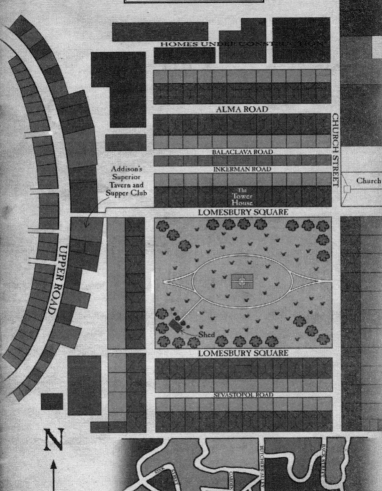

Prologue

BULLET WOUNDS

On the far bank of the river two puffs of white smoke blossomed into the clear, freezing air. The man threw himself full-length into deep snow, fighting for breath. As the shots rang out, he could see his companion still thrashing in the water where the river ice had given way.

Two lead balls hissed into the snow, one to his left, one to his right. They were firing old flintlock rifles. In most hands it would take a lucky shot to hit them at this range, but these were woodsmen who could pick the eyes out of a bull moose at a hundred paces. You could run from an army patrol every day of the week and never get caught, but they should never have tried robbing woodsmen.

Crack! Crack! Two more shots.

The woodsmen were maybe five yards out from the other bank, standing on the ice and taking careful aim, but they wouldn't risk coming any further, not now they'd seen the ice give way. The river had been solid early that morning when the two men crossed, hoping for easy pickings, but now it was thawing in the noon sun.

1

This time the man heard the fizz of the slug past his head and at the same instant his companion cried out, 'They shot me, Mundy. They shot me. I got one in the shoulder.'

There was a moment when Mundy could choose. Up the steep, snow-covered bank of the river and he'd be into scrub, and then a hundred yards further on the thick Canadian forest wrapped you round as tight as a tick in a blanket. He found he'd been counting since the last shot – thirteen – fourteen – the woodsmen were good but with the old muzzle-loaders it was still a count of twenty to reload. If he was going to run, it had to be now.

But Mundy didn't run. He spat quickly and plunged into the icy river. The shock of the water was like a fist to the gut.

'Hold on, Trapper!'

Twin plumes of white smoke again, and this time Mundy felt a blow to his leg, as if someone had punched him high up on the thigh. No pain – not really. But as he grabbed his companion around the shoulders, dragging him towards the shore, he could see the tear in his buckskin breeches and a spreading red stain in the water.

Trapper cried out. It was his wounded arm Mundy had hold of. But there was no time to change his grip. Mundy hurled himself and his companion flat in the snow on the riverbank and two more bullets sang overhead. It was only as he began to struggle up the bank, hauling Trapper after him, that Mundy really began to feel the wound. Even now it wasn't pain: the whole leg seemed to have gone numb.

Crack! Crack! The woodsmen were still firing.

'Get up, Trapper!'

The freezing water didn't have to kill you right away. Sometimes you could pull a man clear and his heart just gave out a couple of minutes after. Mundy knew he had to get his companion moving – now.

'I can't – I can't—' Mundy gripped his companion tight around his wounded arm and the man yelled out in pain: 'You sonofabitch!'

It had worked. The pain had brought him back to his senses. Stumbling, running, falling every other step, the two men pushed in to where the pine and birch trees grew thick overhead. In here it was dark – almost like night. In here they were safe.

'Give me your knife, Trapper.'

Trapper drew the dagger out of his belt. It was roughly the length of his forearm with a curved handle made of moose horn. The blade had been fashioned from the pointed bill of a swordfish, serrated on one edge, smooth and razor-sharp on the other. Mundy saw the other man hesitate – he didn't like parting with his knife, not even for a minute – then Trapper handed the wicked-looking weapon over.

Mundy used the serrated edge to cut a strip from the bottom of his breeches. Then he tied it tight around his own leg right up in the groin above the gunshot wound. The slug had missed the artery, but he was still losing a lot of blood. Then he did the same for his companion's shoulder.

'They could go upriver and use the bridge,' he said, talking more to himself than the other man. 'Didn't ought to go thievin' off woodsmen no how.'

'Weren't no choice.' Trapper's words came in short bursts through gritted teeth. 'They know us too well in town.'

They pushed on silently into the dark forest where the snow lay in a soft carpet underfoot. Mundy's leg still felt numb, making it hard to walk, but Trapper looked the weaker of the two. He had been in the frozen water longer.

Up an incline they skirted a clearing. The sun had disappeared and away to the north above the mountains the clouds were tinged with purple. 'Blue norther comin',' grunted Mundy. That meant more snow later. He led the way down into a steep ravine.

A stream cascaded over the rocks here in summer, but at this time of the year it was frozen. There was no trail, but the watercourse led you right to the bottom. Now Mundy could feel the wound throbbing constantly, sending a shooting pain through the whole length of his body every time he put weight on his right leg.

At the foot of the ravine they cut up the slope on the other side through deep snow. Mundy muttered under his breath, urging himself on: 'Got to keep movin'.'

Every step was a struggle now. Every part of his body cried out to him to lie down and rest, but he knew that if they rested here they would never get up again. Fur-trappers would stumble on their bodies maybe, stiff and frozen; or wolves might get to them first, in which case their bones would be scattered from here to the Gulf of St Lawrence and they wouldn't ever be found.

For a moment he thought he'd passed it. Then he glimpsed

...ar tall pine rising above the other trees on the ridge.
... was no sign of a track. Anyone coming this way by
accident could have walked right past the place and never
known there was a camp in the thick woods. Half carrying his
companion, Mundy clambered up over the rocks to where the
ground levelled out.

They'd built defences here – a line of pits with sharpened
stakes in the bottom, covered over with brush and snow.
Beyond that there were deer traps – young pine saplings bent
over to the ground with a wire noose attached. Step into one of
those and the wire tightened around your ankle, the young tree
shot upright and you went catapulting into the air suspended
by one foot. The trap could pull a full-grown man's leg
clean off.

Not that they'd ever caught a man. The hide-out was too far
back in the woods for anyone to find who hadn't tracked them
there, and they were too good to be tracked. All the same
Trapper never tired of repeating it and the words were fixed in
Mundy's brain too now: 'You need defence. And you need a
back door.' He trod carefully, leading his companion the safe
way through the traps, sweeping the snow back to cover their
footprints. The 'back door' was a vertical rock face beyond the
level ground. Mundy had done the work there, fixing a rope so
the two men could scale the cliff if they had to get out fast, and
then cut it behind them.

The hide-out was built the way the Mi'kmaq built their
wigwams, with skins and strips of birch bark to keep out the
cold and an opening at the top. The trick was to fashion it

so that smoke from the fire got out and the worst of the snow didn't get in. It had taken them two seasons to figure that out.

Inside, the floor was soft with animal pelts and pine boughs. Mundy loosened the tourniquet on his leg and peered at the wound in the semi-darkness. The bullet had missed the bone. He felt round his leg, wincing at the pain. There was no second wound. That meant the slug was still in there somewhere and he or Trapper would have to dig it out.

They'd done it before – heating a blade over the fire and probing into bloody flesh. He found he was shivering and he knew it wasn't just the cold. The shock of a gunshot wound could kill you even if you didn't bleed to death. He needed to get a fire going fast.

'You got lead in ya?' he asked his companion.

Trapper didn't answer for a moment. He was slumped down in a corner of the wigwam. He could have been unconscious. Then he stirred.

'Don't feel good, Mundy. Could be the last job me and you goes on.'

'Fool job too!' Mundy spat out. 'Them hunters ain't hardly no better off than we are. Shouldn't never go robbin' your own kind. Ain't no luck in it.'

The other man ignored this. Instead he seemed to be following his own train of thought. 'You got a wife and little'uns, Mundy. You bin an army man. Won't nobody even care if I die out here in the snow.'

'Army don't care about the likes of me,' said the other man

angrily, striking a flame to a pile of tinder in the centre of the floor. ''Cept mebbe to put me on the peg for eighteen months for doin' nothin'.'

'I done time in every jail from here to the Great Lakes,' said Trapper. 'Ain't nothin' to it.'

The fire was beginning to burn now, sending smoke spiralling up through the hole at the top of the wigwam. Mundy stretched out his wounded leg, trying to keep it raised to slow the bleeding

'Tell me about how you got a wife and little'uns, Mundy,' said Trapper suddenly. His teeth were chattering and his voice sounded weak.

'I told you all that.'

'Yeah. But tell me again. I like to hear about sum'n' better'n this. Lizzie her name is, right?'

Mundy took a drink from a leather water bottle and passed it to his companion. It was better if they rested before he tried digging the slugs out. You needed a steady hand and a slow-beating heart for that. He started to retell the story of his wife and two boys back in England, how he'd left them when the army sent him off to this frozen wilderness halfway around the world.

'Could be three of 'em now. Missus was expectin'. Could have a girl or another little boy. 'Cept he wouldn't be so little no more. She had black hair and dark eyes.'

'What was your boys called, Mundy?'

'I told you.'

'Tell me some more.'

'Matt was the oldest. Then Jimmy – same as me. I always wanted Joe. But Lizzie said it was too plain.'

And as Mundy retold his stories of a family he'd once had in a faraway country he'd once called home, the snow fell silently outside and the two men's blood seeped just as silently into the frozen ground.

Chapter 1

JOE

There was a crack like a rifle shot.

'Oi, you can't do that 'ere!'

Joe ducked instinctively and twisted sharply round. Three big lads were standing on the dirty London roadway ten feet away, glaring at him, while the messengers and shoppers that crowded the narrow street pushed past. The noise had been the sound of three heavy-handled brooms being clashed together like weapons.

Joe stood his ground. Tough-looking kids had been pushing him north of the City all week. It was the fifth time today.

'Weren't nobody here,' he said defiantly.

'We're 'ere, ain't we?' said the tallest of the boys. 'Watchmaker's shop down to the crossroads. That's our pitch. And you're on it!'

Joe took a step backwards, shooting a glance over his shoulder. Through the crowd an old man was hobbling towards him. In his hands he held the same kind of broom as Joe and the three boys – stout wooden handle with birch twigs tied tight with twine around the business end. Seemed like trouble whichever way he went.

'Look,' he said, turning back to the boys, 'I paid for me broom same as you. I got a right to work.'

The tall boy looked down at him and laughed. 'He's little but he's fierce, ain't he?'

They all laughed at that. Then they moved towards him in a group. Joe took another step backwards. He was going to have to make a run for it. Again.

Suddenly one of the boys shot out a hand, stopping the other two. A hansom cab had pulled up beside them, halting traffic. The driver pulled his lever to release the doors of the cab, but the immaculately dressed gentleman inside hesitated, eyeing the filthy roadway between him and the watchmaker's.

Forgetting Joe, the three boys stepped briskly forward. One took the cabman's horse by its bridle, the other two swept busily, clearing the street of horse dung, mud and rubbish. Joe hovered in the entrance to the shop, watching.

Less than half a minute and there was a clear path from the cab to the watchmaker's door. The sweepers made a flourish in the air and tucked the brooms under their arms, as if they were sheathing swords. Then all three swept off their caps in unison and made a low bow.

The gentleman laughed and reached into his waistcoat pocket. He disappeared into the shop, leaving the three boys splitting the coins he'd handed out. One of them looked up to see Joe still standing by the shop door. He lowered his broom and dug the handle sharply into Joe's ribs.

'See you round 'ere again, we knock out your tombstones for marbles. Understand?'

Joe understood.

The boys headed off through the crowd, pushing each other and laughing. Joe turned up the road, holding his side painfully. The old man with the broom was blocking his way. He saw Joe try to dodge past and reached out a hand.

'Easy, boy. I ain't gonna hurt yer. New to this game, eh?'

Joe nodded.

'Ain't got a trade of yer own?'

Joe hesitated. Then he shook his head. It wasn't true. He did have a trade, but he wasn't going back to it.

He'd been a tosher five years and more, searching the stinking sewers of Pound's Field for scraps, and robbed of most of what he earned by an old monster of a woman he'd called Mother. But it was three months now since he'd left Pound's Field and nothing on earth was ever going to get him back to that rat-infested hole again. Couldn't go back anyhow. He'd left owing Mother money. If she ever got hold of him again, it'd be a lot worse than getting his teeth knocked out.

The old man eyed Joe slowly, taking in his decent clothes and boots. 'What you want to go sweepin' for, anyhow?' he said slowly. 'You look like you got a bit put away.'

'Did have,' said Joe shortly. 'Got thieved off of me, didn't it?'

As he spoke, Joe could feel again the sickening sensation of waking up a week back to find his grey cloth bag gone. Inside that bag had been every scrap he'd ever saved from Mother.

He'd kept it out of sight day and night. He'd slept with the bag tied to him under his vest, but that hadn't stopped it going. They'd slipped something in his drink. Must have, to make him sleep through it. There'd been a filthy taste in his mouth when he came round in the morning and it wasn't just the taste of being dirt poor again. Anyway, the bag was gone and it wasn't coming back by wishing.

The old man had been watching him silently. 'Can't work nowhere down here without you're part of a gang,' he said finally.

'How do I join?'

'You can't.'

Joe thought about that for a moment. Then he looked sharply at the old man. 'You ain't part of no gang,' he said.

'Me? I bin on my corner so long nobody bothers me. Crushers know me. Kids know me.'

'You make a livin' at it?' asked Joe eagerly. 'Sweepin'?'

'Sometimes.' The old man pointed to a scruffy-looking mongrel with a white rump and one torn ear that hovered a short distance off, avoiding the passers-by. 'That dog yours?'

Joe looked over his shoulder. The dog's eyes never left him.

'Boy ain't mine. Just follows me around.'

'Same difference,' said the man. 'Might be a help. Might not.'

'How d'yer mean?'

But the man had spotted someone and he was already leaving. 'Find yer own pitch,' he said, limping away as fast as he could.

'Yeah, but where?' Joe called after him. But the man didn't respond.

Joe headed north on Lower Road. A thin, cold rain began to fall. He passed a one-legged man in a ragged uniform. He had a broom. A couple of hundred yards further on there were two more fierce-looking kids who eyed him suspiciously. They had brooms too.

There'd been crossing sweepers in Pound's Field, but Joe didn't remember seeing so many. Maybe he just hadn't noticed. It hadn't mattered back then.

Where Lower Road became Upper Road he passed a line of ragged women and children huddled on the pavement. Joe took a quick look down the side street where a gas lamp burned dimly. They were waiting for a soup kitchen to open: you didn't see a crowd like that anywhere else; and it must have been getting close to five o'clock because arguments were breaking out at the front of the line. They never had food or lodging for everyone.

Joe hurried on. He didn't like hanging around places like that too long. It always felt like bad luck.

Upper Road was wider and straighter than Lower Road but just as dirty, and the area looked poorer. The glovers' shops and haberdashers had given way to pawnbrokers and dingy slop shops. Joe didn't see anyone with a broom, but the chances of any tips for sweeping the street around here seemed pretty slim.

It was getting dark now and Joe's stomach was telling him it was time to take what little money he had left to a cookshop when a carriage passed him at a brisk trot, breath steaming from the nostrils of its pair of jet-black horses. Then two gentlemen swinging silver-handled canes came out of a side street and strode on up the road in front of him. Joe peered through the drizzle at the dark streets. He was an hour's walk north of anywhere he knew, but this was still the East End. Where were the gentry off to in these parts?

Then he saw it.

Up on the next corner, high over the entrance to a tall building, a single enormous gas lamp lit up the night, making the thin rain glow like a shower of gold. There were boarded-up windows in the upper storeys of the building where the crumbling brickwork looked ready to collapse into the street, but the ground floor shone with gleaming plate-glass and gilded plasterwork.

It was a gin shop, one of the biggest and gaudiest Joe had ever seen. Gilt letters on the windows advertised a dozen different brands of liquor and written up over the door in tall black letters was the name of the place. Joe stopped just beyond the reach of the gas light, squinting up at the frontage of the building. He knew the gold leaf and the plasterwork meant money – and lots of it. He didn't know what the sign said, because Joe had never learned to read or write.

'Boy!' he hissed. 'Wait!' The dog stopped.

It was early yet, but the gin shop was doing a roaring trade. Half a dozen burly costermongers staggered out of the gleaming mahogany doors. They'd have been shouting their wares on the street that morning, but it looked as if they'd spent the rest of the day drinking. Two gentlemen with fashionably dressed ladies on their arms stepped smartly out of the costermongers' way and then went inside. A big man in a red uniform held the double doors open and put his hand to his cap in a salute. Joe registered one of the gentlemen slip a coin into the doorman's hand. As the doors swung open, a cloud of pipe and cigar smoke erupted into the cold evening air along with the racket of a hundred people all ordering food and drink and shouting to each other at the same time.

Joe hung back in the shadows, keeping out of the doorman's sight. A four-wheeled brougham drew up in the glowing circle of light outside the gin shop, and a sharp-eyed boy was holding its door open before the horse had come to a halt. A sweeper! Naturally there'd be one working a place like this.

'Welcome to Addison's Superior Tavern and Supper Club! Mind your step there, sir!'

The boy had one of the smart, new-style brooms with a solid head and stiff bristles. Joe had seen them in the market. Tenpence they cost. His had been tuppence ha'penny and that was enough! Joe could hear the boy's voice clearly above the noise from inside the bar. He certainly had the patter.

'Terrible the rubbish in the streets these days, sir! Did you know one hundred tons of horse dung are deposited in our metropolis every twenty-four hours?' The boy snatched the cap off his head and swung round to the lady at the man's side. 'Pardon me for mentionin' such matters, madam.'

The woman looked at the boy coolly. 'Give him something, Lawrence, or he'll probably cover us with the stuff when our backs are turned.'

'Oh, no, madam!' The boy was all outraged innocence as he set about explaining how he and his friend Charlie were the last honest crossing sweepers in London. 'Bob and Charlie wouldn't never play a dirty trick like that, madam!' But Joe could see that all the time his eyes were on the gentleman's hand as it dipped into his trouser pocket and extracted a coin.

'Thank you kindly, sir,' he cried, tossing the coin high into the air.

Joe's eyes followed the tiny silver disc turning over and over, spinning up into the night air until it was almost out of sight. Bob caught the coin in his left hand without looking and slipped it into his pocket. The woman laughed.

'Nice to see you in our 'umble part of town, madam. And I hopes the evening ends well, sir.' Bob winked broadly at the gentleman.

The man raised a hand as if to give the boy a cuff round the head for his cheek, but Bob had already ducked away and was button-holing another well-dressed couple. 'Welcome to Addison's Superior Tavern and Supper Club!'

As the doorman held the doors open again, a ragged little girl, maybe half Joe's age, slipped past carrying an empty bottle and trailing what looked like her mother's shawl behind her. The doorman ignored her. The two toffs Joe had spotted on Upper Road laughed loudly at the child and flipped a coin into the doorman's waiting hand.

Joe had heard about these kind of places, where the rich came slumming amongst the poor, but he'd never seen one before. There was money being made here – outside as well as in. The question was: how was he going to get any of it?

Chapter 2

ADDISON'S

'What's yer game, short-shanks?'

The voice came loud and sudden from behind him. Joe turned slowly with a long sigh, knowing what was coming. Sure enough, he was looking up at a tall, heavily built boy, maybe three or four years older than him, with a tenpenny broom in his hand, just like Bob's. This would be the sweeper's partner, Charlie.

The boy looked down at him, a glint of amusement in his eye. Then he put his fingers to his mouth and let out a piercing whistle. The dog at Joe's feet yapped excitedly at the sound. Charlie aimed a swift kick.

''Ere, Bob,' he called out. 'I caught meself a tiddler. What's yer name, tiddler?'

Joe said nothing. A group of men and women burst out of the bar, singing at the tops of their voices. The red-coated doorman watched them go impassively, then his eyes rested on Joe and the two sweepers.

'I'm watchin' you, Charlie,' he called out.

The tall boy put his hands up, still holding the broom, and

18

took a pace backwards away from Joe. 'We ain't doin' nothin',
Freddie.'

'Mister Frederick to you, you little cadger.'

'Silly me!' Charlie smacked himself on the brow as if in
horror at making such a mistake. 'We ain't doin' nothin', *Mister
Frederick* – Mister Frederick, *sir*, I should say.' The doorman
scowled while Charlie made a great show of doing up a loose
button on Joe's jacket. 'Bob and me is just makin' friends with
– what d'you say your name was, short-shanks?'

'Joe.'

'Joe what?'

'Just Joe.'

'We're makin' the acquaintance of Just Joe, Mister
Frederick.'

'Well do it some place else.'

'Fair enough,' said Charlie. 'Come along, Just Joe. They
don't want to see the likes of you outside a Superior Tavern and
Supper Club. And we want a word with you. Don't we, Bob?'

'That we do,' said the other boy slowly. 'That we do.' Joe
could hear the menace in his voice.

The pair marched Joe on up to the corner, beyond the reach
of Addison's light where the road was quiet. He knew what to
expect. He had a broom and he was on their pitch: he was
going to get a beating.

Joe's eyes searched the darkness for an escape route. The
soot-blackened side of the gin shop rose above them. Ahead,
the bright-red bricks of a new wall led on down a dark side
street. Just next to where they were standing Boy was sniffing

at a jagged crack where the builders had tried to tie the new wall into the old brickwork. Joe could see the same clear divide at his feet. Where he stood the road was unpaved and all three boys were ankle-deep in mud, but just a couple of yards further on a pavement of neat grey slabs began and the road had the new surface of crushed stones they called mac. Beyond that there wasn't much street lighting, but the boy could see dim lines of tall terraced houses against the evening sky. Maybe he could lose these two down there. Maybe not . . .

The problem was, he didn't know the area. Running was easy when you knew where you were. In a strange part of town running was risky. Running got the pursuers' blood up and it could make the beating worse. Joe stayed where he was, eyeing Bob and Charlie warily. The two bigger boys kept a firm grip on him and talked over his head.

'See now, what I like about this one,' Charlie was saying, 'is that he's nicely turned out.'

The tall boy fingered Joe's collar. He'd paid five shillings for the jacket and breeches and then another two bob for boots. It had felt good to own his first set of decent togs – still did, come to that.

'The nobs like a decent turnout.' Charlie was doing all the talking. Now he turned his attention back to Joe. 'See, Just Joe, you think you're going to do better if you look all ragged and pathetic like, but you don't. The nobs just turn their noses up. 'Specially the ladies. What they likes is the kind that looks decent and honest.' He laughed. 'You are honest, aren't yer, Joe?'

Joe studied the boy's face. What did he want him to say? He tried to match the older boy's knowing smile. Bob slapped him hard on the back.

'When you can afford it, eh, Joey?' He laughed. ''E's a fly one, this, I reckon, Charlie. Might be able to make somethin' of him, eh?'

The two boys looked at each other. Charlie winked and Bob nodded his head. Were they going to let him in on their turf outside Addison's? Joe could feel the excitement building inside him. It was the first sniff at earning a living since he got out of Pound's Field. Before someone stole his bag full of gear it hadn't mattered so much. Now it was life or death. They'd want something in return. A piece of what he got probably. But whatever they wanted, this was too good to let slip.

'You gonna let me in on your pitch?'

Bob laughed. 'Oh, no, Joey. There ain't a sweeper in London that'd do that. But we just might point you at a pitch of your own.'

'Where's that then?'

'You're quick, Just Joe,' said Charlie. 'Quick and nicely turned out. That's good. You see down there?' Still keeping a grip on his shoulder, the tall boy spun Joe round and pointed down the side road where the street was clean and paved. 'There's a load of new houses down there. Lomesbury, they call it.' There was a sneer in the boy's voice when he pronounced the name. 'Full of toffs, it is. Now, me and Bob here can't be away from business now, but you come by here tomorra mornin' and we just might steer you right.'

Bob wrapped his arm tighter round Joe from the other side, squeezing hard, but his voice was soft. 'See, you go down somewhere like Lomesbury Square, Joey, and what you got to do is get to know folk. You got to know every housemaid, every cook and coach driver and all the nobs too. And you got to make 'em like you, Joey. Me and Charlie, now, they have a laugh at us sometimes. But they don't like us, do they, Charlie?'

'Don't know why,' smirked the other boy.

'Me neither, Charlie. But a little short-shanks like Joey here – now they just might go for him. So here's the word, Joey. Stay smart. Stay clean. And don't beg. Right? Not ever. You got to make it look like you're doin' somethin' for them or they won't part with a farthin'.'

Suddenly Joe realized they were telling him what they knew about making money from the gentry. He'd never had dealings with gentry. His eyes narrowed in concentration as he tried to memorize every word.

'See, you don't make money sweepin', Just Joe.' Charlie took over. 'Not really. You make money when you're a part of the place – like the weather and the mud and the horse muck, or Freddie the doorman.'

Bob spun him round again, so that he was facing back towards the gin shop. Then he let go, and the other boy suddenly gave Joe a punch on the arm which might have been meant to be playful but hurt. As Joe stepped back, surprised, Charlie grabbed the broom out of his hand and began to pull the birch twigs out of it one by one.

'Who sold you this then, Just Joe?' he said, scattering the

twigs across the road. Once a few had been removed the whole thing began to disintegrate. 'This kind of tuppenny ha'penny rubbish won't last you out the week. You need a decent yard broom like me and Bob.' He handed Joe back the broom handle and the two boys walked away laughing.

'See yer tomorra, short-shanks,' Bob called out.

Joe followed them part of the way back to the gin shop with the dog trotting behind him. He squinted up at the sign over the door. First letter was an 'A'. He could make out that much. Second two were both the same. That must be 'D'. After that the letters just seemed to circle round each other in front of the boy's eyes. He watched Bob and Charlie take money off a couple more toffs out for a night in the East End. Joe couldn't imagine ever being able to talk to the gentry like that himself, but maybe he was going to have to give it a try.

He was getting ready for the long walk home to his lodgings on Crooked-back Lane when the double mahogany doors of Addison's suddenly burst open and a small man in a black suit came flying out backwards and landed heavily in the road where Bob and Charlie had been sweeping. The two boys laughed as the small figure scrambled to his feet and headed straight back towards the bar.

The red-uniformed doorkeeper – Freddie – blocked his way. He said something Joe didn't hear, pointing the way up the road, but the man shook him off, staggering sideways and shouting back at the doorman, who stood head and shoulders taller.

'I don't care who you are.' Freddie was shouting too now.

'You don't get in 'ere again. Now clear off and don't come back.'

The man made as if to charge the door. Then he seemed to change his mind and reeled away from Addison's in Joe's direction. Bob and Charlie cheered. Another group of men were laughing. The dog barked and Joe stepped back as the man staggered past. And then in the glow of the light from the gin shop Joe saw his face.

It wasn't a man at all. It was a boy of about his age. Joe had seen plenty of kids on the street the worse for drink, but this boy had a quality suit on – that was what had made Joe think he must be an adult – and his well-fed face had none of the pinched look of the gin drinker.

A tall figure in a bowler hat suddenly loomed out of the shadows at the side of Addison's, where the new Lomesbury pavement ended and the muck of Upper Road began. Without a word he took the staggering boy by one arm, lifted him almost off his feet and marched him back the way he had come.

Joe followed. He didn't know why. Most likely this was the boy's father and he was taking him home, where he'd get a good whipping for drinking gin and that would be an end of it. But there was something that made Joe want to see for himself what happened.

The road got dark quickly. Further on it looked as if there might be a big open space and beyond that a couple of gas lamps lit up the tall fronts of the houses. But here all was darkness. Just a few yards down the road Joe almost stumbled over the pair.

The man had the boy by the scruff of the neck and he was

pushing him down into the gutter. Joe caught the sharp smell of fresh horse dung. Then his eyes began to adjust to the darkness. The man was rolling the boy on the ground, covering his clothes, his hair and his face in horse muck.

The dog gave Joe away, suddenly barking furiously at his side. Joe hadn't meant to speak. The words just came out.

'Hey, let 'im up! Pick on someone your own size.'

The man straightened up, leaving the boy lying flat out on the roadway. He made a lunge at the dog, but the animal skipped nimbly away, still barking. Then he took a step towards Joe.

Joe raised his arm instinctively to defend himself and realized he was still holding the handle of his broom. He couldn't see the man's face clearly, but he heard him curse. Then he felt the broom handle snatched out of his grasp. The man put it across his knee and snapped it in a single, easy movement, throwing one half at the dog and one at Joe.

'Clear out of it, street trash,' he snarled, 'and take your mutt with you.' Then he picked the boy on the ground up bodily and carried him away into the darkness.

Chapter 3

CROOKED-BACK LANE AND
LOMESBURY SQUARE

There was no light and the way the thirty or so other people in the room snored around him, Joe could tell it was a long time until morning. Later in the night the kids over in the far corner cried in their sleep and voices muttered and cursed, but now there was only the sound of exhausted folk sleeping. Far away Joe heard a church clock strike a quarter to the hour. But which hour?

Joe had never slept too well on Crooked-back Lane. There were no beds in the room, which had once been a stable loft, just two long platforms and two lines of dirty mattresses stuffed with wood shavings. If a heavy man was kipping next to you and he turned over in his sleep, he could crush you. But for the last week, since the night his grey cloth bag disappeared, it had been much worse. Joe woke every half-hour, thinking he felt fingers rifling through his clothes, but it was only the bedbugs crawling and biting. He'd thought of moving somewhere else, but what was the point? He had nothing else worth stealing now and Crooked-back Lane was cheap.

Joe lay on his back and stared up into the darkness, waiting for the clock to strike the hour. If it was four o'clock, he'd get up now. He wanted to be in Lomesbury before the gentry were awake.

He thought about the day ahead, running through all the things Bob and Charlie had told him about sweeping. Get to know folk. Stay smart. Stay clean. Don't beg. Didn't have to tell him that. People had called him a dirty tosher when he'd worked down the sewers, but he'd never been out on the cadge and he wasn't going to start now. Not easy to stay clean in this flop house though, and he couldn't afford the public baths any more.

Joe tried to concentrate on Lomesbury and sweeping, but his mind wandered back to the grey cloth bag. He'd only moved into Crooked-back Lane so no one would figure he'd got money. Blend in, that was the idea, look like all the other poverty-stricken kids on the street. The clothes must have given him away. Shouldn't have bought new clothes. Stupid thing to do. Made him stand out, didn't it? Made him look like someone worth thieving off. Now he was down to sweeping. And crossing sweepers were lower than toshers. Never mind. If that was the only way to make a living then that was what he was going to do.

At long last the clock struck the hour. One. Two. Three. Four o'clock.

Joe slipped off the end of the sleeping platform, careful not to waken the men on either side of him. He felt his way down the middle of the long room, and washed his face and hands in a pail of dirty water by the door. He tried unsuccessfully to flatten out the crop of stiff black hair that always stuck up straight on his head these days like a fistful of paintbrushes. Then he headed down the creaking stairs, brushing at his jacket and breeches.

Boy was awake in the yard, shivering under the gaslight when Joe emerged. The dog must have known he was coming, but he didn't wag his tail. Joe had never seen him do that. But he did prick up the one ear that moved, as if he was ready for the long walk to Lomesbury.

'Come on then, Boy,' said Joe.

The small hours of the morning were bitterly cold, but Joe already felt better out of the stale air of the flop house. He headed briskly along silent Crooked-back Lane, keeping out of the puddles of water and the worst of the mud and rubbish which choked the narrow street.

Even at this hour there was a coffee stall open at the bottom of Lower Road. Joe spent a ha'penny on a scalding mug of black, bitter liquid. It was more carrot and chicory than coffee but it warmed him. He spent another ha'penny on some of yesterday's bread and butter. He gave the crusts to the dog. Then he headed north.

Lower Road had been crowded the day before. At this hour it was empty, except for a few men pushing barrows down to the early market. He stopped a cart loaded with brooms, and the man tapped his foot impatiently while Joe inspected each in turn. Finally he made up his mind.

'I'll take this one.'

The man eyed him sarcastically. 'Sure about that, are yer?'

Joe didn't answer. He counted out five brown ha'pennies and handed them over. That meant he had exactly a shilling left in the world. A shilling would pay for food and lodging for three days – four if he didn't eat too much. After that he would have to sell his boots and then his clothes. One way or another he had to start earning soon.

He walked on, in a hurry now to reach Lomesbury. Little by little the dark sky overhead turned a dirty grey. By the time he passed the side street where the soup kitchen was, the lamp-lighters were on the street, extinguishing gas lamps.

Addison's was locked up tight and there was no sign of Bob and Charlie, but Joe didn't wait for them. He was impatient now to be on his own pitch. He rounded the corner, passed the crack in the wall, stepped onto the neat, stone rectangles of the Lomesbury pavements and came to a dead stop.

By a line of pointed, black railings he stood for a long moment and stared. In spite of all that happened afterwards, Joe never quite forgot his first sight of Lomesbury in the dim light of early morning. A freezing fog hung in the air, blunting the sharp edges of the great houses that rose ghostly on every side. Muffled sounds of traffic and the cries of the first street vendors came from back on Upper Road, but they only seemed to emphasize the silence that enveloped the square in front of him.

Everything looked new: new houses, new railings, new roads, new pavement, new trees planted in the middle of the square. The London Joe knew – the London of Pound's Field and Crooked-back Lane – was all packed tight at odd angles, as though someone had chucked the houses up in the air long ago and let them fall at random in the dirt. But here even the young trees stood in straight lines, and long straight rows of terraced houses peered at each other from a distance as if to say, 'Keep away. Don't come too close.'

For a moment the boy nearly doubled back the way he'd come. Bob and Charlie would be along in a bit. Now that he was here, what they'd told him last night didn't seem enough. He needed to know more about how to behave in a place like Lomesbury Square, otherwise the toffs'd have him out on his ear. They'd call the crushers. They'd get after him with a whip!

He took a step forward. He took a step back. He squinted up at the dim, grey sky. It was wide and open just like Lomesbury Square, the way it never was in London. He didn't like the look of it. He looked down at the little white mongrel that sat on the pavement a few yards away, apparently survey-ing the scene himself. 'What d'yer reckon, Boy?'

His voice sounded oddly loud in the silence of the square. He looked around, checking whether anyone had heard him, but the place seemed utterly deserted. When he looked back, the dog was gone.

Joe scanned the road ahead. There he was, sniffing at some-thing. Probably found some food or— 'No!'

Joe ran at the animal as he cocked his leg against the black railings that fenced off the empty middle of the square. 'No!!' Too late.

He swept some loose sand over the wet patch Boy had

made. Then he swept a couple more yards along the pavement. The smart, grey slabs were clean already, but using the new brush made him feel better.

There was a pile of horse dung in the middle of the road. Joe swept it into the gutter along with some loose stone chippings. Then he went back to his pile of sand and swept that over to join the horse dung. He'd started work. That was good. Now he just needed to get paid for it.

The horse muck made him think of the boy getting chucked out of Addison's and the man who had rolled him in the dirt. Where did they fit into the sharp corners and clean pavements of Lomesbury Square?

He worked his way round the north side of the square, sweeping as he went, though there wasn't much to clear. At first glance the houses all looked the same with their white plaster and immaculate brickwork, but now he could see that one house on this side was even bigger than the rest. It had a square tower at one corner with a pointed roof which rose above the other house-tops into the misty air. On the doorstep a girl in a black uniform was on her knees with her back to him.

Get to know folk. That's what Bob had said.

'Mornin'!'

Joe tried to sound cheerful, but he knew it came out nervous. The girl looked at him. Then she went back to scrubbing the front doorstep without a word.

Three doors down he tried again. Same response. At the corner house another uniformed housemaid was polishing a

31

brass doorknob. Joe stood watching her, trying desperately to think of something to say.

Make 'em like you, Joey.

'Give you a 'and, if you like.'

The girl turned round. In spite of the white cap and black uniform she didn't look much older than him.

'All right.'

She held out the rag she was using. Joe stepped forward awkwardly, took the rag and began working on the doorknob. He polished it until it shone. Then he polished the brass letter box and the brass number beside the door.

'My name's Joe,' he said, handing the girl back her cloth. 'What's yours?'

'None of your business,' said the girl. 'Now buzz off, you little cadger!'

And that was pretty much the story of the morning. Joe watched soberly clad gentlemen with leather cases emerge from shining front doors and head off towards their business, but he couldn't summon the nerve to go near them. Then smartly dressed nursemaids appeared in the square, pushing prams or walking little kids up and down, but he didn't see how he was going to get any money from them. He kept an eye out for the boy from Addison's, but he wasn't even sure if he'd recognize him. It had all happened so quickly last night.

As the morning went on, tradesmen began to appear. Joe held the coalman's heavy dray horse and the fishmonger's broken-down old nag. He helped carry sacks of flour and potatoes and half a hundredweight of bacon and boxes of soap and candles and butter and shoe-blacking. But he had to leave everything at the back door; not a cook or a housekeeper or a footman would let him inside any of the houses. He shifted great bags of grass seed and half a gross of young bushes for the gardener who worked in the park in the middle of the square. But the old man wouldn't let him inside the gate. Heavy-footed policemen came round on patrol twice and Joe kept out of sight on the other side of the square.

'And not a copper coin to show for it, eh, Boy?' Joe squatted down on the pavement. The dog stared at him as if he understood. 'Still, lesson learned: no chink from no tradesmen. That old bloke yesterday was wrong about you though. You ain't no use at all.' Every one of the tradesmen Joe had helped that morning had aimed a kick at the dog.

He was by the new wall that led up towards Addison's. Bob and Charlie would be at their pitch by now more than likely. Maybe he should cut up that way. Maybe not. Better to figure it out for himself.

Joe swept the south side of the square, gathering every last scrap of muck and mud and straw and loose chippings he could find until there was a series of neat piles in the gutter. Then he stood a moment, leaning on his broom. The street looked clean enough to eat your dinner off, but there was no one in sight. No one had even seen him do it. That was no good either.

The sharp sound of hooves made Joe turn his head. A four-wheeled cab – a growler – was pulling up on the north side of the square. He sprinted round and began busily sweeping a path to the front gate of the nearest house. He'd already done this side, but at least there was someone to see him work now, someone who might drop a coin in his hat if he did it just right.

A tall man in a long jacket jumped easily down off the growler's running board and held the door open. Joe stared open-mouthed at his head. He was wearing a wig – all white and curly and covered in powder! Everything in Lomesbury looked strange, but this was beyond strange! Joe figured the man must be bald underneath, but surely he could find a better thatch for his head than that. The man looked down his nose sideways at Joe and curled his lip. The boy realized he was staring and ducked his head, but he stayed where he was.

A pair of tiny, pointed, black patent leather shoes appeared from the door of the cab, then the hem of a lilac silk dress. Joe stepped back with a low bow, tucking his broom under his arm, as much like the boys outside the watchmaker's shop as he could manage. He knew his hair didn't look good, but he snatched the cap off anyway. The lady needed somewhere to drop her coin, didn't she? Or maybe the bald bloke would give him something. Any kind of coin would be a start.

Joe risked a look up from under his eyebrows and the lady seemed to catch sight of him for the first time, because she let out a small scream and staggered slightly. The man had an arm out at once to support her. He guided her through the gate and up the front steps to the house. As soon as she was inside, he wheeled sharply round. His movements had all been slow and rather stately, but now he was back down the steps in two strides, fists clenched, eyes narrowed.

'Clear out of it, street trash! And take your mutt with you!'

Joe backed across the roadway with the dog keeping close to his side. There was a real savagery in the man's eye, as if he hated him just for being there on the street. But it wasn't the face Joe recognized. It was the voice. Last night, behind Addison's, it had been too dark to see faces, but the voice was the same and so were the words. Surely this was the man who had rubbed the drunken boy in horse muck and then carried him away into the dark.

Chapter 4

THE TOWER HOUSE

Joe felt the park fence behind him. It was too high to climb and the railings were too close together to squeeze through. There was no escape there.

But the man didn't come any nearer. He stopped on the kerb and stared long and hard at Joe as if he were memorizing his features. Somehow the wig didn't look so funny any more. Then he did an abrupt about-face and disappeared round the side of the house. Joe breathed a long sigh of relief. If it was the same man as last night, he hadn't recognized him.

Joe peered up at the tall building. It was the big house with the tower. He looked swiftly around to see if anyone was watching: the old gardener was digging in the middle of the square amongst the weeds and rubble, a man with a handcart was hawking door to door fifty yards down the street, but there was no one else about.

He slipped across the road to the black iron railings that ran along the front of the house. He wanted to see where the man had gone. Maybe the boy was somewhere there too. He came face to face with a stout woman in a cap and apron.

The woman put her head on one side and looked him straight in the eye. 'I seen yer,' she said.

'I never – I ain't—' Joe stammered.

'I seen yer sweepin' all along here.'

'Ain't no harm in it.'

'I never said there was harm in it.' The woman laughed. 'That dog yours?'

'He's not mine,' said Joe uncertainly. No one on Lomesbury Square seemed to like the look of Boy. 'But he's with me,' he finished.

'A boy that looks after a dog can't be all bad,' said the woman thoughtfully.

'Don't look after him,' said Joe. 'He's just with me.'

The woman seemed puzzled at that. 'You had your dinner?' she asked after a pause.

'I'm all right. Don't always eat in the day, do I?'

'I'll bet you don't.' The woman looked him up and down.

Joe glanced awkwardly at his jacket and breeches. They'd looked pretty good earlier, but he'd got a tear at the knee that morning and the jacket was starting to fray at the cuffs. They'd robbed him at that slop shop. Five shillings and they'd be in rags in another month! *Stay smart. Stay clean.* That's what Charlie had said and he already looked like a beggar.

'You want a piece of bread?' asked the woman.

'Ain't no cadger.'

'All right. I didn't say you was. You can do somethin' for me then. See this.' She held out a piece of paper. Joe took it, eyeing the writing doubtfully.

'Can't read it.'

'You don't have to read it,' laughed the woman. 'Can you run?'

'Yeah. I can run.'

'Well you run down to Solomon's with that. Tell them it's an order for the Harvey Asylum for Fatherless Children. Now there's four of 'em,' the stout woman went on slowly, 'so you make sure you tell the shop the right one—'

'Soup kitchen, yer mean?' Joe interrupted her. 'Corner of Lower Road?'

'That's right. You're a quick one, ain'tcha? Mr Harvey don't like people calling it a soup kitchen, mind.'

'I seen it.'

'You could get a decent bellyful yourself down there.'

'Me?' Joe looked shocked. 'Them places is full of cadgers and tramps. I don't never go near 'em.'

'All right.' The woman smiled. 'You just run the errand then and come right back.'

'Solomon's?'

'On Upper Road. You know where it is?'

'I'll find it,' said Joe. He hesitated. 'What's your name?' he asked awkwardly.

The woman laughed again. 'My name's Mrs Briggs. I'm cook here for Mr and Mrs Harvey. What's yours?'

'Joe.'

'Joseph?'

'No. Joe.'

The boy made as if to go. He took three steps and turned

back to Mrs Briggs. 'That man,' he began. 'The bald one.'

Mrs Briggs exploded with laughter. 'What bald one?'

'With the wig on.'

'Oh! Mr Bates. Don't mind him. His bark's worse than his bite, as they say. Like that little scruff of yours, I shouldn't wonder.'

'I think I seen him down by Addison's. Has he got a son?'

'Mr Bates?' The woman looked surprised. 'No, he hasn't got a son. He's a single man, he is. He's the Harveys' footman. Been with the family donkey's years and he don't waste his time in gin shops. No more than you should at your age. Now, you stop asking questions and cut along 'fore I change my mind.'

Joe sprinted round the square. He kept his head down crossing the main road – he didn't want Bob or Charlie spotting him now he had an errand to run. A footman. That was a kind of servant. And a single man. So who was the boy then? Perhaps it wasn't the same man. Perhaps he'd got the voice wrong and Bates using the same words was just a coincidence. Joe put it out of his mind. He had a living to earn.

He was back in five minutes. There was no sign of Mrs Briggs.

What was he supposed to do now? Perhaps she'd tricked him – not planning to give him anything for his trouble, same as the rest of them that day. Well he was sick of it. Grand houses or no grand houses, he'd done a job of work and even if it was only a crust he deserved something for it.

Joe went up to the front gate of the house – the Tower House: that was how he thought of it now, though he could see there was another name etched on the gatepost. He met Mrs Briggs coming to meet him. She had a bright new penny in her hand and half a loaf of bread.

'It's only broken victuals,' she said half apologetically. Joe looked blank. 'Left over from yesterday,' explained Mrs Briggs.

''S all right.'

Joe took the money and the bread so quickly he forgot to thank her and hurried off to the top end of the square. Away from the houses where the long wall led up towards Addison's he sat on the kerb to eat. When he'd had all he wanted, he tossed the rest to Boy who wolfed it down hungrily.

A win and a bellyful! Joe laughed aloud – a tiny explosion of air, stifled as soon as it began. Five minutes it had taken him to run to Solomon's and back and she'd given him a win! This was going to be easy after all. He stowed the penny carefully in his pocket and headed briskly back down to the square, looking around for his next job.

He didn't get another tip all afternoon.

As the day began to fade and the fog returned, lights appeared in the windows of the grand houses, and the soberly clad gentlemen with leather cases that Joe had seen leave in the morning came home again. Curtains were drawn across the big bay windows. But in some rooms the curtains weren't pulled straight away and the candles and lamps burning meant he could see right inside in the way he hadn't been able to in the daylight. The ground floor of the houses was raised above street level and all Joe could see from the road was heavy, patterned wallpaper, pictures in gilt frames and sparkling chandeliers.

Then a figure would stand for a moment at a front window looking out – a woman's face, framed in long, brown ringlets, or a gentleman with whiskers and a white bow tie.

There was no one on the street now. Every now and then you could hear a noise that could have been the crowd at Addison's, but the wide open spaces of Lomesbury Square were silent. Joe knew he might as well be heading home to Crooked-back Lane where the houses were packed so close people strung their washing across the street. He didn't feel hungry – not really. The bread at midday would do him till morning and he could save Mrs Briggs's penny and come back tomorrow and try to earn another one.

But Joe didn't leave. There might be cabs or carriages later and he could hold horses' heads and open doors maybe. That was what he told himself. But it wasn't the prospect of another tip or two which held him in the darkening square. It was those rectangles of yellow light and the people who swam into view every now and then, all dressed up in finery that must be every-day to them.

It began to grow darker. The lamplighter came round, but only the two street lights at the far end of the square were working – perhaps the others hadn't been connected to the gas yet – so most of Lomesbury Square became shadowy, and the illuminated front windows where curtains still hadn't been drawn gleamed more brightly.

Joe walked silently down the north side of the square as far as the Tower House where Mrs Briggs had given him the penny and the food, and the footman, Bates, had told him to clear off.

The curtains were pulled across the front window, but in the middle they didn't quite meet. A shaft of yellow light shone out into the darkness.

A chill wind was blowing now. Joe pulled his jacket a little tighter around his thin frame and eased the latch up on the front gate, his heart pounding in his ears. As he slipped through the gate, the boy's face was suddenly lit up by the light from the window. He ducked down into the shadows, crawled up the front steps on hands and knees and made a spring across to the broad windowsill.

He didn't know what he was planning to do. He couldn't remember deciding to open the gate of the Harveys' house, let alone climb up here to spy on them. He lay flat on the window ledge waiting for his heart to slow.

There was an opening the span of both hands in the curtains, but to see through the gap he would have to move into the light. He glanced back towards the road. Only a couple of yards of front garden and a line of pointed railings separated him from the pavement. If he was in the light anyone passing in the street could see him. This was stupid! The crushers had been round the square three times in the day. They'd be round again after dark sure as shufflin', and if they saw him it'd be the magistrate and three months in quod most like.

Joe edged forward another inch. Maybe it *was* stupid, but crushers or no crushers he had to see what happened behind the glass of this tall house with its shining plasterwork and its tower that reached up into the black sky. He craned his neck just a little more and blinked at the light.

The room shone like a magic lantern slide. A coal fire danced in the grate; long candles glinted on polished wood, silver and brass; an enormous bronze lantern, suspended from the ceiling, was reflected in a gilt-framed mirror on the opposite wall. In the corners of the room shadows lingered where the light didn't reach.

As his eyes got used to the brightness, Joe could see more details. A table filled almost the entire length of the room. To the left at the head of the table sat a man with thick side-burns the shape of mutton-chops, which made his long face look even longer. He wore a black suit and a white tie, tied tight around his neck. On either side of him were two more black-suited figures, one with his face turned away from Joe. Then there was a long stretch of table, full of silver candelabra and crystal bowls packed with flowers – and at the far end sat a lady in a shimmering blue dress, her long white fingers resting lightly on the shining white tablecloth. Behind her on the wall hung a huge painting of a man in scarlet uniform, mounted on a rearing horse and brandishing a sword.

Joe recognized the lady. She was the one who'd screamed when he held out his cap for a coin. She must be Mrs Harvey. So the man at the other end of the table was Mr Harvey.

No one moved. No one spoke. The candle flames swayed, but the people were as still as the portrait on the wall. They scarcely seemed real. In front of each of them lay a line of gleaming knives and forks and spoons and two or three crystal goblets that winked in the candlelight, but it looked as if they might sit there all night and never speak or eat or move a muscle. Joe found he was holding his breath.

Then suddenly a door on the far side of the room swung open, and the tall footman called Bates walked in wearing his powdered wig. Surely this grand-looking character couldn't be the man who had cursed at him on the street the night before. Mr Harvey's head turned almost imperceptibly. He may have spoken, but the window glass was too thick for the boy to hear. Then he swivelled round and pointed straight at Joe.

He could have jumped. He could have run. He could have flattened himself on the window ledge at least. But a sick feeling flooded through the boy from his ankles to his head and Joe found himself unable to stir. For a moment all he could see was the sharp crease in the footman's trousers as he stood at the tall window. Joe peered upwards, only his eyes moving, waiting for the sash to be thrown up and strong arms to grab him.

The man stared straight out into the darkness, his eyes darting left and right, but he didn't look down to where Joe crouched. Then he took a step backwards and reached up to pull the curtains closed. It wasn't Joe Mr Harvey had been pointing at: it was the open curtains.

Just as Bates had his hands on the curtains, the black-suited figure whose face Joe hadn't been able to see swivelled in his chair, and Joe was staring straight into the face of another boy. It was as if his own reflection had suddenly appeared behind the glass, except that this boy's black hair didn't stick straight up on end like paintbrushes and his cuffs weren't frayed and his shoes weren't crusted with horse muck – or at least they weren't now. Because in the moment before the room was blocked from his sight, Joe was quite certain: this was the boy who had come staggering out of the gin shop last night and got rolled in the dirt of the street.

Chapter 5

ALEC

Mr Harvey put the tips of his fingers together and sat up very straight at his desk, looking directly into his son's eyes. The early morning light from the tall window behind him made it hard to see his face. 'So, Alexander, do you have anything to say by way of explanation?'

Alec tried desperately to hold his gaze. One – two – three – he managed a count of five. Then he looked down – the way he always did.

In the silence his father let out his usual long sigh, then he spoke again in the same cool, precise voice: 'The facts of the case seem to me to be quite clear, Alexander, and not, I regret to say, unfamiliar. Mr Johnson here observed you returning home after dark the night before last.' The tutor stirred in his chair and cleared his throat self-importantly. Mr Harvey went on. 'You had soiled your clothes in the most revolting fashion, thereby making quite unnecessary work for Mr Bates, who has been a loyal servant to the family since before you were born—'

Alec stole a glance towards the door at the impassive face of Bates.

'Alexander, you are not attending to me!'

His father never raised his voice. This was as angry as he ever sounded. Alec looked instantly back at him. This man – 'Mister Harvey' he always called him behind his back, not 'Father' – this man didn't know the real reason he'd come back covered in horse dung three times in the last month. Alec looked steadily into his father's eyes, holding the secret like a shield. This time he managed a count of ten.

Mr Harvey took a long, slow breath. When he spoke again he was back to his usual calm, measured tones, as if he were telling Bates which wine he would drink that evening or discussing some matter of business the way Alec had heard him at the bank on Lombard Street.

'I would have been happier to deal with this matter yesterday, but unfortunately my presence was required at one of the Asylums for Fatherless Children. So I will now give you a final opportunity to offer an explanation.'

'It wasn't my fault,' muttered Alec.

'Speak up, boy. I am perfectly willing to listen to an honest account.'

'It wasn't my fault!'

'Did someone else cause your clothes to become soiled?'

Alec shot another quick glance at Bates. Then he looked down again. 'Don't know.'

'What do you mean you don't know?' Alec didn't speak. 'Either you soiled your clothes yourself or someone else did it to you. Now which was it?'

Alec said nothing. He should have kept quiet in the first

place. This was just making it worse. Mr Harvey tapped his fingers sharply on the mahogany desk and pulled a gold watch from his waistcoat pocket.

'I can devote no more time to this, Alexander. There are many other matters that require my attention this morning.' He stood up and began to pace backwards and forwards on the thick-piled carpet of the study, hands clasped behind his back. 'You have given a great deal of anxiety to your unfortunate mother, Alexander—'

At the mention of his mother, Alec instantly felt tears pricking behind his eyes. He bit into his bottom lip. He was not going to cry. He tried to concentrate on something else – the crack at the top of the window where his father always left it open just a little whatever the weather outside . . . the houses on the other side of the square . . .

'– your unfortunate mother, who you know is not well. I will not say that your regrettable expulsion from school last year caused her' – he paused an instant, searching for the right word – 'her illness. That is regrettably of many years standing. But I am afraid it may well have compounded her – difficulties. I do not say this to distress you, Alexander, but you are a young man now and a man needs to understand that his actions have consequences.'

Alec bit down harder, fighting his feelings. Why did he have to bring his mother into it? It had nothing to do with her. He could taste his own blood now, but it wasn't working. He was going to cry – like a baby – in front of Bates and Johnny Johnson, and his father would think it was because he was going to be locked up for a couple of hours and it was nothing to do with that; it was to do with – to do with – Alec groped in his mind for what it was to do with but he didn't know himself.

Mr Harvey was standing behind the desk now, using his full height to look down on his son as he pronounced sentence, the words as clipped and precise as always.

'You must understand, Alexander,' he said, 'that any punishments meted out to you are given not in a spirit of anger but with a view to helping you.'

'Helping me?' Alec couldn't prevent himself from interrupting.

'Yes, helping you to reform your ways by sending you to a place of quiet in which you can reflect on your actions. I hope you understand that.' Mr Harvey waited, but Alec had nothing else to say. 'Very well. Now, I had intended confining you, Alexander, for two hours to the room above this one, a room which we have unfortunately had to designate as the Reformatory. However, you have now compounded the original fault of soiling your clothes by attempting a false excuse, which is not manly conduct, so I am extending that period to four hours. The studies with Mr Johnson which you will therefore miss in the morning will be completed in what is usually your leisure time later in the day. I trust this will not inconvenience you too much, Mr Johnson. And now I really must be leaving for my place of business.'

The tutor simpered and seemed about to say something. Alec stood in front of the desk, still fighting tears, and at that moment the door burst open and Bates had to spring to one side as Alec's seven-year-old sister, Felicity, burst into the room. She bounced over to her father and perched herself on the edge of his desk.

'Papa, I want to tell you something.'

Mr Harvey's long face relaxed instantly into a smile and the gold watch went back into his pocket. 'And what is that, my dear little Flicky?'

'It's about Alice, Papa. She has a gentleman follower. She's not supposed to have gentleman followers, is she, Papa?'

'Oh, really, Flicky, that is no concern of mine. Now I really must be going.'

But he didn't go. Felicity picked up the pens on the blotter, she pulled the roll-top mechanism of the desk up and down and she prattled on about the boyfriend she had seen her nurse-maid, Alice, talking to. Mr Harvey bent to trace a line down the side of his daughter's face with one finger. He rearranged a little pink bow that had come loose in her hair. Felicity pulled at his mutton-chop whiskers. Bates looked on and smiled indulgently. Mr Johnson looked on and smiled too. Alec stood in front of the desk, apparently forgotten. He felt the tears recede. His lips tightened. He watched his father playing with his little sister and his face was hard. Finally Mr Harvey seemed to notice he was still there.

'You may take Master Alexander to the Reformatory now, Bates,' he said. 'Give him this book to peruse.' Mr Harvey handed the footman a heavy leather-bound volume.

'Four hours, sir?'

'Four hours, Bates. To be continued for the remainder of the week.'

Joe hurried round the corner. He hadn't woken as early as he'd meant to and it was already broad daylight. He wanted to be sweeping on the square before any of the sober-suited gentlemen left for work. That way they'd see him working again as soon as they came out of their doors. Where the side wall of Addison's didn't quite join the new Lomesbury bricks, Bob and Charlie were squatting on the pavement waiting for him.

'How's tricks, Just Joe?' Charlie was at Joe's elbow in a moment. 'Didn't see you yesterday. Not avoidin' yer friends, are yer?'

'No.' Joe stopped, shouldering his broom. 'Busy, weren't I? Doin' like you said.'

'Gettin' rich?'

'Got a win from the cook at one house.'

'A win!' Charlie looked impressed.

Joe took a breath. It was better if he said it himself. 'You want your whack, don'tcha? 'Cos you put me onto it? It's fair enough. I don't mind.' He tried to make it sound as if he meant it.

'My whack?' Charlie sounded shocked. 'Are you suggestin' me and Bob would take some of your hard-earned off of yer?'

'Don't yer want it?'

'No.'

'What do yer want then?'

'You bin keepin' the wrong company, Just Joe. We don't

want nothin', do we, Bob?' The other boy didn't say anything. 'We just want to see how our new friend's gettin' on.'

Joe looked from one boy to the other. They wanted something. That was certain. But if it wasn't money, then what was it?

'Where d'you get the win then, Joey?'

Bob's voice was very casual. It was the first time he'd spoken. He put one arm around Joe's shoulder and walked him down towards the square.

'The one with the tower. Over the other side.'

'Find out the cook's name, did yer?'

'Briggs.'

'You done well, boy.'

Joe went on hurriedly: 'Family's called Harvey. Footman named Bates.' Then he stopped, eyeing the two bigger boys, realizing he was talking too much. 'Why d'you want to know?'

Bob didn't answer straight away. He still had his arm around Joe's shoulder and he was squeezing just a little now, the way he had outside Addison's. Suddenly he spun round in a quick movement and he had Joe's broom in his hands.

Joe lunged forward. If the boy was going to pull it apart the way he had the other one, it would be another tuppence ha'penny gone and he was losing money faster than he was earning. But Bob stepped back, holding the broom up high out of Joe's reach.

'You want your tuppenny ha'penny broom back, Joey?' Joe made another grab. Bob was too quick for him. 'You want your tuppenny ha'penny broom and a pitch like me and Charlie got?' The dog was giving his shrill little bark now. Bob lashed out with Joe's broom and Boy scrambled away, slipping on the pavement that was wet from overnight rain. Bob laughed. 'You ought to teach that mutt of yours to do tricks, Joey. Toffs'll pay money for that kind of stuff. 'Specially if they got a ladybird with 'em.'

Charlie caught Joe from behind as he made another lunge for the broom. 'Now, don't get yerself excited, boy.' His voice was soft and soothing. 'Bobby and me wants to help you out. Get you one of those nice new brooms like we got. Get you set up in a better pitch up west maybe – outside one of them big stores.'

Joe stood still now. He couldn't fight these two. The only way he was going to get his broom back was to find out what they wanted. Charlie dropped his voice still lower, bending until he was almost whispering in Joe's ear. The joking tone he usually used was gone. Suddenly he was deadly serious.

'You got to know some folk already on the square, ain'tcha, Joe?'

'Some.'

'Know a few of the houses, eh?'

'A few.'

'That's right. Now all you got to do is keep yer eyes open. Find out when people come and go. Which doors is open and which is locked. Where they keep the key safe inside and where they keep it under the mat. Hear anythin' knock, Joe?'

So that was it! Joe knew what the boy was driving at, but he played dumb, waiting for Charlie to come right out with it.

Charlie didn't seem to be in a hurry. His voice was conversational now, as if he were changing the subject altogether. 'You ever wonder why the street changes so quick up on the corner there?'

'It's new, ain't it.' Joe's eyes flickered between the two boys. He edged sideways, trying to get within grabbing distance of his broom.

'Yeah, it's new, Just Joe. What d'you reckon was here before?'

'Fields and stuff. I don't know.'

'Weren't no fields, Joey.' It was Bob who spoke. His voice was quiet like Charlie's, and to Joe's surprise he simply put the broom back into his hands unharmed. 'Used to be market gardens all over here. And houses. My whole family lived in one stinkin' little room right about where we're standin' now. Flattened the whole lot, they did.'

''S right, Joe. My old man worked six months of the year plantin' cabbages and such. Know what he does now?' Charlie paused for effect, but he wasn't expecting Joe to speak. 'Nothin'.'

'So we're plannin' to even things up a little, ain't we, Charlie?' Bob had his arm around Joe again. 'You never heard of Robin Hood, Joey?'

'Robbin' what?'

Bob and Charlie laughed. They were almost directly outside the Tower House now. The housemaid scrubbing the front doorstep glanced up for a moment, but when she saw the three boys she turned straight back to her work.

'Robin Hood,' said Charlie. 'He took from the rich and gave to the poor, didn't he? Well we're the poor, and so are you, Just Joe.'

'Ain't wrong to take money from rich folk, Joey,' insisted Bob. 'Robbin' your own kind ain't no good, but the rich – well, that's fair game, ain't it?'

'I ain't comin' in on no robbery.'

'Yes, you are, Joey,' said Bob softly. 'You just don't know it yet.'

'We want a house that's ripe for pickin',' Charlie went on. 'Could be your Tower House here.' He let his eyes wander for a moment up the tall frontage of the house. 'Could be another. You're gonna scope the place out for us. Understand?'

Joe looked sharply from one boy to the other. Bob still had him by the shoulder and the other boy loomed very close, but surely they wouldn't start anything here on the square.

'I ain't comin' in on no robbery,' he repeated.

Joe's voice was just a little louder this time and he half turned towards the house. The two bigger boys looked around anxiously, but the maid on the doorstep had gone.

'You think these toffs is your friends, Joey,' Charlie hissed. 'They ain't. They'll give you a win one day and a kick in the face the next. I know, all right? You stick with yer own kind.'

He stepped quickly in front of Joe, so that for a moment he was directly between him and the houses, then he drove his right fist into the pit of the smaller boy's stomach. Joe doubled up without a sound, gasping for air. The dog began barking again, making quick charges at the two bigger boys' ankles.

'Don't you want to make a little chink, Joey?' Bob pressed his face up close, as Joe clutched at his stomach, struggling for breath. 'Got a bag of money hidden away, have yer?' The boy's voice was heavy with sarcasm.

Joe curled into a ball, making himself a smaller target on the ground. A bag of money! What a joke! He had had a bag of money, or stuff that was worth money anyhow. As the two boys towered over him the image of the grey cloth bag was so clear he could have touched it. With the gear inside that bag he wouldn't be here now, about to get a kicking from a couple of footpads. He let his mind wander back to the dreams he'd had of a new way of life, and he waited for the boots to land. But they never came.

'Hey, what d'you two little muck-snipes think you're up to?' It was Mrs Briggs. 'Clear off out of it, the pair of yer!'

Bright red in the face except where flour clung in patches, the woman was standing at the front gate of the Tower House, waving a rolling pin above her head. Bob and Charlie laughed so hard they both took a step away from Joe. The boy slid backwards on the ground, feeling with his hand for the broom. Lomesbury wasn't a good place to make a run for it – the new streets were too wide – but it looked like his best bet.

Then Bob and Charlie stopped laughing. The tall figure of Bates, the footman, was standing behind Mrs Briggs. He wasn't wearing his wig, and Joe had time to notice the man wasn't bald after all. Bates didn't say anything. He didn't have to. The heavy riding whip in his right hand spoke for him.

Mrs Briggs called out again. 'I said, clear off! Go on, the pair of yer.'

Bob and Charlie turned as one and stalked off down the street, hands thrust deep in pockets. The footman took a step towards Joe and the boy backed away involuntarily. But Mrs Briggs put out an arm to stop the man. 'It's all right, Mr Bates. I know this one.'

'Oh yes?' The man took a long look at Joe, his mouth curled into a sneer. 'And I reckon I know his type.'

'He's been runnin' errands for me, haven't you, Joe?'

'Yes, Mrs Briggs.' Joe scrambled to his feet.

'And I got one for you this mornin' and all. Only you'd better stay out of the way of them two ruffians. You need to get yourself a proper guard dog, boy. Not that scrawny little tyke.'

Joe laughed soundlessly, his face screwing up until his eyes disappeared. 'What d'yer want doin', missus? Me and Boy'll run it for yer.'

'Same as last time. Few extra provisions for Lower Road tonight.'

'Soup kitchen again? What's he bother with them cadgers for, your Mr Harvey?'

'That ain't no concern of yours, boy,' put in Bates. But Mrs Briggs seemed happy to talk about her master's good works.

'He's a great worker for charity, is Mr Harvey,' she said proudly. 'There's three Harvey's Asylums now in the East End and another over near Holborn. He even goes and serves out the food himself sometimes.'

'Gentry might do better spending more time on their own

sons,' said Bates, addressing the cook as if Joe weren't there. ''Stead of wasting it on charity boys.'

'You're right, Mr Bates,' Joe piped up, Bob's advice ringing in his ear – *make 'em like you* . . . Maybe it wasn't too late to make even the stone-faced Bates like him. 'Now me, I ain't no charity boy. I got me a trade, ain't I?'

He picked up the broom. Mrs Briggs smiled, but Joe saw the footman's lip curl. It was a waste of time. Bates was never going to like him and deep inside Joe didn't care. He could still see the man standing over a boy half his size, grinding his face in the dirt. The picture stirred something close to anger in Joe.

'I'll just fetch my list,' said Mrs Briggs, going back through the side gate. 'There's not much,' she called over her shoulder. 'You can carry it down to Lower Road, if you like.'

Joe watched Mrs Briggs go. He looked at the footman, Bates, still watching him, his whip by his side, from just inside the pointed iron railings of the house. This man was a servant who waited at table on the family – including the son. How could he have been treating the boy the way he did? It made no sense.

Joe looked away awkwardly and began to make a show of sweeping the street. There was fresh horse dung to clear. Maybe he could do a deal with the old man who worked in the park in the middle of the square. He might pay for a regular supply of manure. But there was a penny coming from Mrs Briggs for sure – could be more if he took the stuff to the soup kitchen himself. As he swept, he could feel Bates's eyes on him. Joe kept his gaze on the road.

'Here you are then, Joe.'

As Joe crossed the road for the list, he saw Bates lean down and say something in the woman's ear. The expression on her face changed. She looked uneasily at Joe.

'P'raps you'd better just hand over the order, Joe,' she said. 'Let the delivery boy take it to Lower Road. Don't want to put him out of a job, do we?' she finished with a forced laugh.

'Fair enough.'

Joe started down the street. He knew what it meant. Bates had said something to her – something that meant she wasn't going to trust him. He'd taken maybe ten steps when he heard the footman's deep, sneering voice quite clearly in the morning air.

'Don't ever trust that street trash with anything, Mrs Briggs. I know the type. They'll rob the nose off your face.'

Joe looked back into the man's eyes. They were filled with contempt. Then he hurried away on his errand.

Chapter 6

A FACE AT THE WINDOW

From high in the tower Alec watched the boy leave quickly with the dog at his heel. The animal's shrill bark had drawn him to the window and he'd witnessed the whole scene – the three boys, Mrs Briggs and Bates – without really understanding what was going on. He'd seen the smallest boy fall to the ground clutching his stomach. He'd felt his own fists clench, wanting to be part of the fight. He saw himself on the ground with the small boy; he saw himself standing with the other two. He wasn't sure which picture he preferred.

The other two boys had gone, and now this one was going, hurrying off with the dog scampering behind him. With his broom hooked over his shoulder he looked like he was heading off on some adventure. Alec wished he was going with him. The sweeper boy was free to come and go as he pleased, whereas he was stuck up here in what his father insisted on calling the Reformatory for four hours every day for the rest of the week!

But it wasn't this that made Alec clench his teeth tight

61

until the muscles of his jaw ached. It was the thought of 'dear little Flicky' climbing onto his father's knee as he was being marched out of the room. 'I can devote no more time to this, Alexander.' That's what 'Mister Harvey' had said. 'There are many other matters that require my attention this morning.' Yes, thought Alec bitterly, like rearranging the poison dolly's little pink bow!

He dug hard into the window frame, using the broken tip of a knife, and a tiny splinter of wood landed on the floor at his feet. The room was full of locked trunks and packing cases tied with string – all the stuff the family had never unpacked when they moved into the new house a year ago. He'd found the broken knife one day under a box.

He began digging into the next layer of wood.

It had started as a kind of revenge: if there was no way of getting back at his father then at least he could do some damage to this hateful room. But then gradually his attention had focused on the heavy brass lock that made it impossible to open the Reformatory's single window. Now he was working his way into the timber on one side of the lock. How long until he could chisel it out altogether? Another month of mornings up here? Another year? One day he'd have that window open and then . . .

Alec saw himself out on the window ledge. He felt the cold March wind blowing in his face, trying to send him toppling three storeys down to the street below. He felt the roughness of the bricks on his hands as he clambered inch by inch up towards the roof. He felt his fingers slip, the brickwork tearing at his fingernails; his feet couldn't find a hold; he fell over and over, down and down; he landed face up, impaled through the back on the sharp, black railings at the front of the house. He was squirming on the spikes, blood oozing from fatal wounds. His mother, roused from her darkened room for once, was crying on the front step. His father was straining desperately to lift his dying son's body . . .

The blade slipped as he gouged at the woodwork, sending a splinter into his thumb. Alec threw the knife away and slumped down on the floor, sucking at his bleeding hand.

He'd built the packing cases into walls so that the centre of the room was like a tiny cell on its own. For a while he just sat there, face screwed up in a scowl, arms clamped rigidly around his body. Then he picked up the book his father had given him and looked at the title page – *Lectures to Children by John Todd*.

He threw the book across the room and burrowed in amongst the packing cases where he hid his stack of illustrated penny papers. 'Penny dreadfuls', Johnny Johnson called them. He'd caught Alec with one and taken it to Mr Harvey. Alec had denied furiously that he had any more of 'this accursed, cheap literature' and got two hours in the Reformatory for his trouble. In fact he had dozens of them hidden up here: *The Skeleton Band*, *Tyburn Dick*, *Jack Sheppard*. There was a street hawker who sold them on Upper Road sometimes, just down past Addison's.

Alec pulled the latest instalment of *The Boy Burglar* out of his pile. The Boy Burglar drank 'dog's nose' in a public house with mobsmen twice his age. Then he swiped a bagful of precious gems and leaped from a rooftop to escape the crushers. Alec disappeared into the story and for a while he forgot he was in trouble with his father again and that later that evening at dinner there would be twenty questions on *Lectures to Children*, none of which he would be able to answer.

He finished the story and went back through the pictures again, examining every tiny detail of the Boy Burglar's latest escapade. One of the crushers had foiled his daring burglary, and the Boy Burglar had taken a terrible revenge on the man, tying him to an anchor with his own handcuffs and then watching as the river rose and the man was drowned. The last picture in the paper showed just the dark tip of the policeman's hat above the moonlit water as the Boy Burglar laughed in his hiding place on the dock. Alec could see himself crouching there behind the barrels as first Johnny Johnson and then his father sank beneath the dirty waters of the River Thames.

He stood up and looked out of the window again. The road was empty. Out on the newly-laid gravel paths of the park in the middle of the square, Felicity in her pink bonnet was playing with a shuttlecock under Alice's watchful eye. Alec saw the pink bonnet disappear slowly under the river water too.

The sound of a key turning softly in the lock interrupted his fantasy and a face appeared round the corner of the door.

'Got another of those magazines you like, Master Alexander.' It was Bates. 'Thought you might be hungry too. Sneaked a piece of pie out of the kitchen.'

Alec took the penny dreadful – another *Starlight Sal* – and bit into the pie with a muffled 'thanks'. Bates stood uneasily in the doorway, glancing behind him down the stairs.

'I'd let you out, Master Alexander,' he said, 'only your father—'

'What's dog's nose?' interrupted Alec, his mouth full of pie.

'I don't know.'

'Yes you do. I heard someone ordering it at Addison's.'

Bates closed the door hurriedly. 'You got to stop going to that place, Master Alexander. One night I'm not going to be there, and then your father—'

'Oh, my father's a bowl of pot scum!' It was one of Starlight Sal's favourite expressions.

Bates sighed heavily and sat down on one of the boxes to watch Alec eat. The footman had been a friend ever since Alec could remember. He'd given rides on his shoulders up and down the back stairs in the old house in the City and he'd been getting Alec out of scrapes since the boy was ten. Alec could talk when Bates was there, just as he could talk rings around Johnny Johnson when he had him on his own. It was only when his father was in front of him that he couldn't seem to come out with anything except some stupid lie that just got him into trouble.

'You're a coward, Bates,' said Alec, still chewing. 'All you think about is your job.'

'Working man that doesn't think about his job soon finds he hasn't got one,' pronounced the footman solemnly. 'Anyway,' he went on, 'I'm thinking more about you than my job. You and the family. Young gentleman like you shouldn't be drinking gin. Gin's only good for street trash.'

'I've only got a drink out of them once,' said Alec angrily. 'Wretched barmaid won't serve me.'

'Well you acted like you was drunk as a lord night before last.'

'I know.' Alec laughed. 'I don't know why. I watch them all slurping down their Cream of the Valley and Real Knock-me-down and I feel as if I'm full of the stuff myself.'

'Gin's a curse, Master Alexander. I seen enough of it when I was a nipper. Blue ruin, my old man used to call it.'

'I can't imagine you having a father, Bates. Did he hate you like Mister Harvey hates me?' Alec had a way of hissing out his father's name between clenched teeth.

'He was a hard man, my father,' said Bates grimly. 'Quick to use his fists and his belt. And I was the better for it. Boys need a strong hand if they're to grow into strong men. And your father doesn't hate you. Might not seem it to you, but he's got your best interests at heart.'

'Is that right?' said Alec shortly. 'So it's in my "best interests" to be locked up in here for the next week, is it?'

'If you done wrong, yes,' said Bates simply. 'Stay away from Addison's and you won't have to come back covered in muck to hide the smell and you won't be in trouble.'

Alec laughed. 'That's the only good part. The punishment's for getting my nice suit dirty. What do you think Mister Harvey would do if he knew where I'd really been, Bates?'

The footman got up quickly, glancing nervously at the door. He obviously didn't want to think about what might happen if Mr Harvey ever found out Alec had been inside Addison's

Superior Tavern and Supper Club and that he, Bates, had known about it all along. He picked up Alec's empty plate and gathered some crumbs that had fallen on the floor. Hiding the evidence, thought Alec with another laugh – just like Tyburn Dick.

'Stay out of trouble, Master Alec. For my sake?' The tall footman was almost pleading. Then he was gone.

Alec heard the key turn back in the lock. He was alone again. He settled down with his new penny dreadful. Starlight Sal was drinking brandy and planning a 'hoist' with The Panther in her boudoir in a thieves' den in Pound's Field. But even this tale of London's legendary criminal heartland failed to hold him, and Alec was drifting off to sleep when the sound of a horse in the street drew him to the window again.

The boy was back, holding the door of a hansom as Mr Harvey came briskly out of the front gate. Finally he was leaving for work, an hour after he'd said he had to! As his father climbed into the cab, Alec saw him reach out and press something into the boy's hand. It had to be money.

He thought about how he had to go to the study every Saturday morning to receive his allowance for the week and how what he got depended on the report from Johnny Johnson and what his father thought of his 'conduct' for the week. How much easier to hold a cab door and have a coin pressed into your hand!

As the cab pulled away, Joe checked the coin in his hand. A silver sixpence! He was making a living out of just one house.

All he had to do was keep out of Bob and Charlie's way and he was on velvet. He tossed the coin in the air, unable to believe his luck, and right up at the top window in the Tower House a movement caught his eye.

Someone was looking straight down at him. It was hard to be sure, but it looked like the boy he'd seen at dinner with the family. That must be his room high up in the tower. He slept up there in a soft bed and there'd be boxes full of – what? Joe wasn't sure what a boy like that would fill boxes with. All he could imagine was silver spoons and glass scent bottles: the kind of stuff he'd dreamed of finding in the sewers in his days as a tosher. He raised his hand in a tentative greeting. A hand appeared briefly alongside the face in the window. Then the face was gone.

Chapter 7
STRONG ARMS

It wasn't just the walls and the silver and copperware that shone in the candlelight; the faces of the people seemed to glow as well. Joe shifted position on the window ledge for a better view, and for a moment the curtain blocked out the dining room and his own reflection floated like a pinched and grimy ghost behind the glass. He took a look over his shoulder.

There were more people coming and going in the street this evening – some kind of party on the other side of the square with carriages and loud laughter and music. But they were all too interested in their own concerns to bother with the figure crouched outside the Harveys' window.

Joe had been there every night for a week now. Some nights the curtains were pulled tight shut; some nights, like tonight, he could see everything. But either way he hadn't been spotted yet, either from inside or outside the house. He'd worked out what time the crushers made their evening patrol around Lomesbury Square. They were as regular as the Harveys at their dinner – first patrol when the soup came in, second patrol a couple of minutes after the little girl appeared. The rest of the time Joe had come to think of himself as invisible.

Bates was moving slowly behind the boy's chair – Joe had argued it out every way with himself, but tonight he made up his mind he'd been wrong about these two: it must have been someone else he'd seen in the street outside Addison's. The footman poured a cloudy liquid into the boy's glass, and Joe twisted awkwardly on the ledge to copy the boy, reaching out a hand for an imaginary drink and lifting it slowly to his lips. The boy gulped deeply. Joe swallowed with him.

Mr Harvey's face stiffened and his nostrils flared as if a bad smell had suddenly filled the room. Even with his face pressed as close to the glass as he dared, Joe still hadn't been able to hear anything from inside because no one ever raised their voice. But Mr Harvey must have said something, because when the boy took another drink he did it quite differently, sipping delicately at the glass. Joe did the same.

Bates was at Mr Harvey's shoulder now, pouring wine. The ruby-red liquid cascaded into the glass, catching the light, and a single drop splashed onto the white tablecloth. Mr Harvey looked up sharply at the footman and the boy raised his hand to his mouth, half concealing a smirk. Joe copied him. Mr Harvey's head swivelled towards his son and the smile disappeared abruptly. So did Joe's.

It was like a game they played each night around that long table with its starched white tablecloth, but Joe couldn't fathom the rules. He could imitate the boy, or try to, but he couldn't understand what lay behind it. Mr Harvey looked angry with his son sometimes – that face as if he'd smelled something bad – but Joe couldn't work out what the boy was doing wrong. Wasn't he supposed to smile? Why did it matter how he drank?

And there were other things about the glowing picture that puzzled Joe, things he hadn't noticed at first. At the far end of the table Mrs Harvey sat tonight – as every night – almost completely motionless, the painting of the man on the horse looming over her shoulder. Her long fingers rested on the tablecloth as if she were about to play the piano. Her eyes looked placidly at the scene in front of her. Her lips moved occasionally, as if forming words. But if she was speaking Joe couldn't hear her and nor apparently could anyone inside the room, because they paid her not the slightest attention. Also, she never ate – anything. One after another, dishes that made saliva dribble from the corner of Joe's mouth were placed in front of her, and one after another Bates cleared them away untouched. Why?

Mr Harvey seemed to gesture sometimes in her direction, and at first Joe had thought he was saying something about his wife. But after a while he realized the man was pointing past the silent woman at the picture on the wall behind her and talking about that.

He was speaking to the man next to him now. Joe had decided he couldn't be a member of the family but he hadn't summoned the nerve to ask Mrs Briggs who he was, so he called him 'the bendy man', because while he listened to Mr Harvey the man's back bent and swayed as if the words were having some kind of physical effect on him. Once again Joe thought he caught a trace of a smile hiding in the corners of the boy's mouth. There was laughter inside him, but it seemed he was meant to hide it.

Sometimes Mr Harvey would simply shoot a glance to his right without speaking and the boy would try abruptly to adjust what he was doing – pick up a different fork, spoon the soup more slowly, remove his hands from the white tablecloth and fold them in his lap. And always Joe tried to do the same, perched on his windowsill in the darkness.

He found himself wondering if all families were like this – full of silences and angry glances and hidden meanings. Joe had never known his father, and his mother and brothers had died of tramp fever too long ago for him to remember much about them. The old monster he'd called Mother was the nearest thing he'd ever had to a family. But he'd got away from her and Pound's Field and he was better off – better off on his own. Wasn't he?

At the end of the meal a little girl in a shimmering blue dress, looking like a miniature copy of her mother, was led into the room by a nursemaid in uniform. Joe had seen the girl playing in the square, and he'd seen the nursemaid slipping off to talk to a man once or twice.

The girl always appeared at the same time, but Mrs Harvey's face didn't alter. Joe would have guessed she was blind if it hadn't been for the scream when she saw him that first day in the square. But the sight of the little girl seemed to transform Mr Harvey into a different person. His solemn face broke into a smile – a smile Joe had never seen at any other time. He fed the girl from his own bowl with a tiny silver spoon, and Joe saw the boy's face go rigid. He knew what that look meant all right. The boy hated her.

It was Joe's signal to leave. The girl and the sugary-looking pudding meant the foot patrol would be by in the next five minutes. He jumped noiselessly down from the window ledge, eased the gate open and hurried across the road to recover his broom from behind the park railings. The police weren't waiting for him. But someone else was.

Two pairs of strong arms lifted him bodily and a forearm was clamped across his face before he could cry out. The grip was so tight around his mouth Joe couldn't breathe and he was gasping for air as he felt himself hurled down onto the roadway. At once a knee was in the small of his back and his face was pressed down flat into a pile of horse manure he'd swept himself that afternoon. He was choking on it, breathing it in, desperately fighting for air. Then he heard Charlie's voice.

'Just Joe got a little caper of his own planned, has 'e?'

Joe struggled to answer, but he couldn't catch a breath, let alone speak.

'We seen yer, Joey.' Bob was there too – of course he was. 'We seen yer spyin' through the winder.'

'What they got then, Joe?' demanded Charlie. 'Plate? Candlesticks? How you aimin' to get in?'

Again Joe struggled to make a sound.

'I can't hear yer, boy.'

Charlie lifted Joe's face out of the pile of horse dung for a moment and the boy took a long, rasping breath, then another, then he was back face-down in the filth.

'Now, you got one chance to say somethin' we want to hear, Joe. One chance. And then Bobby and me is goin' to take this pile of horse muck and shove it down your throat. You follow me?'

Joe managed to nod his head.

'Right. One chance, mind.'

Charlie let him up long enough to catch his breath.

'What's their name?' demanded Bob.

'Harvey,' gasped Joe, spitting filth out of his mouth.

'Business?'

'Don't know—' Joe felt his head being pushed back towards the road. 'Office in the City somewhere,' he said desperately. 'Bankin' maybe. I don't know.'

'They must be loaded,' said Charlie, his voice heavy with greed. 'This is gonna be beautiful!'

'You got a dark lantern, ain'tcha?' said Bob sharply. 'Someone inside.'

Joe knew what he meant, but he pretended not to. He'd got his breath back and his brain was functioning properly again. Bob and Charlie wanted something out of him: that meant they wouldn't hurt him badly unless they were sure they couldn't get it. All he had to do was spin it out until the crushers came by, and they were due any minute.

'It's that fat woman, ain't it?' insisted Bob. 'I seen 'er talkin' to yer.'

'She's just the cook. I ain't got nothin' planned. Honest—'

Before he could finish, Charlie had his face pressed down

into the muck again. Joe didn't struggle. If he just went limp, Charlie didn't press so hard and he could sneak a breath now out of the corner of his mouth. Couldn't be more than a couple of minutes more. Then Bob spoke again.

'This is takin' too long, Charlie. Crushers could be by any time.'

Joe's heart sank. The pair knew about the police patrol. Were they going to take him somewhere else?

'I got a better idea,' Bob went on. 'Hold him up, Charlie.'

Boy had been jumping around yapping furiously, trying to nip in and sink his teeth into the burly lad who held Joe down, but Bob's boot had kept him at a distance. Now, as Charlie lifted his face out of the horse dung again, Joe could see that Bob had got hold of the dog. The animal fought desperately in the boy's grasp as Bob held him upright by the scruff of the neck with his left hand. With his right hand he had a length of wire twisted around the animal's throat.

'I'm gonna count to three, Joe.' Bob already had the wire so tight that Boy could no longer bark. His tongue was lolling out of his mouth. His eyes were wide and bloodshot – terrified. 'One –'

'Wait!' Joe struggled frantically in Charlie's grasp.

'– two –'

'Leave him be!'

'Last chance, Joe.'

'All right.'

'I can't hear yer.'

'All right! Let him go!'

Bob slackened the wire around the dog's neck just a little, but he didn't let him go.

'Talk fast, Just Joe,' muttered Charlie, pulling the boy upright and backing him against the park railings. 'What's the plan?'

'It's the cook,' stammered Joe. 'She trusts me, see?'

'Does she now?' Charlie's voice was gloating.

'Yeah,' Joe went on quickly. 'I know where she hides the key to the side door, don't I? It's a stroll-in.'

'A stroll-in!' repeated Bob delightedly.

'When?' demanded Charlie.

'The family's my mark,' said Joe warily. 'Why should I let you in?'

'Because we're friends, Joe,' purred Charlie.

'And because if you don't,' added Bob, 'I'm going to throttle this nasty little mongrel, cut him up and feed you the pieces.'

'All right,' said Joe. 'Tonight then. I'll meet yer.'

'Where?' demanded Charlie.

'Here. Outside the house. Midnight.'

'Right. That's better.'

Finally Charlie let go of the boy, and at the same moment Bob flung the dog from him. Joe caught the animal awkwardly in his arms, holding him tight against his side, feeling the dog shiver uncontrollably in his grip.

'Don't be late now, Joe,' said Charlie. 'Remember: there'll be no warnings next time.' And with that they were gone.

Joe watched them leave. Then he started back towards the Harveys' house. There was a lot to arrange before midnight.

Chapter 8

BREAK-IN

A steady drizzle was falling as the church clock began to strike twelve. In the daylight Joe had hardly noticed the chimes from the new church, but in the stillness of midnight they sounded unnaturally loud. Cracks of light still showed from the upper windows of some of the houses on Lomesbury Square, but in the Tower House all was dark.

Quick footsteps were approaching and Joe ducked lower where the bare branches of a line of young trees touched the park railings. Boy whined softly. Joe put his hand on the dog's muzzle to quiet him. It was Bob and Charlie.

'You're late.' Joe's whisper was clipped, hard and businesslike. Tonight he was in charge and he wanted to make sure the other two got the idea right away. 'You two are goin' to foul this caper up, ain'tcha?'

'No we ain't,' said Charlie.

'We got held up,' added Bob.

'Call yourself cracksmen. I heard you kickin' up a breeze halfway down the street.'

Bob and Charlie crouched down close to Joe. They were both carrying large canvas sacks.

'That mutt of yours is more likely to blow the gab than I am,' muttered Charlie.

Joe ignored this. 'You got them dirty great sacks,' he snapped. 'Where you plannin' to fence the swag then?' There was no answer. 'You ain't even thought about it, have yer?'

'Time enough when we've done the job, ain't there?' said Bob weakly.

'Coupla green boys, you are. But luckily for you I happen to know just the right person?'

'Oh yeah?' Charlie sounded sceptical. 'Who's that then?'

'Mother,' said Joe shortly.

There was an awe-struck silence.

'What, down by the docks?' gasped Bob finally. 'Pound's Field Mother?'

Joe looked away to hide a smile. The name had worked its magic. They were three miles or more from Mother's home ground, but even this far out everyone had heard of the woman who ran the part of east London known as Pound's Field.

'You never said you knew her,' said Charlie.

'No. Well I know how to hold my gas, don't I? Now, you hold yours. And get your boots off.'

'What?'

'Get your boots off. It's quieter.'

The two boys looked at each other.

'We're gonna do this my way, or we're not gonna do it at all,' said Joe levelly.

Bob and Charlie began to remove their shoes. Joe smiled tightly in the darkness. They had accepted him as leader. The dog let out another tiny whine.

'Don't worry none about him,' hissed Joe. 'He knows what to do. Don'tcha, Boy?' The dog snuffled excitedly and flattened himself against the pavement, but he made no other sound. 'Come on. Let's do it. 'Fore you two lose yer nerve. Wait there, Boy.'

Joe led the way, cutting straight across the road and slipping through the front gate. Bob and Charlie followed close behind, shoes hanging round their necks by the laces. The dog stayed by the fence as Joe had told him. The three boys edged down the path at the side of the house. A dozen brick steps down and they were at the side door – the servants' entrance to the house. Joe slipped his hand under the doormat. Sure enough the key was there. He fitted it silently into the door and the key turned easily in the new lock.

Joe made a signal for the other two boys to follow, pushed open the door and edged into the darkened passageway. He'd expected a lamp or maybe even a gas jet burning, but the place was in total darkness. He put a hand out in front and a hand behind to check Bob and Charlie were there, and the three boys stood still, waiting for their eyes to adjust to the blackness. It seemed to take for ever. Joe could hear the quick, nervous breathing of the other two boys. Charlie moved to close the door behind them, but Joe put out a hand to stop him. He wanted the side door of the house open.

The basement passage was still black ahead, but the polished floor at his feet gleamed faintly now in the darkness. Joe felt his way forwards, feet silent on the bare wooden boards. With shoes on they would have been certain to make a noise. On the right the door to the kitchen was open and a glow of light showed where the fire burned low. Mrs Briggs probably kept it going all night. They passed a closed door on the left. One or more of the servants could be sleeping down here. They tiptoed past.

Ahead, stairs led upwards. Joe checked quickly on Bob and Charlie, and then led the way again, easing his feet softly onto each step. The other two boys were heavier. A sharp creak seemed deafening in the silence of the darkened house. The three boys froze. No sound came. The house was asleep.

At the top of the stairs Joe wrapped his hand carefully around the doorknob and turned it so slowly he could hardly feel it move. The door catch was as silent as the lock in the side door had been. He eased his weight against the heavy wooden door, and Bob and Charlie followed him into a carpeted hallway.

The glass in the upper half of the front door showed grey to their right. There was just enough light to see their own dim reflections in a huge, gilded mirror which ran half the length of the opposite wall. There was an odd smell in the air, a smell Joe recognized from somewhere. He looked back to check the door they'd come through was still open. Then everything seemed to happen at once.

It was the barking that woke Alec. His brain had tried to make

it part of his dream: the sweeper boy's mongrel was yapping at him, trying to stop him from doing something – something bad . . . Then he was awake and the barking was downstairs and it was real. He took the stairs four at a time. The hall should have been in darkness. Instead, a single lantern lit up the scene.

The dog he'd seen in the street, the one he'd just been dreaming about, was tearing around the floor making a furious racket. Over by the door that led down to the basement two scruffy-looking boys had their hands thrown up in front of their eyes against the lantern's glare. Framed in the doorway behind them was the tall figure of Bates. A grim smile of satisfaction was on the footman's face as he held the two boys struggling helplessly in an iron grip.

'Street trash!' Alec heard him sneer.

The dog suddenly stopped barking, trotted across the plush carpet and stood looking up at another figure whose face was in shadow. Alec guessed at once who it was. Why didn't he run? Bates had both hands full. The sweeper boy could make a break for it, maybe up the stairs and out of a window – that's what the Boy Burglar would have done.

But the sweeper boy didn't run. And then it was too late. A hand came out of the darkness and gripped him by the neck, and Alec could see who was holding the lantern. It was Mrs Briggs. The boy twisted in her grip, looking up into the cook's face.

'Joe!' Her voice was shocked, disgusted. 'Joe, what are you doin', boy? All the kindness we've shown you and this is the way you repay the family!'

The boy said nothing. He hung limp in the cook's grasp with the dog still gazing up at him.

'Stupid mutt! Told yer, didn't I?' The taller of the other two boys had spoken.

Bates growled in his ear, 'Less of it, my little baby blagger.' And with a quick movement the footman banged the two boys' heads sharply together. Alec flinched in surprise. 'Now, I've got someone for you three to meet.'

A uniformed policeman came through the door behind Bates, swinging his truncheon loosely in one hand. The two older boys stopped struggling. Alec noticed their bare feet and the boots hanging round their necks: it was a trick the Boy Burglar used.

'Crusher!' one of them moaned. 'Where'd you spring from?'

'I fetched him,' said Mrs Briggs quickly. 'And Mr Bates too. Heard that dog downstairs, I did.'

Alec crouched out of sight by the banisters, wide-eyed, as the policeman produced a pair of brass handcuffs and fastened the two boys' wrists together. All the fight seemed to have gone out of them and they made no attempt to resist. He gave them a sharp shove in the back and they disappeared down the back stairs.

'I'll take this one along myself.' Bates's deep voice had real relish in it as he stepped forward to take Joe out of Mrs Briggs's grasp.

Alec had an impulse to run across the hall and intervene – to grab the boy himself and – and what? Help him escape? Or march him off to his father and claim he had captured him single-handed? He stood up. He was going to do something. But before he could take a step, Mrs Briggs's face broke into a broad grin and her sides began to shake and tears started to stream down her cheeks, and the sweeper boy's face screwed up and his eyes seemed to disappear. Alec realized they were both laughing.

Bates raised a fist and crossed the hall in two strides. 'What you laughing at? I'll teach you to come thieving round here, you little ramper.'

A voice from behind him made Alec jump and stopped Bates in his tracks. 'Leave him, Bates. The boy has done us a service. Is that not right, Mrs Briggs?' It was Alec's father.

'It is, sir.' The cook wiped her eyes with the corner of her apron. 'I'm sorry, Mr Bates. I couldn't say while those two villains was still here. Young Joe told me all about their little scheme earlier tonight and I told Mr Harvey.'

'And I summoned a constable,' continued Mr Harvey, 'but I deemed it best no one else should know. If those two ruffians discovered this boy had – "blown the grab" is the expression, I believe – he might have faced reprisals. Is that not right – er – Joseph?'

'Joe, sir.' Joe ducked his head awkwardly. 'Thank you, sir.' Alec could tell at once the boy hadn't understood what his father had said. Joe's eyes darted quickly round the hallway, resting for an instant on Alec in the shadows of the staircase. But when he spoke it was to Mr Harvey again. 'It's "blow the gab", sir.'

'I beg your pardon?'

' "Blow the gab". Give the game away. You said, "Blow the grab." '

'Did I? Well, whatever the correct terminology, you have been most enterprising and we have apprehended a pair of criminals.'

Alec realized his mouth was hanging open and he closed it abruptly. The feeling that he'd walked straight into the pages of *The Boy Burglar* was so strong he shook his head to check he really was awake. His father seemed to notice him for the first time.

'Since you are here, Alexander,' he said in his slow, emphatic voice, 'you may learn a lesson, I think. This boy – Joseph – has shown intelligence and courage, characteristics which I have great hopes you will one day learn yourself. The moral is, I think, that despite their lack of advantages the lower classes may have a native wit that puts their betters to shame at times.'

Alec shook his head in disbelief. Somehow the whole thing had turned into another lecture. What had he done wrong? He looked across the hall at the boy who called himself Joe. Why couldn't he, Alec Harvey, be held up as an example of intelligence and courage instead of this – 'street trash' Bates would have called him? But there was something in Alec which couldn't let him see Joe like that. The boy stood there, looking down at the floor, shuffling his bare feet, giving the dog a pat on the head. Alec wanted to go and stand beside him, to pat the dog himself, to be a part of the scene, not just looking on.

'I knew about it, Father,' he blurted out suddenly. 'Er – Joe told me all about it.'

Mr Harvey frowned and his eyes narrowed. 'When did this happen, Alexander?'

'It happened – it happened . . .' Alec stammered hopelessly. Why had he said it? Of course he hadn't known what was going on. It was like saying it wasn't his fault he'd got his clothes filthy. Somehow these things just came out of his mouth when his father was looking at him. He was already locked up half the morning. What would it be now?

He could see his father's face harden. He heard the long breath in through the nose that always ended in a heavy sigh of disappointment and another judgement. But before his father could say anything, Joe spoke.

'I seen him at the window. I seen him and I – I give him a signal – like.'

'A signal?' Mr Harvey looked surprised.

'Yeah. You know?' Joe waved his hand vaguely. 'Like that.'

Mr Harvey's frown deepened.

'I see through you, Joseph, but I do not blame you. You are a good-hearted boy, but you make a mistake in trying to cover for another's falsehood.' He rounded on Alec. The boy knew what was coming. He hardly needed to listen. 'As for you, young man, I very much regret to say that your morning sojourn in the Reformatory, which was due to end tomorrow, will now be extended for a further two days. As ever, the punishment is for your own good. It is imperative that you should grow into a man who values truth above all things, but I regret very much that the evening should have ended in this manner. Mrs Briggs' – he turned to the cook – 'make sure

Joseph doesn't leave the house with an empty stomach. Bates, go down to the police station and inform the constable that we wish to prosecute those two malefactors to the uttermost limits of the law. Alexander, go to bed.'

Alec walked slowly back up the stairs to his bedroom. He thought about Joe eating in the kitchen with Briggsy chattering away at him. The dog would probably be getting something to eat too. He would have given anything to be there, to have been part of Joe's plan, pretending to burgle the house and getting the other two boys caught instead. It was brilliant!

Alec felt a stab of envy go through him. Why couldn't he do something clever like that? Why couldn't he show 'intelligence and courage' instead of this—? Again Alec baulked at Bates's 'street trash'. And the boy had corrected his father. That'd been good. *It's 'blow the gab', sir.*

In the silence of his bedroom Alec laughed aloud at the memory. Then he remembered how his mornings in the tower room now stretched on into next week and the laughter died. Still, there was one good thing: he'd have plenty more time to work on that window lock.

Chapter 9

AN INVITATION

Last night's drizzle had turned to steady morning rain. Alec watched a couple of delivery vans come and go. Beyond the railings in the middle of the square old Barlow, the gardener, was already at work, digging in the sodden ground. Better to be out there in the rain than stuck up here for another morning. He was supposed to be writing an essay for Johnny Johnson about his namesake, Alexander the Great. Instead he slumped down amongst the boxes and picked up an old issue of *The Boy Burglar*.

There had been real boy burglars in the house last night – a real adventure. And he had wanted so much to be involved he'd told a stupid lie and now here he was again. Alec threw the paper down, went back to the window and removed the rag that concealed the damage he'd done around the lock.

He began to chisel steadily at the wood. The windowsill outside was wide enough to stand on, but would he be able to reach the roof of the house from there? It was hard to tell without getting the window open. A splinter of wood came away under his broken knife blade.

If he could just get out he would do something; something to make his father praise him the way he'd praised the sweeper boy, Joe. Or better still he would get some kind of revenge. He would break into his father's study and steal something valuable, something he really cared about – his books or his velvet jacket or his silver cigar box – and he would destroy them. Smash them into pieces.

Alec dug hard into the wood and the blade snapped in half. He cursed. Now it would be even harder to work with.

Then he spied Joe down in the road. He was running off with the dog at his heels, gone on some errand probably. The sweeper boy had tried to back him up last night, tried to get him out of trouble. He'd acted like a friend. Alec had had friends at school – friends his father wouldn't let him see now – but he couldn't imagine them trying to get him out of trouble like that or him doing it for them. What had made the boy do it? And why hadn't his father locked him up too for telling a lie? What Joe had said was a lie just the same as what *he*'d said, wasn't it?

The boy was running back around the square now with a four-wheeled growler following. That's what he'd gone to fetch. Someone must be going out in the cab. But from which house? It couldn't be theirs: his father had already left for work, and anyway he always took a hansom. They'd got rid of the family carriage years ago because his mother hardly ever left the house any more. In fact, these days she scarcely came out of her room. The only time Alec saw her was at dinner, when she sat like a ghost, and they all pretended it was normal the way she mumbled to herself and never ate. Like the stink. It wasn't as strong up here but you could still smell it. Builders had been all over the house and they couldn't find where it came from. So now they all just pretended it wasn't there. Why did they do that? And why did he pretend too?

The cab stopped right under Alec's window. It was for their house. His mother was going shopping or visiting like she used to. Perhaps she was better. Perhaps her illness had gone and there would be no more of that medicine she was always taking and she would go back to being the smiling, sweet-scented woman he remembered bending over him at night when he slept in a tiny bed in the nursery in the old house. That was before 'dear little Flicky', the poison dolly, came along and the illness started. Alec craned forward, desperate now to catch a glimpse of his mother.

The front door opened and Joe watched Mrs Harvey emerge, with Bates a pace behind holding an umbrella. The last time Joe had seen her outside the house was his very first day on Lomesbury Square when she'd screamed at the sight of him. She came down the front steps painfully slowly, holding the railing with one gloved hand and shielding her eyes with the other. She looked even paler in the daylight than in the candlelit dining room. At the front gate she stopped, eyeing the dirty pavement doubtfully.

Joe snatched the cap off his head. Then he stuffed it in his pocket and began brushing furiously at the pavement. He soon had that clean enough. But the growler had stopped well away from the kerb, and rain and the tradesmen's wagons had made a mess of even the freshly laid roadways of Lomesbury Square. Joe worked so hard that one of the willow strips that held his broom together began to come apart. At this rate it would be useless by the end of the day and buying another broom would mean no money for food tonight. Lomesbury Square was barely a living, so should he try and take over Bob and Charlie's pitch? As he swept the road, Joe thought about the way Bob had talked to the swells outside Addison's and decided he couldn't do it.

Bates tapped his foot and pursed his lips, but Mrs Harvey waited patiently for Joe to finish. At last the boy was satisfied. He stepped back with what he hoped was his most graceful bow and stole a glance up at the silent lady. Mrs Harvey's hat had a short veil that partly concealed the upper half of her face, but Joe could just see her eyes. They weren't looking at him. In fact, they weren't looking at anything. They stared vacantly into the distance, and what might have been a faint smile played around the corners of her mouth, as if she were thinking of something far, far away.

'Missus.' No response. 'It's as clear as it gets, missus.'

Bates stepped forward. 'All right,' he said in a low voice. 'Don't want you on the monkey around Mrs Harvey.'

'Ain't on the monkey,' Joe came back instantly. 'Ain't never bin no beggar!'

At the sound of his voice, Mrs Harvey turned her head towards the boy. Joe wondered if she was going to scream again. But instead the faint smile became just a little more definite.

'Mr Harvey and I were wondering' – the words emerged in a gentle, far-off voice; Joe had to strain forward to hear what she was saying – 'if you would care to take dinner with us this evening.'

Joe dropped his broom.

'What?'

She began again. 'Mr Harvey and I were wondering . . .'

The gentleman last night had used words Joe didn't understand. Perhaps he'd misunderstood this too. Perhaps he hadn't heard right. Joe looked at Bates. The man's mouth was hanging open. He looked up at the cab driver. His mouth was hanging open as well. Perhaps he had heard right after all.

'Thank you, missus. You mean with Mrs Briggs and—'

Mrs Harvey interrupted placidly, the faint smile still on her lips. 'I mean with us. Shall we say seven o'clock?'

Before Joe could respond, Mrs Harvey stepped out onto the path he'd swept in the road. She had her hand on the door of the cab when she seemed to change her mind. She turned uncertainly to the footman.

'Bates?' The smile was gone and there was a hint of something else in her voice – something like fear.

'Yes, madam.' He was instantly at her side.

'Bates, I believe I may have forgotten to take my' – she paused – 'medicine this morning.'

'No, madam. I saw you measure the drops myself.'

Mrs Harvey looked at him. For the first time her eyes seemed really to come into focus. 'In that case,' she said, pronouncing the words slowly but very distinctly, 'the dose was insufficient. I shall return to my room.'

'Yes, madam.'

And without another word she climbed slowly back up the steps to the house. Joe and the cab driver watched her go.

'Don't stand staring like a pair of windows!' snapped Bates. 'A lady can change her mind, can't she?' He looked quickly at Joe. 'And don't you be taking advantage, street trash. You showed me up last night and I ain't one to forget. Ever!' And he followed his mistress to the front door.

The cab driver cursed quietly. 'High and mighty,' he growled. 'Climb up in the world and then kick the ladder away behind yer. That's his type.' He spat onto the roadway. 'Don't you pay him no heed, boy. Get on now!' The driver set his horse moving.

Joe stood where he was, shaking his head in disbelief. He hadn't heard what the cabbie said and he'd barely registered Bates's words. His mind was in a whirl. He'd got hold of the wrong end of the stick somewhere. Must have. It wasn't possible that this lady had just invited him, the boy everyone in Pound's Field had called Joe Rat, to eat amongst all that polished wood and gleaming silverware. It just wasn't possible.

The rain had stopped falling by noon. Mrs Briggs called Joe into the kitchen and gave him some bread and cheese. She even had some scraps for Boy. The dog hovered outside the door, whining anxiously: he didn't seem to want to follow Joe inside.

In the end Mrs Briggs set a dish down on the step and the animal ate there.

'Yes, up in the dining room. That's right. With the family.' Mrs Briggs smiled down at him as he ate at the kitchen table. 'It's to say thank you for what you done last night. Just like Mr Harvey to do a thing like that.' It was true then. Joe still hadn't quite believed it. He grinned up at her, stuffing another lump of cheese into his already full mouth. Bates was standing in the doorway.

'Another charity case,' he growled. 'You want feeding, boy, get down to the soup kitchen with the rest of the street trash.'

Mrs Briggs tapped the side of her nose and winked at Joe. 'He's got a bug in his breeches about last night.' She looked over at Bates, scarcely able to suppress her laughter. 'Shoulda seen your face, Mr Bates, when the master popped out, "Leave him, Bates. The boy has done us a service."' The cook pulled a long face as she imitated Mr Harvey's solemn tones. Then she burst into laughter.

Bates scowled. But it was Joe he was looking at. Suddenly the boy didn't feel hungry any more. He left the last of the bread and cheese and headed back out into the square. The reality of eating at the Harveys' candle-lit dinner table had finally struck him.

The closest thing to a family meal Joe had ever known was stuffing his belly in Mother's kitchen with the old monster's bodyguards. He thought about the rows of knives and forks on the Harveys' white tablecloth and his heart sank. He thought about the strange, hat-shaped cloths they put on their laps, the way they cut the meat into tiny morsels with their knives, the way nothing ever spilled out of their mouths. He thought about Mr Harvey shooting off dirty looks at his son. But even that wasn't the worst of it. Bates would be serving the food, prowling round the table, looming over him with that face like thunder. He couldn't go through with it. He'd prefer another night with Bob and Charlie. He'd have to go straight back and say he wasn't coming.

No. He couldn't do that either. He looked down at Boy, who had followed him as far as the gate to the Tower House.

'I could just not turn up.'

The dog put his head on one side.

That was no good. He'd never get another tip again. What in the wide world was he going to do?

Chapter 10

JOE AND ALEC

The sky had cleared and Joe was trying to forget the evening ahead by sweeping the pavement along the north side of the square, when the door to the Tower House opened and 'the bendy man' came down the steps carrying a pile of books. Close behind him walked the boy Joe now knew as Alexander.

He was wearing an odd black hat with a tassel, and his face looked grim. Joe swept a path for them across the road to the park gate. The bendy man looked down his nose sideways at Joe, who hurriedly snatched off his cap. Alec seemed to ignore him completely – fed up after last night's telling off, thought Joe – but as he passed, he half turned his head and Joe could have sworn he'd winked at him.

'Mr Johnson, sir.' The boy's voice was excessively polite, but Joe thought he caught just a hint of something else in it. The bendy man stopped in the act of unlocking the park gate. 'Mr Johnson, sir, my father admires this urchin's intelligence, courage and enterprise.' Urchin? Joe had been called a few things in his time but never urchin. 'Do you not feel it would

96

be charitable of us and instructive for him if we were to enter into conversation?'

Mr Johnson looked hard at Alec, then he took a pair of spectacles out of the top pocket of his black frock coat and looked hard at Joe. Joe spat quickly on his hand and brushed it across the top of his head, knowing it wouldn't help. Nothing would flatten out his hair. That was another reason he couldn't sit down in the Harveys' dining room.

Out of the corner of his eye he saw Alec put his hand up to his mouth to hide a smirk, just the way he did at dinner. The boy was laughing at him and he'd called him an urchin and then he'd said something else Joe hadn't understood which had a nasty sound to it too. Joe felt his fists clench instinctively. Then Alec suddenly peered over Mr Johnson's shoulder and pulled a face so exactly like the appraising look the bendy man was giving him that Joe had to cough hard to hide a splutter of laughter. He couldn't make the boy out. Was he laughing at him or trying to make friends?

'You see, Mr Johnson' – Alec was talking again now, manoeuvring the bendy man and Joe towards the park gate – 'my father believes the lower classes have a native wit despite their disadvantages.'

Mr Johnson opened his mouth to say something, but Alexander was still talking. 'In fact, Mr Johnson, the poet John Keats spoke with an accent not unlike this undersized beggar.'

'Ain't no beggar.'

Joe was almost inside the park, a place he'd never imagined getting into, but he wasn't going to let that go.

'I beg your pardon, Master Joseph. You are a crossing sweeper, I believe, which means, Mr Johnson' – Alec rounded on the man – 'that he knows what every horse in London has been fed in the last twenty-four hours.'

'How so, Alexander?' The bendy man, Johnson, looked bewildered by the stream of words coming out of the boy's mouth.

'Horse dung, Mr Johnson. We are talking horse dung!'

'I beg your pardon!'

'I sweep it, see,' put in Joe, catching on. 'I sweep up the horse dung, so I know what they've ate.'

'Quite!' exclaimed Alec. 'He knows what they've ate!'

Again Mr Johnson was about to speak, and from his face it wasn't going to be anything pleasant, but this time they were interrupted by another voice.

'You can't come in 'ere! And keep that scruffy mutt of yours out too, you little muck-snipe!'

It was Barlow, the gardener, who guarded the half-acre in the middle of the square as if it belonged to him instead of the residents of Lomesbury. He came along the gravel path towards Joe, hefting a spade in his hand like a weapon. Then he realized who the boy was with and pulled off his hat hurriedly.

'Beg pardon, Master Harvey, Mr Johnson. Didn't know the boy was with you.'

'He's not,' said Mr Johnson.

'Of course he is,' said Alec. 'Don't be such a snob, Johnny.'

'How dare you! I shall speak to your father at once.'

'But my father considers this to be a boy of intelligence, courage and enterprise, Johnny.'

It was too late. Johnson was gone. Alec watched him march up the steps into the house. His face fell. 'More trouble with Mister Harvey,' he muttered. Then he turned to Joe with a quick laugh. 'Still, Johnny won't find him until this evening. You know my problem, Master Joseph?' he asked.

'Can't keep yer trap shut?' suggested Joe.

Barlow practically exploded at this. 'You watch your lip, you little gutter-snipe!'

Alec laughed. 'He's right, Jeremy Barlow!' Then the laughter was instantly gone. 'At least, that's part of the problem.'

Alec relapsed into a brooding silence, eyeing his home with a bitter twist to his mouth. Joe was struggling to think of something to say, when the other boy suddenly clasped an arm around his shoulder.

'You don't mind my friend walking in the park with me, Jeremy Barlow, do you?'

Joe heard the challenge in the boy's voice, and his eyes swivelled to the gardener. Barlow didn't want him there. Joe knew that. But he also knew the old man wouldn't say so to Mr Harvey's son. The gardener's grip on his heavy spade tightened; his gaze fell on Boy, who was waiting outside the railings, nose straining at the smells which came from the freshly dug earth. 'Not the dog though, Master Alexander. Please.'

'Very well, Jeremy Barlow: not the dog. In any event,' Alec went on, 'he would interfere with my plans. Come on, Master Joseph.'

Alec marched Joe off across the broad, muddy expanse where Barlow had been sowing grass seed, talking at the top of his voice.

'Rumour has it, Master Joseph, that you have been invited to dinner tonight. What have you done to deserve this awful punishment?'

Joe looked down at the deep footprints they were making in Barlow's carefully raked soil. He twisted round in Alec's grip with a gesture of helplessness at the gardener. The old man scowled and walked away.

'Well? Why the prison food?' Alec stopped and faced him impatiently. He was head and shoulders taller than Joe.

'It's 'cos of last night,' said Joe. 'Sorry I didn't – I mean, sorry you—'

'Sorry I failed to keep my trap shut? I don't know what it is, Master Joseph: I'm all right with Johnny and old Jeremy Barlow, but as soon as Mister Harvey has his fishy eye on me I can't seem to—' He broke off angrily. 'I can't seem to do or say anything right.'

Alec strode off towards the other end of the square. Joe hurried after him. 'Why do you call him that?'

'What?'

' "Mister Harvey". Isn't he your real father?'

Alec laughed. 'Oh, he's real enough. Though actually I did used to wonder if I was picked up from the Asylum for Fatherless Boys. You know – adopted?'

'I ain't never had a father,' said Joe.

'You don't know when you are well off. Take my advice, Master Joseph,' said Alec, 'don't ever have one.'

'Nor a mother since I was a young'un.'

'Any sisters?'

'No. I had two brothers. They died.'

'You are a lucky crossing sweeper, Master Joseph,' observed Alec dryly. 'I have a full set.' They reached one of the new gravel paths Barlow had made. Alec stopped, looking back at the Tower House. 'The mother is what they call a permanent invalid.'

'She looked like she was a long way off,' said Joe, remembering the pale lady who had invited him to dinner that morning.

'She has this – medicine she takes. But it seems to make her worse not better.'

For a moment Alec looked a long way off too, just like Mrs Harvey. Then his mouth turned down at the corners and he took the strange-looking flat hat off his head and began pulling the tassels out of it one by one. 'And then there is dear little Flicky—'

'Flicky?'

'Felicity . . .' The name came out in a long hiss. 'The apple of Mister Harvey's eye. I call her the poison dolly because she poisoned my mother.'

'Poisoned her? How d'you mean?'

'By being born.' With a sudden movement Alec sent the hat skimming across the ground at a blackbird. 'Missed! Stupid thing, isn't it, Master Joseph? Johnny makes me wear it for lessons. It's called a mortarboard. But this afternoon I am going to do something very clever with it. And you are going to assist.'

Alec picked up the mortarboard from where it had landed and led Joe on down the path, chattering all the way. He talked about hats and birds and teachers and books. Joe had never heard anyone talk so much. As he tried to follow the stream of words, Joe thought of the silent figure he'd watched through the dining-room window. That boy sat bolt upright at the table, trying to imitate his long-faced father. This boy rabbited on like a street patterer selling snake oil in the market, and then suddenly he looked as if he hated everyone and everything around him. It was like two or three different people. On the other hand he'd never talked to a boy with such a white starched collar or such shiny leather shoes, so perhaps it was just that he didn't understand him properly.

'Can I call you Alexander?' he asked shyly.

'I had rather you did not,' said Alec. He'd stopped and was digging in his pockets for something.

'Oh.' Joe tried to sound as if he didn't care.

'Mister Harvey is a great admirer of Alexander the Great. I am a great disappointment.'

'Why?'

'Because I look unlikely ever to conquer half the known world and all I've managed so far is to get myself expelled from school. So I would prefer it if you called me Alec.'

Joe's face twisted into a quick smile. 'Right.'

At the other end of the garden, tucked away behind a row of young bushes, was a newly-built shed belonging to the gardener. It had a wooden porch running round the front and a long box on the wall with plants inside. Joe liked the straight, square lines of the building and the way the new hinges on the door shone. He would have liked to take a look through the window, but Alec was already busy on the ground a few yards away by a line of young trees. When Joe came up to him, he was down on hands and knees, propping his hat upright with a stick.

'What d'you mean by "expelled from school"?' Joe began.

But Alec ignored the question. 'Observe closely, Master Joseph,' he pronounced. 'We take a piece of quite ordinary bread.'

From his pocket Alec produced one of the rolls the family ate at dinner and Joe's stomach suddenly felt empty. He had never eaten bread that looked like that. Even Mrs Briggs hadn't given him anything as soft and white and fresh. He stifled a cry of horror as Alec began to crumble the roll in his hands, scattering the pieces on the ground.

'What?' Alec glanced up at him.

'Nothing,' said Joe weakly.

'We position the bread beneath the hat, you see.' Alec went back to what he was doing. 'Than we attach to the stick a length of household twine.'

With a dramatic gesture as if he were performing a conjuring trick, Alec pulled a long length of string out of his pocket, tied one end to the stick and then backed away carefully, paying out the string as he went. He crouched down by Barlow's shed.

Joe went up onto the front porch and peered through the window. The shed was big. The bare wooden floor inside was swept clean and tools hung neatly on hooks around the walls. There was a cane chair and a table. Joe turned to Alec.

'What's your room like up in the tower, Alec?'

Alec laughed shortly. 'That's not my room. It's a Reformatory.'

'A what?'

'A place for reforming the wicked.'

'Like a prison, you mean?'

But Alec suddenly stiffened and gestured furiously at Joe. 'Down!'

Joe squatted down next to him and his eyes followed the line of the string. A blackbird had landed under the young trees and was pecking at the soil.

'You after blackbirds? You can't eat 'em.'

'I don't want to "eat 'em".' Alec imitated his voice. 'I want to catch 'em.'

'What for?'

'For fun, Master Joseph. Don't you ever do anything for fun?'

Joe thought about that for a moment. 'How d'you mean?' he asked finally.

'Well, what do you do when you're not working in Lomesbury Square?'

'I'm always workin'. 'Cept when I'm asleep.'

'Well then, this is your chance to have fun,' said Alec. 'Do you want to hold the string?'

'Not really.'

The two boys crouched side by side in the shelter of Barlow's shed. Joe would have taken a look round the back, but he knew Alec would tell him to keep still. After a while he summoned up the courage to say what was on his mind.

'Alec?'

'Shh.'

'You know you don't like bein' called Alexander?'

'Shh.'

'Well, d'you mind not callin' me Joseph? See, only Mother ever called me that.'

'Your mother?'

'Not my real mother,' said Joe hurriedly. 'Her I used to call Mother back in – Pound's Field.'

Joe looked around uneasily. Lying in the old stable loft on Crooked-back Lane, he'd dreamed about Pound's Field, seen himself fleeing through its dark alleys and filthy lanes, but he didn't like speaking the name of the place aloud in daylight.

'Pound's Field?' Alec gasped, forgetting to keep his voice down. A small bird which had been pecking at the loose bread near his hat flew off in alarm. 'That's where all the' – a crowd of images from *Starlight Sal* sprang into his head – 'the mobsmen are and the blaggers. I liked the way you told Mister Harvey last night, Master Joseph – Joe,' he corrected himself at once. ' "It's blow the gab, sir." ' Alec tugged at his forelock and did his best to imitate Joe's voice.

'I don't talk like that,' said Joe.

'Yes you do. It's a real place then?'

'What?'

'Pound's Field.'

'Course it's real,' said Joe, sorry now he'd ever mentioned it.

'Will you take me there, Joe? To meet Mother?' Suddenly Alec's voice was very urgent.

'Take you where?'

'Pound's Field. Let's go there now. Before Johnny comes back. I want – I want—' Alec was suddenly lost for words. What was it he wanted? He wanted everything – he wanted anything – anything outside Lomesbury Square and the life he knew. 'Don't you sometimes just want your whole life to explode?' he demanded finally.

'No,' said Joe simply. 'Anyway, can't never go back round Pound's Field even if I wanted to – which I don't. Left owin' money. The old monster'd have me in the river soon as look at me.'

'It sounds brilliant!'

'The river?'

'The whole thing.'

'You're jokin'!'

The two boys settled down again. After a few minutes another bird landed under the trees. It hopped around for a while, pecking at the ground, but going nowhere near the hat. Then it flew off. Joe turned to look at the other boy.

'Alec?'

'Hello.'

'Can I ask you something?'

'You can!'

'First night I come up this way, I seen a boy. Up by Addison's. He looked like you. Only he was drunk.'

'Drunk?' Alec looked appalled. 'Do you mean intoxicated with strong drink, Master Joe?'

'Yeah. He were bung-eyed and reelin'.'

'And are you suggesting' – Alec turned straight to Joe, his face a picture of outraged innocence – 'that I, Alec Harvey, was "bung-eyed and reeling", as you put it?'

'Well' – Joe was already wishing he hadn't asked – 'it's just there was this man too—'

'A man?'

'He looked like Mr Bates.'

'And what was he doing?'

Joe could hardly bear to go on. 'He was rubbing you in horse muck.'

'Rubbing me in horse muck! Are you mad? What would Bates be doing rubbing me in horse muck? Are you sure you were not bung-eyed and reeling yourself, Master Joe?'

'I must have got it wrong,' said Joe hopelessly. 'Must have bin someone else. No offence meant,' he added desperately.

'And none taken,' said Alec. Then the expression on his face suddenly changed. 'Actually,' he went on, 'what I said is not quite true.'

'You mean it was you?'

'Yes.'

'And Mr Bates?'

'Yes.' Alec hesitated. 'Except—'

'Except what?'

'He makes me do it.'

'Who does?'

'Bates.'

'He makes you?'

'Yes. And then he covers me in horse dung.'

Alec hung his head as if the memory were too painful to bear. Then he sneaked a sideways look at Joe. The other boy's face was a picture of shock and amazement. Alec stifled the urge to burst out laughing. He'd meant to tell Joe the truth. But the truth was too dull a story to tell a boy who came from Pound's Field. Besides, there was something about the look of wide-eyed amazement on the other boy's face that made Alec want to see just how fantastic a lie he could make him swallow.

'But how does he make you, Alec?' demanded Joe. 'And why d'you let him do that to yer? He looks like a nasty bit of work, but can't you – can't you tell Mr Johnson or your father or—?'

'He knows where the body's buried.'

'What body? Are you havin' me on?'

Alec could see at once he'd gone too far. 'I can say no more,' he said dramatically. 'My lips are sealed – with blood,' he added, borrowing a phrase from Starlight Sal.

'But—'

Alec held up his hand. 'Hush! Look!'

A blackbird had hopped right over to the hat. It pecked at the ground. It tilted its head on one side, inspecting the white bread.

'This is it! This is it!' whispered Alec excitedly. He held his breath. So did Joe.

The bird hopped sideways and pecked at the bread. Alec jerked on the string. The two boys leaped up and ran to the trees. The hat was flat on the ground. Alec lifted one corner and peered underneath. Nothing. The bird had been too quick. Alec swore.

'Don't look so shocked. You've heard worse in Pound's Field.'

'That's different.'

'Is it?' Alec rearranged the hat and they both went back to their hiding place. 'Tell me about it.'

'What?'

'Pound's Field.' The way he said the name seemed to give it an air of mystery and excitement.

Joe looked at him. He hadn't told anyone at the flop house in Crooked-back Lane about his time in Pound's Field. It hadn't been safe. But he'd got his tosh thieved off him anyway. So what was the harm in it here? This boy wasn't going to go nosing on him to Mother and it was stupid to think there was bad luck in mentioning the place, as if talking about it could somehow drag him back there.

So, as they crouched and watched the birds come and go, always just avoiding Alec's trap, Joe told stories of his time as a tosher working in the London sewers and giving all he got to the woman he'd called Mother. 'The old monster' – that's what he called her to the boy in the stiff white collar and shiny shoes. At first he felt uneasy and kept trying to change the subject, but Alec always drew him back to the dark lanes and alleys of Pound's Field, which seemed to fascinate him, and in the end

Joe found himself embroidering his stories, trying to make his life sound even more desperate and dangerous than it had been. He told Alec about the time he'd had to hide in a madman's house with a girl from the country and escape down an underground river from a dozen pursuers – really it had been half that number – and Alec's eyes grew wider and wider. He particularly seemed to like the part when Joe had nearly been eaten alive by rats.

'Have you ever read *Tyburn Dick*?' asked Alec when Joe's story came to an end.

'Ain't much for readin'.'

'You mean you can't read?' Joe shook his head. 'Don't learn. Reading is a substitute for doing. You've never been to school either?'

'No.'

They were things Joe wouldn't normally admit, but with this boy he felt different.

'Very wise. School is like prison except you're supposed to enjoy it.'

'What did you mean by "expelled from school", Alec?'

'You asked that already.'

'And you didn't answer.'

'Didn't I?' Alec drew a deep breath. 'That's why I have lessons at home with Johnny. They threw me out. Mister Harvey was "most displeased".'

Alec pulled a long face like his father. Joe laughed.

'How come they threw you out?'

Joe had never been inside a school and had only the

dimmest idea of what went on in one. He pictured Alec landing on a pavement somewhere and someone throwing his flat hat after him like the night outside Addison's. But had that been Alec and Bates or not? First this boy said one thing, then he said another. You never knew when he was serious and when he wasn't.

'I stole the headmaster's cat.'

Joe let out a short laugh. This had to be a joke. Then he looked at the boy's face. It was deadly serious.

'I never liked the little brute,' Alec went on quietly. 'It scratched me on the hand once. So I picked it up one day and shut it in a cupboard right up in the top of the school where no one ever went.'

'What happened to it?'

'It died.' Alec's voice was flat and matter-of-fact. 'I opened the cupboard three days later and it was dead. Only then one of my so-called friends blew the gab and here I am.' He finished with a wave of the hand.

There was a silence. Alec stared intently at his trap as if that was all he cared about in the world, and Joe watched him. He liked talking to this boy with his shiny shoes and his stream of clever words. But he didn't like his story about the cat. It had been an accident. Alec hadn't meant the cat to die. Only he didn't seem bothered that it had died. Perhaps it was time to forget about Alexander Harvey and get back to his own world on the street with his dog and his tuppenny ha'penny broom.

Joe was already on his feet when it suddenly came back to him that he was supposed to be sitting at dinner with this boy later that evening. He'd been worrying about nothing else since morning, but here in the park he'd forgotten all about the candlelit dining room. Now here he was, standing next to the one person who could help him.

'Alec?'

'What?' The other boy started. When he turned, he looked surprised to see Joe still there next to him, as if he had been far away in his thoughts.

'This dinner . . .'

'What about it?'

'I ain't never sat at a table like yours,' said Joe hesitantly. 'Well, like yours probably is anyway.' He didn't want the boy knowing he'd been spying through the window at him. 'I was wond'rin'—'

'Helpful hints for the inexperienced diner!' exclaimed Alec delightedly. 'Of course, Master Joe. Only too happy.' He dropped the end of the string and seemed to forget all about trapping birds. 'Well, where do we begin? Start of the meal. Sit down. Try not to fall off your chair.'

'Reckon I can manage that,' laughed Joe, but Alec was still talking.

'Lots of knives and forks on the table in front of you. Basic rule is: start at the outside and work inwards.'

'Work inwards,' repeated Joe, deciding he would have to try to memorize all this.

'First course: soup. Rule one: if it's too hot, don't blow on it, wait for it to cool down. But' – Alec held up two fingers – 'rule two: don't wait too long or you'll be last to finish and that means you're holding everybody else up. Very bad form. Rule three: spoon it from the wrong side of the bowl. Second course: fish. Rule one:—'

'Hold on,' interrupted Joe. 'How d'you mean: the wrong side of the bowl?'

'The wrong side of the bowl,' said Alec impatiently, 'means the wrong side of the bowl. OK?'

'OK.'

'Right. Second course: fish. Don't use a knife. Fork only for fish.'

'Fork only for fish,' repeated Joe, the worried frown on his face deepening.

'Then there could be stuffed this or stuffed that – all pretty straightforward. Then meat course. Right. Conversation during meat course. Very important this: never talk about the animal you're eating. So, if there's mutton on the plate, no stories about dear little baby lambs you've seen skipping around the farm. What else? Don't dip your bread in the gravy. Don't eat too fast. Don't eat too slow. Don't breathe so anyone can hear you.'

'Don't breathe?'

'Don't pick your teeth. Don't speak with your mouth full. Never use a spoon for anything except soup. Cross your knife and fork on the plate when you've finished so Bates knows to take it away.'

Joe stopped listening for a moment, imagining the footman's beady eye on him. Then he realized he'd missed a lot of what Alec was telling him.

'. . . you won't be offered wine, but if you are you can't say no. On the other hand, you don't have to drink it. That's about it. General advice: don't cough, don't sneeze, don't blow your nose. Chew everything thirty-two times—'

'Thirty-two?'

'Thirty-two. And watch your feet: don't sit on them or wrap them round your chair or stick them out in front of you so they touch someone else's. Oh, and don't slurp your drink or tip your tea in the saucer.'

'Right,' said Joe doubtfully. 'Er – tell me about the knives and forks again, will yer?'

But Alec was suddenly on his feet and heading over to the trap. 'This is hopeless! We're going to try something different.'

He picked up the hat and most of the bread. When Joe came up to him he was soaking a single crust from a tiny phial of clear liquid.

'What's that?' Joe asked.

'It's a drop of Madame's medicine,' whispered Alec conspiratorially.

'Whose?'

'My mother.'

Alec put the wet crust down on the grass and drew Joe back to the hiding place with him.

'What about the hat?' asked Joe.

'Don't need that now. Watch.' The two boys settled down once more behind the shed. 'One last thing,' whispered Alec. 'About tonight. If you like the food, don't say so.'

'Don't say you like it?'

'No. Don't say you like it. Eruct.'

'Pardon.'

'Eruct!' explained Alec. 'Belch!'

'Belch?'

'You know.' Alec swallowed a mouthful of air and demonstrated. 'A decent belch shows you appreciate good cooking. The family won't do it, but guests are expected to.'

'Are you sure?'

But Alec didn't answer. A red-throated robin had come hopping over to the bread. Accustomed now to the free meal, it pecked eagerly at the bait. Then it hopped away. For a moment nothing happened.

'It's not working,' hissed Alec angrily.

The bird fluttered its wings and took off. It managed a few yards. Then it came crashing to the ground. It struggled upright again. Then it fell down, feathers twitching. Then it was still.

With a cry of delight Alec leaped to his feet and sprinted over to the bird. The creature must have sensed his approach because it made a final effort to escape, fluttering its wings hopelessly but barely moving across the ground. Alec reached out and scooped it up in one hand.

'Got him, Joe! Got him!' He gripped the tiny bird around the neck. 'Shall I finish him off?'

Joe was on his feet. 'Hey!' His voice stopped Alec. 'Ain't no sense to that. You ain't gonna eat it.'

Alec made a twisting motion with his hand, as if to snap the bird's neck. Then he laughed. 'You've got a soft heart, Joe.'

He tossed the bird to one side. It lay still on the ground for a moment. Then its wings twitched and its feathers ruffled and suddenly it was up and flying unsteadily across the square and out of sight. Joe watched it go with a sigh of something like relief.

Chapter 11
The Candlelit Table

The room smelled of polish and candle wax and something else Joe couldn't quite put a name to. Nobody spoke. In fact no one had spoken since they sat down on the padded leather chairs and that felt like an hour ago. The tick of the tall clock in the corner seemed to echo in the silence. The boy's eyes scanned swiftly round the table and his heart hammered inside his chest, beating out a rhythm to the clock's ticking. Everyone sat perfectly still and upright with their hands folded in their laps, looking straight in front of them. He tried to do the same, but as the silence and the waiting went on and on, he became more and more certain that he was about to shout something out – something loud and rude and completely inappropriate.

'What?' Joe felt himself slip on his leather chair as he turned sharply to Mrs Harvey, who was sitting right next to him.

She'd said something – he was almost sure of it – but when he scanned the table again, no one else was paying the slightest attention to the pale lady with the long fingers. Still, her lips were definitely moving and this time Joe caught a few words.

'. . . and salt for our guest . . . long journey . . . not quite well. I'm afraid you'll have to forgive me . . .'

Her lips went on moving but the words were quite inaudible now and she wasn't looking at him. Her eyes were fixed in front, but she didn't seem to be looking at her husband at the far end of the table either. In fact she didn't seem to be looking at anything. Now the lips froze into a fixed half-smile. Still and silent, she reminded Joe of one of the dummies outside the wax museum. He could see the candle flame reflected in the tiny black pupils of her eyes. Then he realized he was staring. That couldn't possibly be good manners.

The clock chimed the hour and at the same moment Mr Harvey's voice came so suddenly that it made Joe jump again. 'Bates, you may serve our guest first.'

Bates had come in without Joe even noticing, and now the footman was approaching in his powdered wig with an enormous, silver bowl that Joe recognized and a look on his face that the boy also knew only too well. The bowl said, 'Soup.' The face said, 'Street trash! Street trash at the table and I have to give it food!' Outside the kitchen door a scruffy mongrel was wolfing down off-cuts from the mutton joint – at least it had the decency not to come into the house – but this crossing sweeper was sitting in the dining room at the family table! And he, Francis Bates, was expected to wait on him.

Joe thought about Alec's story. Perhaps the footman did somehow force him to go and drink gin at Addison's. The man looked capable of anything. Joe spat on his hand and tried once again to flatten out his thatch of black hair. No success. Bates watched the performance and his expression flickered from distaste to disgust.

The soup was a clear, brown liquid, startlingly dark in the white china bowl. A smell of meat mingled with the other aromas in the room – beeswax and – what? It was something Joe knew . . . It wasn't in the kitchen downstairs where he'd eaten bread and cheese with Mrs Briggs at midday, but now he remembered noticing the smell last night as he crept into the darkened hallway with Bob and Charlie. Alec's phrase came back to him. *He knows where the body's buried.* Was that what he could smell? A corpse? Couldn't be.

He picked up a spoon at random and stirred speculatively at the soup, searching for solid matter. Then he realized Mr Johnson was watching him, so he put the spoon down again.

Five bowls stood steaming on the table now, but no one started to eat. Joe was getting the idea. You had to wait for some kind of signal. Maybe the clock would chime again or Mr Harvey would say, 'Go!' or Mrs Harvey would say something else. This was going to be easier than he'd thought.

There was no signal. But when Mr Harvey picked up his spoon, Alec and Mr Johnson picked up theirs. So Joe picked up his. Then he realized he'd got the wrong spoon and put it down hurriedly, knocking over a glass. Luckily it was empty. Work from the outside. That's what Alec had said. How could he forget?

Joe took the big round spoon in his hand and dipped it nervously into the bowl. Mrs Harvey didn't glance at her soup or touch her spoon, but no one commented. Joe watched Alec out of the corner of his eye. What was it the boy had said? *Spoon it from the wrong side of the bowl.* But what did that mean? Then he saw Mr Johnson dip his spoon carefully into the far side of his bowl. Mr Harvey was doing it too. The wrong side meant the other side!

For the first few mouthfuls Joe imitated the others, but the soup tasted so good he forgot almost at once and began to spoon it hurriedly into his mouth. His left arm slowly encircled the bowl in an instinctive movement to prevent anyone stealing it. He didn't look up again until all the soup was gone. Bates was poised by the table with the silver tureen. No one else had managed more than a couple of spoonfuls.

'It's good, Mr Bates,' said Joe nervously.

'Give the boy some more, Bates,' Mr Harvey called from the far end of the table, which looked about twenty yards long from where Joe was sitting.

Joe had a second bowl of soup. Then he had a third. And another bread roll. White and soft and smothered in rich, yellow butter, the roll seemed to dissolve in his mouth. It was the same as the bread Alec had used as bait for the birds. You could scarcely call it by the same name as the coarse black stuff Joe was used to.

After the third bowl Joe let out a soft belch, the way Alec had told him, to show he had appreciated the food. No one seemed to notice, so he did another a little louder. He thought he saw just a faint smile of approval at the corner of Alec's mouth, but no one else paid any attention. The soup really had been delicious. He felt full and almost at his ease for the first time since he'd stepped into the candlelit room. To his right Mrs Harvey still murmured softly to herself from time to time, but Joe was learning to ignore her like everyone else.

As Bates cleared the bowls away Joe surveyed the room. The fire burned and the candles shone. The flashing eye of the horseman in the painting glared down at them from behind Mrs Harvey's head, and in the corners there were shadows where the light didn't quite reach. It all looked just the same as it always did. Except that tonight he wasn't outside with his face pressed to the glass: tonight he had stepped through the glass and he was part of this family with their enormous house with the tower and their gleaming silver and copperware and their servants. Just in front of him was the window where the curtains didn't always quite meet. They were open tonight. Leaning forward Joe caught a glimpse of his reflection floating outside in the darkness and at that moment he realized what the other smell in the room was.

It wasn't a dead body. It was drains. Not the overpowering stench of the sewers he'd worked back in Pound's Field, but just a trace, hiding behind the polish and the candle wax and the food.

Joe looked quickly around the room again, wondering if anyone else could smell it. Perhaps they didn't notice it any more – like they didn't notice Mrs Harvey talking to herself. When he'd peered through the glass from outside, Joe had never imagined a smell like that might be lingering in the candlelit room.

Another plate was in front of him. Bates was serving more

food. More! Of course – six or seven courses, Alec had said, and Joe had watched the family eating often enough to know the meal could go on for hours. But somehow in the excitement of tasting that delicious soup he'd forgotten there might be anything else.

He peered uncertainly at the pool of thick, yellow sauce in front of him. Egg custard, he decided, with something underneath. He picked up a knife and probed under the yellow sauce. Could be fish . . .

Fork only for fish!

Joe put the knife down in a hurry and picked up a fork. No! That was wrong too. No one else had got theirs yet. He dropped the fork on the floor.

No one was looking at him. Or at least no one except the painted man on the horse who had the kind of eyes that seemed to stare straight at you wherever you were. Mr Harvey was talking to Mr Johnson, saying something Joe couldn't follow. Mrs Harvey never blinked, and Alec hadn't spoken since they sat down. As Joe bent to pick up the fork, he watched the other boy for a moment and again he had the odd feeling that there was more than one Alec Harvey. There was the boy in the park with the words spilling out of his mouth and then there was this boy who sat as stiff as a board like his father, with his eyes fixed in front of him like his mother.

No, he was wrong. Someone *was* looking at him and it wasn't just the steely-eyed soldier on the wall. Bates was watching him with the silver fork in his hand and he could read his mind as clearly as if he'd spoken aloud. 'Street trash on the lift!'

The man thought he was stealing it. Joe put the fork back on the table and stretched out his legs, trying to look unconcerned. Bates scowled. Then Joe remembered . . .

Watch your feet!

He pulled them in hurriedly, hoping whatever he had touched under the table hadn't been Mrs Harvey. But he was afraid it had been, because she was talking again and this time the voice was just a little louder.

'. . . and salt for our guest who has had a very long journey. Unfortunately I am not quite well. I'm afraid you'll have to forgive me, Mr—?' Her brow furrowed, as if she were trying to remember something.

Around the table everyone went on as if Mrs Harvey were invisible. Joe felt he really had to say something. She was trying to remember his name.

'Joe,' he said. 'My name's Joe.'

Mrs Harvey's eyes rested on him for a moment but she didn't seem to have heard. Her lips parted and a strange hissing sound emerged through her teeth, which finally turned into a word.

'Sssssalt?'

'What? Oh salt. Yeah. Thanks.'

Mr Harvey told Alec to pass something – Joe didn't understand what he said – and suddenly there were two beautiful silver bowls in front of him, each with a tiny spoon resting inside.

Joe felt Bates's eyes on him again. He knew what the man was thinking. He took a spoonful from each of the silver bowls and tipped it hurriedly onto his food. Then he realized he had curled his feet up under him. He wriggled quickly, trying to sit properly, the way Alec was sitting, upright, hands only appearing above the table when he ate. He wriggled too quickly, slipping on the polished leather seat and banging his head hard on the back of the chair as his legs went from under him.

'. . . salt for our guest!' Mrs Harvey's voice emerged as a thin, high wail before relapsing into muttering and Joe clambered back onto his chair.

His face flushed hot. '*Try not to fall off your chair*,' Alec had said, and he'd laughed. He might not get all the knives and forks right but he could sit on a chair, couldn't he? And now he'd fallen on the floor at Mrs Harvey's feet. This time she had actually looked at him, but her eyes didn't seem to focus.

'Got salt, thanks,' he managed.

Joe ate what was on his plate as fast as he could. It wasn't custard on top and he wasn't sure what was underneath, but whatever it was he'd put a great deal too much salt and pepper on it. He wasn't quick enough to stop Mr Harvey telling Bates to give him some more, so he took a drink of water and ate another plateful, hoping he hadn't slurped at the water, fearing he had.

An enormous dish of meat and vegetables was being placed in front of him when Joe realized Mr Harvey was talking to him.

'. . . presumably you have one.'

'What? I mean, pardon?' said Joe, correcting himself at once. Then he realized he'd shown no appreciation of the yellow food, so he let out a loud belch. Alec spluttered into his handkerchief in what Joe took to be a sneeze. His father inhaled sharply through his nose, and his eyes narrowed.

'Alexander!'

Alec's expression fell at once and he looked down at his lap. Joe could remember the boy telling him you weren't supposed to sneeze, but surely he couldn't help it. Mr Harvey's face appeared to grow even longer than usual as he went on talking. Joe could follow some of what he said. Alec could follow it only too well.

'I have invited Joseph here this evening, Alexander,' said Mr Harvey, 'partly as a way of thanking him but chiefly as an example to you of the duty the rich and fortunate owe to the poor and unfortunate. I have managed, I flatter myself, to follow this duty in the public domain with the Asylums for Fatherless Children and other charitable works. Bringing a member of the lower classes to our family table continues that duty in the private domain. However, this boy' – he indicated Joe, and Alec saw how his father's face softened – 'this boy is also an example, Alexander, of the manly virtues of self-help and resilience. Would you not agree, Mr Johnson?'

The tutor's head inclined slightly and his back bent as if he were bowing to Mr Harvey. 'Certainly, Mr Harvey,' he purred. 'I would certainly concur, and might I add—?' But Mr Harvey hadn't finished.

'Joseph has not had your advantages, Alexander. He has not had the privilege of attending an expensive school, a privilege which you unfortunately squandered. He has never received individual tuition from a distinguished scholar such as Mr Johnson—' The tutor glowed. Alec stopped listening. He kept his eyes down and dug his fingernails into the palm of his hand out of sight under the tablecloth.

Joe had gone back to his food while Mr Harvey turned his attention to Alec. His stomach already felt dangerously full, but he worked his way through the meat and potatoes. *Don't dip your bread in the gravy.* Not much danger of that. Joe doubted if he would ever want to eat another piece of bread as long as he lived. Then he realized Mr Harvey was talking to him again. The man was so far away at the other end of the table Joe found it hard to focus on what he was saying, and he used so many words he didn't understand.

'What I was asking, Joseph, before we were interrupted' – his eye went sideways again to Alec – 'was what your second name is. We know you only as Joseph.'

'How d'yer mean, sir?' Joe knew he sounded stupid, but he wasn't sure what the man wanted him to say.

'Well,' said Mr Harvey, his voice patient, soft: Alec could only remember hearing him talk to the poison dolly like this, 'what is, or was your father's name?'

'Don't know, sir. They used to call me Joe Rat back in Pound's Field, but that ain't my real name.'

'I imagine not,' said Mr Harvey.

'He was a soldier, my father, sir,' added Joe suddenly. 'I remember that.'

'Indeed? A soldier?' Mr Harvey's gaze strayed for a moment to the huge portrait on the wall behind his wife's head.

'Yes, sir.'

'That's most interesting. In which regiment?'

'Don't know, sir. But he went to—' Joe searched his memory. He didn't remember his father. He had gone for a soldier before Joe was born. But he could still remember his mother talking about the man. He didn't like to think about those days – back before he went out on his own. But he felt he had to tell Mr Harvey something. Suddenly a word came floating out of his past. 'New-something, it was. New Brun – Brunny . . .'

'New Brunswick?' suggested Mr Johnson.

'That's it! New Brunswick. That's where he went. Across the ocean, Ma said. Army wouldn't let Ma and me brothers go. So we was left behind.'

Joe told his story – how they had lived in the Whitechapel Workhouse where his mother had done the laundry, how she had told them their father had been killed in the army, how she and his two brothers had died of cholera and he'd ended up in Pound's Field with a woman he called Mother. He left out the fact that she was the biggest villain in the East End and that she'd sent him toshing down the sewers.

'Remarkable! Quite remarkable!'

Mr Harvey pushed back his chair and got up from the table, leaving his food unfinished. Everyone was silent as he paced the length of the room, apparently lost in thought. He stopped under the portrait which filled the end wall from floor to ceiling, and stood contemplating the picture for what seemed like ages. Joe looked more closely at it too. Behind the scarlet-coated horseman was the smoke and flame of cannon fire and a plunging waterfall, but you hardly noticed that. It was those eyes you saw – hard and sharp and staring straight at you. It was only now Joe realized that behind his curled moustaches the horseman had the same long face and piercing eyes as Mr Harvey.

Suddenly Mr Harvey whirled round and addressed himself to his son. He had obviously come to some important decision. 'I am going to give you a practical example of what I was speaking about, Alexander.' He glanced towards the portrait. 'An example of which I believe the colonel would have approved.'

Alec wasn't listening. In fact he hadn't even noticed his father get up from the table. His mind was full of Joe's story of the workhouse and Pound's Field. It was more of what he'd told him in the park that afternoon, but here in the family dining room it seemed like a tale from another world, away from the dull safety of Lomesbury. Alec's heart pounded as he saw himself alongside Joe, escaping from the workhouse, living rough on the streets, being part of Mother's gang . . .

'Alexander, you are not attending!' Joe saw Alec wince at his father's rebuke. 'I was saying that I am about to give you a practical example of the rich doing their duty towards the poor in the private and personal domain.' He directed his penetrating gaze back at Joe. 'Now, Joseph, was your mother ever told officially that her husband had been killed?'

Joe quickly swallowed a mouthful of mutton and vegetables, trying not to choke. 'Don't know, sir.'

'But the posting was definitely to New Brunswick in British North America.'

'Think so, sir.'

'And you were confined to the Whitechapel Workhouse where your mother worked as a laundrywoman?'

'Yes, sir.'

Mr Harvey was making notes in a little book now. Joe looked past him at the red-coated soldier on the rearing horse. The more you looked at the painting, the more it could have been a picture of Mr Harvey himself.

Mr Harvey finished writing and put the notebook away. 'That's most interesting, my boy,' he said. 'Most interesting.' Then he noticed where Joe was looking. 'The portrait, Joseph, is of my late father, Colonel Richard Harvey, at the Battle of Queenston Heights in Upper Canada. That battle took place some forty years ago and more than two thousand miles from your father's posting, but on the same wild continent. The colonel would have wished me to do everything possible to assist the son of a British trooper. Did you know my son is named after a soldier named Alexander the Great, Joseph?'

Joe saw Alec wince again, and just for a moment, as Mr Harvey had talked about the colonel, he'd thought Mrs Harvey's placid face had hardened too. But now it was just as blank and impassive as ever.

Joe finished the mutton and vegetables. Then he struggled with a roast bird of some kind, trying desperately to copy the way Alec cut it so easily into mouthfuls with his knife and fork. And all the while, Mr Harvey talked loudly about British colonies and army regiments and the Atlantic Ocean; Mrs Harvey sat swaying imperceptibly on her straight-backed chair, eating nothing, muttering softly, ignored by everyone; and in Joe's nostrils the smell of drains seemed to grow just a little stronger.

A vast, quivering pudding was being carried ceremoniously into the room by Mrs Briggs, and little Felicity – this time in a frilly pink dress – was hovering at her father's side waiting to be fed, as Joe leaned back in his chair and let out a belch which rumbled up from deep in his bloated stomach and exploded into the candlelit dining room.

'Not quite well!' exclaimed Mrs Harvey, starting back in her chair so that for a moment Joe thought she was going to fall just as he had. Felicity screamed. Out of the corner of his eye Joe saw Bates lift a hand as if he might step over and clip him across the head in spite of Mr Harvey and dinner and everything, and at the same moment Alec burst into uncontrollable laughter.

'Alexander!'

Joe looked round the table, smiling weakly. Then he stood up with some difficulty. 'Reckon I'd best be off.'

'Dessert is about to be served,' said Mr Johnson sharply.

'Better not, beggin' your pardon, sir.' Joe put one hand to his mouth as he felt his stomach turn over inside him.

Mr Harvey stood up as well. 'We'll bid you goodnight then, Joseph. I too shall have to be going out quite soon. Perhaps you would be kind enough to find me a hansom cab as you go. You can expect me to be energetic in the matter of which we spoke.'

Joe didn't know what he was talking about, but he thought he ought to say thank you again anyway. He walked unsteadily round the table and shook hands with Mr Harvey and Mr Johnson. Then he shook hands with Alec, whose shoulders were still trembling with mirth. Last of all he went to Mrs Harvey, but she didn't seem to notice him standing beside her chair, and he hadn't the nerve to pick her white hand up and shake it. So in the end he shook hands with Mrs Briggs and a startled Bates instead, made his way to the back door and hurried away as fast as he could with Boy at his heels.

He got as far as the corner. Then he reached out, gripping the park railings with both hands, and his stomach heaved and he threw up every scrap of the Harveys' rich food onto the pavement until his belly felt as empty as early morning.

Outside Addison's Joe picked up a hansom and sent it round to the Tower House for Mr Harvey, but he didn't go back himself in hopes of a tip. Somehow he didn't want to end this evening with his hand held out.

He walked slowly back towards his dingy lodgings on Crooked-back Lane. On the corner of Upper and Lower Roads the gas lamp was burning as usual down the side street, but the soup kitchen looked locked up tight for the night. A woman clutching a baby to her breast pushed Joe out of her way and hurried over the cobbles. She probably thought he was looking for a roof too and wanted to get in ahead, but Joe didn't reckon her chances. It was late and you needed a ticket to get into most of those places.

He was turning away when a hansom rounded the corner at

a fair clip and pulled up outside the silent building. As Joe watched, the unmistakable figure of Mr Harvey climbed out of the cab. This was where he'd been going. Mrs Briggs had said he sometimes worked at his Asylum for Fatherless Boys himself and here he was. Joe was more surprised to see Bates climb out of the cab after him.

Mr Harvey tugged sharply on the iron bell-pull that hung by the front door of the building and Joe took a step forward. He was going to denounce the footman. He couldn't have done it back in Lomesbury Square, but here on this quiet and dingy side street he felt braver. 'He makes Alec drink gin and rubs his face in horse muck.' The words were forming on his lips. That would pay the stony-faced footman back for all the times he'd sneered and called him street trash.

But before Joe could take another step, the woman with the baby had fastened onto Mr Harvey's coat and a stream of pleadings and complaints was spilling out of her mouth: '. . . the wee one, your honour, he's so weak and we ain't got nowhere and nothin' and his father abandoned us, sir, and . . .' It went on and on.

She was still speaking when the door swung open and a stream of light spilled out onto the wet cobblestones. Perhaps it was the door opening, perhaps it was the arrival of the cab or the sound of the woman's voice, but suddenly the quiet street was full of ragged people – men and women, but mostly children.

Joe waited for Bates to call them street trash, to order them to 'clear off'. But if the footman was even thinking of doing it,

Mr Harvey had spoken first. He raised his hand and a hush that was little short of miraculous fell over the ragged crowd. 'You will all be taken care of,' he announced in a loud voice. 'There is food and shelter for all fatherless children here and for their mothers.' And with that he went through the door and the crowd pressed in after him with Bates doing his best to make them go one by one.

Joe turned quickly away. The moment for talking to Mr Harvey had gone. The sight of all those half-starved, undersized children filled Joe with a sort of superstitious dread, as if going near them might be enough to turn him into one himself. These kind of kids called themselves 'errand boys' but they were nothing more than beggars, most of then sent out onto the streets by parents who were too idle or too drunken to earn a living themselves. Joe didn't blame the beggars. He just didn't want to end up like that himself.

Back in his own dingy lodgings on Crooked-back Lane Joe paid a farthing for a tallow candle in the kitchen. His stomach turned over uneasily at the sight of the lodgers wolfing down bread and mouldy-looking cheese. Then he climbed the stairs to the loft.

The long room was full of the sound of people sleeping. Joe picked up the bowl of dirty water by the door and carried it carefully down the centre of the room to his space on the sleeping platform. Then for an hour he picked bed bugs out of his mattress by the light of his candle, dropping the little reddish-brown insects one by one into the pail of filthy water. He'd never bothered before and he knew it was more or less a waste of time: the sleeping figures on either side were so close his mattress would be infested again before the night was out. But the gleaming, polished surfaces of the Harveys' candlelit dining room were still fresh in his mind, and he couldn't fall asleep as he usually did with the bugs crawling on him.

When the entire surface of the water was covered with a struggling mass of legs and bodies, Joe gave up and stretched out on the mattress. Bugs or no bugs he had to rest. For a while he lay listening to the heavy snoring in the room, thinking about Alec Harvey. He would be in bed in his own attic room in the tower, surrounded by— Then he remembered. Alec had told him it wasn't his room. It was a prison. Was that true? Was anything the boy said the truth? Joe fell asleep imagining gleaming chains and locks, and Bates standing guard with a drawn sword just like Colonel Harvey's.

Chapter 12

Joseph Mundy

It had been raining heavily – soaking April rain that greened the young grass shoots in the park in the centre of Lomesbury Square but turned the roadway into a sticky mess. Joe was soaked through but that wasn't what was bothering him. He'd cleared a path outside every one of the houses on the north side of the square that morning and not a single front door had opened and not a cab or carriage had arrived. In other words: no tips. His broom was already caked with mud. Another hour of this and it would be useless. That would be tuppence ha'penny gone and nothing to show for it.

Joe and his dog hovered by the park railings, but the young trees didn't offer much protection from the rain. From across the square came the slow clip-clop of a single horse and a rumble of wheels. Joe didn't turn round. A month ago he'd been new to this game. Now he knew the sound of every vehicle that visited Lomesbury and the animals which pulled them. This was a delivery van. No chance of a tip there.

He was just making up his mind to give it up for the morning and find a dry spot to wait out the rain when the front door of the Tower House swung open and Mr Harvey was standing there himself, scanning the street. It was three weeks since Joe had eaten dinner in the candlelit dining room. There'd been no suggestion of repeating the experiment and, to be honest, Joe wasn't sorry. He preferred the broken victuals in Mrs Briggs's kitchen.

'Joseph, I want you.' Mr Harvey had spotted him.

'Message is it, sir?' The boy hurried across the road.

'No. I want you in my study at once. Come straight in.'

Joe's eyes widened in surprise. He snatched off his cap and stayed where he was. 'Don't reckon – I mean, I ain't—' He looked down uneasily at his soaking clothes and his boots caked in horse muck.

'Ah!' Mr Harvey seemed to notice the state of the boy for the first time. 'Well, perhaps you had better go round to the servants' entrance, Joseph, and – er – clean up a little first.'

Joe hurried round to the side of the house and walked straight into Bates, leaning against the wall outside the back door with an umbrella, his pipe stuck in his mouth. The man raised a leg to block Joe's path.

'What you after, street trash?' he snarled, looking down at the boy. 'Cadgin' another meal? Ain't dinner time yet.'

'Mr Harvey wants me,' said Joe briskly.

'What for?' demanded Bates.

'Don't know.'

Joe tried to duck under the man's leg, but Bates was too quick for him. He caught the boy by the shoulder and lifted him easily with one hand. If the dog had been there he would have barked, maybe even bitten the man, but Joe had told him to wait in the street.

Bates held the boy off the ground, eyeball to eyeball, legs dangling in mid air. 'I know you, street trash,' he grated. 'I know your type. I heard what you said when you was eating like a pig at the family table. Joe Rat they called you in Pound's Field, did they?'

'Ain't nobody calls me that no more,' said Joe, sorry he'd ever mentioned the name or the place. Bates ignored him.

'That was a nice game with those two other little blaggers, Joe Rat—' Joe flinched at the name. 'But you don't fool me. I know you'll end up thieving off the family. All right? Don't know how yet, but I know you'll try it.' The footman's voice was very low, but it carried an unmistakable threat. 'And when I catch you at it, Joe Rat, you're going to wish you'd stayed in Pound's Field where you belong. You follow?'

Bates lowered Joe slowly to the ground. He straightened out his jacket and brushed him down. Then he cuffed the boy hard across the back of the head and Joe skipped backwards just in time to escape a boot up the backside. Suddenly he'd had enough.

'I know you too, Mr Bates,' he rapped out. 'You make out like you care about the family but I know what you make him do.'

'What you talking about, boy?' snapped Bates irritably. 'What I make who do?'

'You know what I'm talkin' about.' Joe edged sideways. He still had to get past the man and through the door. 'You ain't nothin' but a bully, you are.'

Bates made another lunge for him, 'You're soft in the head, street trash!' But this time Joe saw it coming and he was through the back door before the man could touch him. The footman cursed him from the doorway, but he didn't bother to follow.

Joe hadn't had the chance to clean his shoes, so he slipped them off, quickly shook the rain out of his clothes and padded along the passage in bare feet. It reminded him of the night he'd entered that house for the first time with Bob and Charlie. That pair would be well into a stretch in Pentonville by this time, while he, Joe, the one they'd called Ratboy back in Pound's Field, had eaten at the same table as Mr and Mrs Harvey and their son, and now he was being summoned to the master's study. He wondered what the gentleman wanted him for.

At the top of the back stairs he pushed open the servants' door to the hallway and inhaled the scent of polish and quality wax candles which pervaded the entire house. It would have been as far from the stink of bed bugs and unwashed bodies he slept in as Joe could have imagined, if it hadn't been for that slight odour of drains which lingered behind it all. Did the Harveys really not notice the smell?

Mr Harvey was waiting in the hall. He looked excited. He led the way upstairs to a long landing with several doors leading off it – bedrooms, Joe imagined. The gleaming banister was cool to the touch and so smooth and shiny he could see his reflection in it.

A second set of carpeted stairs took them to another landing where a narrower, spiral staircase continued upwards. Joe guessed it must lead up to the tower room – the room where he had first glimpsed Alec at the window. He would have liked to see inside that room – to find out whether it really was a prison like Alec had said or if that was just one of his jokes like telling him to belch at the dinner table. It had been the morning after the famous dinner before Joe worked that one out.

Instead Mr Harvey unlocked a heavy oak door and led the way into a square room with a patterned carpet on the floor. Books and pictures covered two of the walls from floor to ceiling. The other two walls had tall windows, surrounded by dark wood panelling.

'Come in. Sit down, Joseph,' said Mr Harvey, seating himself behind an enormous desk which seemed to fill half the room.

Mr Harvey began shuffling through a pile of papers while Joe looked round for somewhere to sit. There was a chair with the same kind of slippery leather seat as the ones in the dining room. He decided against that. There were two armchairs, elaborately embroidered with pictures of birds and animals. They both looked as if no one had sat on them since they were made. Joe decided to stay where he was.

At long last Mr Harvey looked up. He was holding a sheet of paper and he was smiling.

'Directly after your dinner with us, Joseph, I put in motion certain enquiries, as I suggested I would.'

'Oh.' Joe remembered a lot of questions about his father, but he didn't know what 'enquiries' Mr Harvey was talking about.

'I began by entering into communication with the principal of the Whitechapel Union Workhouse. I recounted the story you told me of your mother working in the laundry there and sadly dying of cholera along with your two brothers, and he was able to identify you as Joseph Mundy.'

'What? I mean: pardon?'

'Does the name mean nothing to you?'

'What name?' As soon as Mr Harvey had spoken the word 'workhouse' Joe had stopped listening. 'I ain't goin' back to no spike,' he said quickly.

Mr Harvey took a breath and began again. 'I apologize, Joseph. I may be going too fast. I realize all this will come as something of a shock, but good news follows. Your name' – he spoke slowly, spelling the words out – 'according to the records, is Joseph Mundy. Do you not recollect it?'

'Monday? You mean like Tuesday?'

Mr Harvey spelled the name.

'I ain't never heard of it,' said Joe, his eyes narrowing anxiously. What kind of good news was the man talking about? 'I ain't going to no workhouse,' he repeated.

Mr Harvey sighed heavily. 'Sit down please, Joseph,' he said.

Joe took a chance on the leather chair.

'Whether you remember it or not, your name appears to be Mundy. But perhaps more importantly your father, according to workhouse records, did indeed enlist in the army as Private James Mundy and was posted abroad to New Brunswick, as you recalled your mother telling you, some twelve years ago. But – and now comes the good news of which I spoke – an exchange of letters between myself and the authorities in Fredericton, New Brunswick, reveals that, though missing from his regiment, Private Mundy was never officially listed as killed, and that a man with his identification papers is now lying dangerously ill of a fever in a British army hospital in Fredericton.'

Joe struggled to follow the man's words. 'Who's ill?' he blurted out. 'What's it got to do with me?'

Mr Harvey tapped the desk sharply and for a moment the expression on his face reminded Joe of one of the dirty looks he shot at Alec at the dinner table. Then the man stood up and went over to a picture on the wall. It was another portrait. This picture was smaller and there was no horse, but it was obviously the same man as the officer on horseback in the dining room. Mr Harvey had had a story about that one, but Joe couldn't remember what it was. All that came back to him now was the feeling that he was about to explode from vast quantities of rich food. He swallowed uneasily.

'He was a fine officer, my father,' said Mr Harvey, his back still turned to Joe.

That was it. Colonel Harvey. Now Joe remembered.

'I dare say,' Mr Harvey went on, 'I could still recount by heart the stories my mother told me of his campaigns. Unfortunately he was only rarely at home and I had little opportunity to hear them at first hand.' He turned to Joe. 'It was a disappointment to my father that I was unable to follow him and my older brother into the regiment. I was said to have a weak chest as a child.' Mr Harvey looked down at the floor. 'A very grave disappointment, I fear.' And for a moment the man didn't look like Mr Harvey, the banker, or the man who sat long-faced at the head of the dinner table, or even an adult at all. In fact, Joe realized with a shock, at that moment he looked just like Alec after a telling-off. Then he recovered and the look was gone. 'But we are straying from the point, Joseph.'

Mr Harvey sat down once more and placed the tips of his fingers carefully together on the desk in front of him. 'What I am trying to explain, Joseph,' he said slowly, 'is that you are not a "fatherless boy" after all, like the many unfortunates I deal with. Your father is not dead, and in the spirit of personal charity of which I spoke at dinner I have taken the liberty of arranging for his passage back to England by the steamship RMS *Endeavour*. The vessel will reach the London Docks in slightly less than two weeks' time.'

Joe felt his mouth open and close but instead of words coming out, suddenly his mind was full of the image of St George's churchyard in Pound's Field where his mother and two brothers lay in an unmarked grave. He dreamed of that grave some nights, saw the cholera victims piled in one on top of the other like rubbish, saw the quicklime, thick like snow over the dead bodies so they'd rot away underground real quick. He shook his head to get rid of the picture. His mother and brothers were dead. There was nothing to be done about that. It was so long ago he didn't remember what they looked like. But this man was saying his father was still alive. How could that be?

'I still don't understand, sir. I'm sorry.'

He knew it must sound stupid, but it was true. He didn't understand.

'Either your mother was given a false report, Joseph, or' – Mr Harvey tapped his fingers together, searching for the best way to phrase what he wanted to say – 'or she told her children their father was dead because he had – deserted his family.'

'Deserted?'

'Left his family.'

'You said deserted. That's what soldiers do, ain't it? When they run away?'

'No, no.' Mr Harvey looked flustered now, shuffling the piles of paper on his desk and stroking his whiskers. 'No, I'm not saying that. What I'm saying—' He took a deep breath. 'All I am saying, Joseph, is that your father, Private James Mundy, is on his way back to England and, assuming he survives the voyage, that I have arranged for him to receive professional nursing at my expense here in Lomesbury Square. I believe it is something of which Colonel Harvey' – his voice faltered as his eyes went back to the portrait on the wall – 'of which my late father would have approved.'

'This Mundy – he's ill?' queried Joe.

'The letter I received is a little unclear.' Mr Harvey held up a sheet of paper. 'But it appears that he suffered a bullet wound in the course of – well, in the course of his duties, and that has led to a fever. But I have good hopes that he will recover himself once he is in the hands of my personal physician.'

Joe was too bewildered to say anything else and Mr Harvey summoned Bates in the end to show the boy the way out. The tall footman scowled as soon as the study door was closed behind them.

'What did the master want with you, Joe Rat?' he demanded. Joe looked at him, but he couldn't find the words to answer. Bates gave a snarl of disgust. 'Get on with you then,' he snapped. 'You know the way out. I'm watching you, mind.'

Joe made his way down the first flight of stairs, holding onto the banister for support. As he reached the landing on the first floor, he caught a glimpse through an open doorway of a high-ceilinged room with tall windows, curtains billowing in the spring breeze. There was sunshine coming into the room. The rain must have stopped. Mrs Harvey was sitting at a low table, staring intently at her reflection in the mirror.

That was when Joe realized he hadn't even thanked Mr Harvey upstairs in the study. Apparently the gentleman had found his father alive and now he was paying to bring him back to England and set him up in the house here until he was better and all because he was a soldier and Mr Harvey's dad had been a soldier too. Was that what he'd said? Anyway, here was Mrs Harvey and Joe felt he had to say something.

'Just wanted to say thanks,' he called out weakly through the open door. There was no response. The draught from the windows blew a scent of rose petals out onto the landing, masking the smell of drains that reached the upper storeys too. 'You and Mr Harvey' – Joe raised his voice a little – 'you bin good to me and my – well, him they call my father. Missus?'

Still there was no reaction. Couldn't she hear him? Mrs Harvey reached a white gloved hand towards the mirror so slowly it looked as though she might never reach it. Joe felt his own hand stretching out too, as if to help her. At long last, after what seemed an eternity, her fingertips touched her own reflection. Her lips moved but no sound came out.

Joe watched, fascinated, as her hand went to a small glass phial which stood on the table. Still the movements were painfully slow, as if the effort was almost too much for her. Behind him Joe heard the muffled sound of Alec's voice reciting something in a foreign language. He must be having a lesson with Johnson somewhere. The strange chanted words seemed to match the movement of Mrs Harvey's hand. Finally her fingers closed around the phial. She drew out the cork and measured the liquid drop by drop into a glass of water.

'Got bottles of that stuff hidden all over the house.' It was Bates's voice. Joe looked up to find the tall footman standing over him. He was watching Mrs Harvey too. But he was talking to himself, not Joe. In fact he seemed to have forgotten for a moment that the boy was there at all. 'Dangerous stuff, mind. Too much and it's pure poison.'

Joe thought of Alec in the park and the way the bird had just keeled over on its side and lain still as if it were dead. Was this the 'medicine' he'd talked about? It looked like the same kind of bottle. What would it do to Mrs Harvey?

Bates caught Joe's eye and drew back sharply, pulling the bedroom door closed. But before he did, Joe was in time to see Mrs Harvey raise the glass to her lips and swallow its contents at a single draught.

Chapter 13

Bones

'Blasted stuff!' Jeremy Barlow straightened up, easing his back. 'Ground's full of rubbish.' He stabbed his spade into the soil again and began levering out what looked like a muddy old blanket. Joe stepped forward to help. 'Look at that!' growled the man. 'Old coat. Place is like a dump!'

Barlow had three dozen boxes of bright-red geranium plants lined up on the grass next to the flower bed they were digging. Joe had helped carry them into the square that morning. He was getting sixpence for the day, and he was supposed to help put them in the ground too, but the old gardener hadn't let him touch one yet. All he'd been allowed to do was dig horse muck into the earth and collect the weeds and rubbish that kept coming out of the ground. They'd found watercress and potato plants and old tools, a pair of boots with laces still in them, a stack of broken bricks and crockery and enough animal bones to fill three buckets.

Alec picked up the old coat and began brushing the mud off it. He'd been there since midday, when lessons finished for the morning: he'd even tried his hand at digging.

'Still in one piece,' he said, holding the filthy garment up. 'Why is Lomesbury Square like a cross between a burial ground and an old clothes shop?'

'Used to be a market garden,' said Joe. 'Houses too.'

'Really?' Alec looked surprised. 'How do you come to know so much about the history of Lomesbury, Master Joe?'

'Don't know much,' said Joe evasively and went back to clearing rubbish. It was Bob and Charlie who'd told him what the area was like before the gentry moved in, but he didn't want to bring their names up.

''S right,' grunted Barlow. 'There was houses here and stuff growin' all the way up to the little river.' He gestured away to the north. 'Flattened the whole lot, they did. Progress!' He spat on his hands and went back to digging.

'Bad luck on the people who lived here,' said Alec. He slipped the muddy old coat on over his beautifully pressed suit, then he plunged his hands into the pockets and spun around on the spot. 'How do I look?'

Joe let out a short hiss of laughter. 'You look like a tramp.'

'Excellent!'

'Mr Harvey'd have a fit, Master Alexander.' Barlow sounded worried. 'You'll be losin' me my job.'

'Mister Harvey be damned!'

Alec flung the coat down amongst the rubbish and Barlow went back to his digging, looking relieved. For a while he and Joe worked in silence and Alec watched. Then Barlow's spade hit stone again. Joe looked down into the trench the old man had dug. There was a line of bricks across it, still mortared together, like part of an old wall. Barlow leaned on his spade and mopped his brow. But when he spoke it wasn't about the rubbish in the ground.

'Word has it you got a father comin' yourself from across the seas, Joe.'

'Seems like it,' said Joe uncertainly.

'Hear they've turned Frank Bates out of his room too,' the old man chuckled. 'Bet he was pleased.'

'My advice is send him straight back where he comes from,' put in Alec. 'He can take Mister Harvey with him and we can both move into the Fatherless Boys' place.'

But Joe wasn't listening. He looked at Alec. 'Don't know about havin' no father,' he said slowly. 'Seems like they can be pretty hard on their own kin sometimes.'

'You never said a truer word, Master Joe,' observed Alec bitterly.

Barlow looked long and hard at Alec. 'Your father's a gentleman,' he said with emphasis. 'Now, my old man, he was a bad 'un.' His voice was suddenly so quiet Alec had to take a step forward to hear what he said. 'Long stick and a short temper: that was my dad. Drank like a dozen sailors and fought like a mad dog. Old lady used to say he didn't know what he was doin', but he knew all right. I still got the scars on my back.'

'Can I see?' asked Alec immediately.

'No, yer can't,' snapped Barlow. Talking about his father seemed to have angered the old gardener. 'Your father ain't never took his belt to you, has he?'

'No,' admitted Alec grudgingly.

'Well, then,' said Barlow, 'you ain't got nothin' to complain about, have yer?'

'Mr Harvey said I'm to go down and meet him off the ship,' said Joe, still following his own train of thought. 'Next week. In a hansom. Ain't never bin in a cab before.'

'Well,' said Alec brightly, 'then at least you get a ride out of it. Now' – he stood up suddenly, digging into the pocket of his waistcoat and producing a coin – 'here's sixpence, Mr Jeremy Barlow with the scars on his back – a tanner is the word, I believe. Is that right, Master Joe? That's what you're paying this young man, isn't it?'

'Only 'cos your father says I got to,' grumbled Barlow. He was back at his work now.

'Be that as it may,' Alec went on, 'here is what you were going to pay him. I want him for an hour and then you can have him back later. How's that?'

Barlow took the coin, spat on it and rubbed it with his sleeve. Then he put it in his pocket. 'Fair enough,' he said, and he drove the spade in again. 'Ain't much use anyhow.'

'Come on, Master Joe!' Alec was already on his way across the grass towards the gate. Then he stopped suddenly and came back to pick up the filthy old coat and the largest of the bones. Joe was still hesitating, looking from Alec to Barlow. 'Come on!' insisted Alec, and he marched off towards the gate without looking to see if Joe was following.

'I'll be back, Mr Barlow,' said Joe. 'I'm still good for my tanner even if you got his.'

Barlow studied the boy's face for a moment. 'Won't come to no good hangin' round the likes of him,' he growled. Barlow had always been carefully respectful of young Master Harvey. It was the first time Joe had heard him say anything critical about the boy. 'That lad's head is too full of wind and his pockets is too full of money. Makes a bad mix. No matter who his dad is.'

Joe didn't know what to say to that. 'I'll be back,' he repeated.

'Suit yourself,' said the man, bending to his work once more.

The dog was waiting outside the gate: Barlow still wouldn't let him into the park. Alec had given him the old bone and Boy was gnawing furiously at it, his face and paws already covered with mud. Joe could see Alec halfway round the other side of the square, heading for Upper Road. He had Joe's broom over his shoulder. Joe hurried in pursuit: he couldn't afford to lose a broom.

Alec was waiting for him at the side of Addison's. He'd wrapped the old coat around him and he was doing a kind of dance on the pavement, skipping and sweeping at the ground. There was a look in his eye Joe hadn't seen before, a wild look that said he might do anything.

'Got any money, Joe?'

Joe was so surprised he let out a snort of laughter. 'You askin' me for money?'

'That was my last sixpence in the world. Mister Harvey stopped my allowance.'

'Well I ain't got none till Barlow pays me.'

'Good! In that case we shall have to earn it.' Joe looked blank. 'Come on. I've seen the two lads outside Addison's Superior Tavern and Supper Club. We can do what they do. That is if they are not here today.'

Joe laughed again. 'Bob and Charlie? They won't be there. They was the two blaggin' your house.'

'Were they? I didn't recognize them. Excellent! In that case we shall take Bob and Charlie's place.'

Joe put out a hand to stop him. He'd thought about trying to take over the pitch outside Addison's before and given up the idea. 'I can't work them places,' he said.

'Why ever not?'

'Ain't got the patter for it. Bob and Charlie, they could flash the gab for the nobs. Make 'em laugh.'

'Ah!' Alec beamed. 'But you forget, Master Joe: though I now look like a street urchin, I *am* a nob. I *can* talk to these people. Come on. We are going to make your fortune. Bring the dog.'

Joe looked down. The ragged terrier was there as usual. Joe followed Alec unwillingly round the side of the building and out onto Upper Road and the dog trotted after him, teeth still clenched around the enormous bone.

There was the usual daytime traffic on the street – heavy wagons, omnibuses heading in and out of the City, cabs hurrying past: the bustle and noise were shocking after the quiet of Lomesbury Square. Although it was broad daylight the enormous gas lamp above the entrance to Addison's was burning, and the plate-glass windows and gilded plasterwork of the frontage shone like the sun that was missing from the sky.

Alec had already taken his stand outside the gin palace. As Joe came up to him, he was sweeping the roadway in front of three heavily-built men and a stream of words was pouring out of his mouth. Joe realized with a shock that the boy was trying to talk like Bob.

'Cor-blimey-guv'nor-and-did-you-ever-see-this-kind-of-dirt-on-the-streets-of-our-fair-metropolis? Spring-is-here-and-with-it-cometh-the-horse-dung-gentlemen-and-without-the-crossing-sweep-you-is-goin'-to-get-your-lovely-boots-all-mucky-oh-yes-I-should-say-so!'

The men stood hands on hips, watching the boy who was blocking their route into the public house. Joe guessed they'd been working a market somewhere as porters since early morning. Now they were looking to drink some of their wages and they didn't want some kid getting in their way.

Alec finished sweeping, bowed low and stood back with his hand out. 'Gentlemen, you may proceed!'

Joe knew exactly what was coming next.

The men didn't say anything. One of them grabbed the broom out of Alec's hand with an easy movement, and shoved it between the boy's legs. Another grabbed an end, and the pair carried Alec to the road, riding on the broom. They dumped him in the gutter without a word and strode into Addison's.

Joe hurried to help Alec up. The only good thing was that there was no sign of Freddie, the red-coated doorman. He was probably only on duty in the evening.

'That ain't no good.'

'Why not?'

Alec was brushing some of the muck from the gutter off him, but there was hardly any point as the coat he was wearing was already so filthy.

'You won't never get nothin' off blokes like that. It's got to be toffs. 'Cept I reckon they only come round after dark.'

'Nonsense!' Alec had recovered now. 'You are a defeatist, Master Joe. Toffs will come if I want them to.'

He picked up the broom and stood at the side of the road like a guard on sentry duty, scanning each cab that passed, as if willing it to stop. Sure enough, it couldn't have been more than a minute before a hansom drew up.

Alec spun round with a cry of triumph: 'See!' Then he was over to the cab in an instant and sweeping at the road so hard Joe was sure the broom would fall apart in his hands. The same stream of nonsense was spilling out of his mouth, only this time he delivered it in a strange foreign accent.

'O-*mon-dieu*-guv'nor-and-cor-blimey-and-these-our-dirty-streets-of-fair-metropolis-oolala! Spring-is-'ere-and-a-young-man's-fancy-turns-to-horse-dung-*messieurs*-and-wizzout-ze-crossing-sweeper-you-is-mucky-boots-all-over-oh-yes-I-should-say-so!'

The two gentlemen stood for a moment staring at the bizarre figure in the filthy coat. Then one of them suddenly let out a hearty laugh, reached into his pocket and tossed a coin high into the air. Alec caught it as easily as Bob had ever done and marched over to Joe.

'There you are. Smooth as you like.'

Joe laughed, excited by the other boy's confidence. Maybe he was right. Maybe he could take over Bob and Charlie's pitch. If Alec could make money here, acting like an idiot, then why shouldn't he? That way he'd have a steady income of his own. Next week when James Mundy came – he still couldn't think of him as his father – when this man arrived he'd be able to show him he had a way of making a living. He wouldn't look like he was just cadging off the Harveys. But Alec had other ideas.

'Now,' he said, making for the mahogany doors of the public house, 'we celebrate!'

Joe was too slow to stop him. The double doors were already swinging shut again. He followed Alec into the pub and the dog slipped in after him, just as the doors were closing.

Chapter 14
THE BLACK DROP

Considering the way it glowed on the outside, the gloom on the inside of Addison's Superior Tavern and Supper Club came as a surprise. The windows were so covered with advertisements for different brands of gin that scarcely any light could get through. A gas lamp burned dimly in the ceiling. There was nowhere to sit.

In one corner of the cavernous room the three porters who had dumped Alec in the street were standing around an empty barrel with big pewter tankards in their hands, talking in lowered voices. There was no sign of the two gents who had given Alec money, but Joe could see that beyond the bar was another room, and they had probably gone in there.

There were other figures in the bar: a group of silent women with glasses in their hands, a little girl standing on tiptoe to reach the counter. But the place was almost empty and an odd kind of hush hung over everything.

Alec was standing at the long counter which stretched almost the whole way across the room. The barmaid had her back to him, serving the little girl. Joe hovered by the door, waiting to see what happened.

'Sixpence worth of Old Tom,' said Alec, slapping his coin down.

There was a long mirror behind the bar. The barmaid must have been able to see Alec's reflection, but she didn't turn round.

'Sixpence worth of Old Tom!'

Alec shouted this time, dropping his attempt to sound like a kid from the streets and pointing imperiously at one of the enormous painted casks above the bar. The men in the corner glanced up from their drink. Joe noticed one of them nudge another and point over at Alec. The barmaid turned slowly, folding her arms.

'You bin told,' she said shortly. 'Now hop it.'

'Dunno what you mean.' Alec tried unsuccessfully to put on an accent again.

'You don't fool me, just 'cos you got a dirty coat on. I know you and I ain't servin' you no drink.'

Alec looked her steadily in the eye. 'I've got money. You just served a child half my age. Now give me a drink.'

The barmaid picked up a small brass bell and rang it, looking over towards the door at the back. Calling for someone, thought Joe – Freddie probably. She leaned on the bar so that she was speaking right into Alec's face.

'She come in here regular for her old mum and she don't never make no trouble. You come in here and you always make trouble.'

She rang the bell again, harder this time. No one came. One of the porters slammed his tankard down hard on the barrel in front of him and strode across to Alec.

'What you think you're at, Little Lord Muck? First you're comin' flash outside. Now you're kickin' up a breeze while me and my mates has a drain. You're from Lomesbury, ain'tcha?'

'What if I am?'

Alec threw off the dirty overcoat and rounded on the porter, glaring straight up into his face. The man could have reached out and squashed him with one fist, but he was so surprised by the belligerent look on the boy's face that for a moment he did nothing. Joe hurried over to the bar and stood next to Alec.

'Look,' he said, 'he don't mean nothin'. He just talks too much.' Joe turned to the barmaid. 'Give him a glass of ale or somethin' and we'll go. All right?'

'And who are you?' demanded the barmaid.

'I ain't nobody,' said Joe. 'I'm his friend.'

Alec jerked round to look at him. There was surprise on his face.

'I'll sell you a drink, but I ain't servin' him,' said the barmaid.

'I don't drink,' said Joe. 'Ain't no sense in it. No offence,' he added, turning hastily to the porter.

The man's eyes narrowed. He looked from Joe to Alec and back again as if uncertain which of the two boys to hit first. But at that moment the double doors to the street swung open and two more men came in, talking at the tops of their voices, and suddenly the whole atmosphere in the bar changed. One of the women was laughing. The newcomers seemed to know the three porters and were soon standing drinks all round. Joe tried to pull Alec away from the bar.

'You lied to me, didn'tcha?'

'What?'

'You told me Bates made you come here.'

Alec laughed. 'And you believed me!' His eyes were blood-shot and gleaming with excitement, as if he had already been drinking gin.

'Why d'you lie to me, Alec?'

Alec shrugged impatiently. 'You sound like Mister Harvey.'

'Well either way this ain't no good,' said Joe urgently. 'You're gonna get in trouble here, Alec, and I'm gonna get the blame for it, sure as shufflin'.'

'Now you sound like Bates!' Alec's voice was full of scorn. 'All you're worried about is your tips and your broken victuals.'

Joe ignored this. Of course he was worried about food and money. Who wouldn't be? But the mention of Bates's name brought back something else. If the footman hadn't made Alec come here, then the stuff about knowing some secret and rubbing him in the muck was probably a lie too. And he'd run his mouth off at the man like an idiot.

'Come on,' he insisted, taking the other boy by the arm. 'We're leavin'.'

Alec shook him off. 'I'm not going until I get a drink.'

Joe sighed heavily. 'A drink?'

'Yes. And it's got to be for me, not you.'

'Right.'

The barmaid finished serving, and Joe got her attention again. 'Could I—? I mean, could he—?'

The barmaid looked down at him. 'I thought you said you didn't drink.'

'Could we have two glasses of water, please?'

The barmaid looked at Joe as if he'd gone mad. Then she called out to the whole bar at the top of her voice. 'Two glasses of water here for Little Lord Muck and his friend!'

A shout of laughter filled the pub. The two men who had given Alec money came through from the saloon to meet a group of other gentlemen. One of the porters collapsed on the floor without a sound, flat-out drunk, and people stepped over him, crowding towards the bar to see what was going on. The place seemed to be full all of a sudden, and through the throng came Freddie, the doorman, buttoning his red coat.

'What's up, Meg?' he asked the barmaid.

'Took your time, didn'tcha? It's this one again.' She indicated Alec with a nod of her head. 'Got a friend with him this time and a stinkin' little dog.' The doorman took a look at Joe. Then he took a look at Boy. Then he dragged phlegm from the back of his throat with a long, rasping noise and spat into the sawdust which covered the floor. 'And they're both drinkin' water!' The barmaid laughed as she set two murky-looking glasses in front of Joe and Alec.

Alec stared around him at the crowd of people. Everyone was watching. He'd got the attention of the whole bar and this time he hadn't had to start a fight or insult one of the drinkers.

But they were laughing at him, were they? Because all the barmaid would give him was water? Even Freddie in his stupid red coat was laughing now, and everybody was shouting for 'Water! Water!' by which they meant gin. Well, he would show them. He'd show the whole lot of them.

He reached into the pocket of his jacket and drew out the little glass phial he'd taken from his mother's room a month ago. Then, making sure as many people as possible saw what he was doing, he took out the stopper and let three drops fall into his glass of cloudy water and three into Joe's.

' 'Ere, what you doin'?'

'It's medicine, Joe. Drink up. It'll do you good. Cheers!'

Alec lifted his glass to the watching crowd and swallowed the entire contents. He was delighted to hear a cheer from the on-lookers. But as he went to put the phial back in his pocket, Freddie, the doorman, grabbed it from his hand, took out the cork and raised it to his red, bulbous nose, sniffing deeply.

'The black drop,' he announced to the bar.

There was another cheer and shouts of, 'Give us a bit, Freddie.'

The doorman took no notice. 'Where d'you get this, Little Lord Muck?'

'It's medicine. If you must know, my mother takes it for her – for her – illness. Drink up, Joe.'

Alec waved his hand at the other boy, encouraging him to drink. Joe's face was already hazy in front of him.

'Medicine, he calls it.' Freddie laughed and pocketed the phial. 'That's the black drop, little fella. Opium!'

Opium? Joe had heard of opium – how if you took enough, it sent you into a sleep you couldn't wake up from and how once you started you couldn't ever do without it. Could that be the medicine Mrs Harvey took – the reason why she sat at table at night so silent and still and never eating a morsel of food?

Freddie was still laughing full in Alec's face, but the laugh was ugly now. Alec got a sight of a mouthful of blackened teeth. 'Mummy likes it, does she, Little Lord Muck?'

'Don't you talk about my mother, you—'

Alec took a wild swing at the man without aiming and would have fallen to the floor if Freddie hadn't caught his wrist. The doorman squeezed hard. Alec watched, fascinated, as his wrist turned white and his hand began to turn red. It should have hurt, but he felt absolutely nothing. He felt a long way away, as if the whole thing were happening to someone else. Then he saw those blackened teeth again, but he couldn't make out what the man was saying to him.

'Your mother is an opium addict, Little Lord Muck, and you just swallowed enough to lay you out for a week! Here' – Freddie seized the other glass – 'let's give the rest to the dog and see what happens.'

Boy had pressed himself up against the foot of the bar next to Joe, keeping tight hold of his bone, avoiding the heavy boots all around him. The doorman bent down and placed the glass of water carefully on the floor a couple of yards in front of him.

The biggest cheer yet went up from the drinkers in the bar as the dog dropped the bone and trotted across the floor. A chant started up: 'Drink! Drink!! Drink!!!'

Boy put his muzzle into the tall glass. But Joe was too quick. With a sudden movement he lashed out with his foot and sent the glass flying across the room, shattering on the floor. There was a groan of disappointment and then a louder voice.

''Ere, you made me wet!'

It was the biggest of the three porters.

The man headed straight for Joe, the other drinkers falling back on either side, blocking the way to the door. The boy looked quickly around the room. There was no way out. The man was almost on him when Alec, who had been staring blankly in front of him, suddenly seemed to come back to life. Above the noise of the bar Joe could hear his voice.

'What did you say about my mother?'

This time when Alec swung he made contact, catching Freddie off balance and sending him sprawling. As he fell, Freddie caught the porter with his shoulder and sent him flying too. The big man struggled to his feet, staring around him, eyes wild and bloodshot. He'd forgotten about Joe.

The boy took his chance. There were still a dozen people cutting him off from Alec, but there was a route through to the door. Joe took it.

The hazy London daylight made his eyes blink after the gloom inside Addison's. He ran round the building and onto the neat stone rectangles where Lomesbury began, not noticing that for once the dog was not behind him. Two minutes, maybe less, and he was hammering on the door of the Tower House – the side door. He couldn't fetch Mr Johnson for something like this – let alone Mr Harvey!

Mrs Briggs answered the door, hands sticky with cooking as usual. 'Joe, what's the matter? What—?'

'Bates,' Joe gasped. 'Need Bates.'

The footman was standing in the passage behind her. 'What do you mean, "Bates"? You don't call me "Bates", you little—'

'Alec, Mr Bates. You better come. It weren't my fault. I told him not to go in. He's—'

But the footman was already gone, pulling on his jacket as he ran down the road straight for Addison's with Joe struggling to keep up. He knew where Alec was.

Bates had disappeared when Joe reached the double mahogany doors again. A strange howling noise came from inside the gin shop, and, as he pushed open the doors, Joe expected to see a brutal fight in progress with Alec and Bates in the middle and probably the dog too. But the sight which met his eyes was completely different.

The drinkers were lined up on either side of the room, glasses in hand, and stretched out on the floor between them, arms crossed on his chest like a corpse, lay Alec Harvey. The filthy old coat had been draped carefully over his legs, a pair of candles was at his feet, and sitting by his head was a scruffy-looking mongrel with a white rump, a torn ear and an enormous bone, head thrown back, howling at the ceiling.

Joe stood and stared in disbelief. To his left Bates stood and stared too. Apparently the sight had stopped the footman in his tracks as well. One man was laughing so hard the tears were pouring down his face. Another was doubled up on the floor, holding his sides. Many of the drinkers had their heads thrown back and were joining in Boy's unearthly howling, creating the din Joe had heard from outside.

What had looked like an ugly fight when he left Addison's had turned into a joke, and apparently all because of the dog. But was Alec actually dead? Had the stuff he'd swallowed killed him?

As soon as he got over his initial shock, Joe rushed to the boy and bent down beside him. Alec's mouth hung open and his breath smelled odd, but he was breathing. Seeing Joe, the dog stopped howling and the crowd stopped their racket too and went back to their drinks. Joe felt himself pushed to one side as Bates scooped Alec up and carried him to the door.

'Don't want to see that kid in here again, Frank.' It was Freddie, the doorman, from over by the bar.

Bates didn't answer. He carried Alec outside. Joe pushed through the double doors with Boy behind him and almost tripped over the man. He was down on hands and knees in the roadway, rolling Alec in the pile of dirt he'd swept himself maybe half an hour back. 'Sorry, Master Alec,' he was saying. 'No other way to hide the smell.'

And finally Joe understood. The horse muck was to mask the stink of gin and tobacco. Bates was protecting the boy the only way he knew how, protecting the family as he saw it, protecting even Mr Harvey from knowing what his only son got up to.

'I thought you was hurtin' him, Mr Bates,' said Joe, desperate now to apologize to the man. 'I didn't know . . .'

But when Bates looked up at him, there was the same ugly

expression on his face and the same words on his lips. 'Clear out of it, street trash.' Then he went on, 'You'd drag the whole family down to your level if you could, wouldn'tcha? Well, I'm here to stop yer!'

Joe tried to protest, to explain, to say he was sorry, but it was too late. Bates was gone, with Alec cradled in his arms.

Chapter 15

SKINS

From the cab window the City was a blur of noise and movement. The big wheels rattled and scraped on the roadway, and rich folk and poor, tall buildings and slum streets flashed by so fast Joe couldn't tell one from another. He'd never been in a hansom before. He'd watched a thousand speed by and swept up the horse muck after they passed, he'd hailed them for Mr Harvey and the other residents of Lomesbury Square and collected a penny for his trouble, but he'd never sat inside one.

'Look! There's a sweeper like me!' He pointed, but the figure was already past. Then he turned to Mr Harvey, sitting silent and upright next to him: 'Sorry, sir. It just all looks different like.'

Mr Harvey inclined his head slightly. He didn't speak, but on the other hand he didn't tell him off or shoot him one of the dirty looks he gave Alec. With Joe he behaved the way he did with the cadgers at his Fatherless Children place – never a cross word or an angry look. But with his own son . . . Joe realized with a shock – Alec and his father, they were the same. They were both like two different people from one moment to the next. And now he, Joe, was on his way to meet his own father off a ship. He wondered if James Mundy would be like him. Or was it the other way around? Was he like the father he'd never met?

'Stripe me!' Joe seized hold of Mr Harvey as the cab swerved smartly round a block in the traffic without the horse breaking stride. 'Sorry, sir!'

There'd have been dirty looks enough if Mr Harvey had known about Addison's last week. In fact, more than likely it would have been an end to helping old soldiers and their sons and Joe would have been barred from Lomesbury Square for good. But Bates obviously hadn't told Mr Harvey. The footman had blamed Joe to his face for getting Alec into trouble, as if he hadn't been the one to run and fetch help, but he hadn't said anything to anyone else. Couldn't. Otherwise he'd be dropping Alec in it too.

There'd been no sign of Alec anywhere outside the house for days. Maybe that room at the top of the house really was a prison and Mr Harvey had him locked up there. Still, there was nothing Joe could do about it. 'Gentry go their way and workin' folk follow.' That was what Barlow said.

The cab had slowed now. Looking ahead Joe could see the roadway wasn't paved here and the ground had been churned to a mire by heavy wagons. There was something familiar about the street too – the soot-crusted brick of the buildings, the boarded-up windows, the narrow alleys that led off into darkness even in the middle of the day . . .

Pound's Field! They were in Pound's Field! They were at the top of Flower Street and he hadn't even noticed. The horse was going slower and slower. Now they were coming up on Nimms's gin shop and the loose grating in the gutter that led down into the sewers. It was his nightmares come to life in broad daylight! '*Get back where you belong,*' Bates had said, and somehow Pound's Field had drawn him back.

Bates must have done it – told Mr Harvey about what happened at Addison's, put the blame on Joe Rat. They weren't going to the docks at all. Mr Harvey was bringing the street trash back to Pound's Field where it belonged, back to Mother.

'I ain't goin'!' Joe pushed at the wooden shutters of the cab in blind panic. 'You let me out!'

'Control yourself, Joseph.' Mr Harvey's grip on his arm was gentle but very firm. 'A measure of apprehension is quite understandable in your situation, but you are the son of a soldier and you must show courage.'

But Joe wasn't listening. 'What we doin' here? It weren't my fault. Why d'you bring me?'

'I do not understand you, Joseph. What was not your fault?'

'With Alec!'

'Alexander?' Mr Harvey's brow furrowed. 'What about Alexander? Do you know something about my son soiling another good suit of clothes?'

'I— He— What?' Joe's brain was starting to work again. 'No.' Had Bates blown the gab or not? 'What we doin' in Pound's Field?' he demanded finally.

'Really, Joseph!' Now Mr Harvey sounded exasperated. 'We

are on our way to the London Docks. Unfortunately we pass through this particularly insalubrious section of Whitechapel on our way.'

'Oh!' Joe let out a long breath and sank back in his seat. 'I see. We're just passin' through like. That's all right.'

'I am glad you approve of the arrangements,' said Mr Harvey, sounding more like the man who told his son off for drinking the wrong way at table. 'Now, sit up straight. You will be meeting a trooper in the Queen's army soon and you will want to make a good impression.'

Joe pushed himself upright. He was an idiot. Of course this was the way to the docks. And he'd nearly blown the gab himself by going on about Alec. Mr Harvey didn't mean him harm. But that didn't mean there wasn't danger here. Mother had eyes everywhere in Pound's Field and if he was spotted she'd know within ten minutes that the boy who owed her money was back within her grasp. He should never have come in the first place. He made a show of flattening out his hair, trying to hide his face with one hand.

Where Flower Street joined River Lane the cab came to a complete stop, blocked by the flow of heavily-laden wagons that went up and down the main road. Turn right and you were down to St Saviour's Docks. Straight ahead a narrow lane led to the old warehouses no one used any more. They should be turning left away from Pound's Field towards the London Docks, but the traffic was too thick.

'Go on!' Joe mumbled under his breath, willing the cabbie to push his horse through the throng, feeling the panic rising again inside him. 'Go on!' But the vehicle didn't move. He couldn't stand another minute of this: he was going to have to make a run for it.

Suddenly amongst the crowd of pedestrians Joe caught sight of a woman he knew: she'd sold tapes and laces behind the church and paid her whack to Mother just as he had. She was staring straight at him. In fact, everyone was staring at him! This was it. It was coming now. A shout. A chase. A kick to the stomach. And he'd be looking into the old monster's face again, breathing the rank smell that came off her, waiting for her to pronounce judgement.

Then he realized. The tape seller's eyes were blank. She looked at him, but she didn't know who he was. He studied the other faces that were turned his way and he understood. They weren't looking at him. No one in Pound's Field expected to see Joe Rat riding in a cab. They were looking at the gentleman in his hansom and the horse-drawn ambulance behind them, and maybe at the scruffy little white dog that had followed them all the way from Lomesbury.

There was a break in the traffic and the driver cracked his whip sharply, turning left away from Pound's Field and on past the immense walls of the London Docks. Joe breathed a little more easily. Perhaps his nightmares hadn't come true. Perhaps he really had escaped Pound's Field after all.

The cab dropped them at the dock gates and waited in the street with the ambulance, while Joe and Mr Harvey continued on foot. Back in Lomesbury the spring sun had been shining brightly, but a thick haze hung over the docks, blanketing the forest of ships' masts, the tall chimneys belching black smoke and the vast warehouses which rose on every side, blotting out the sky.

Just inside the gates a group of men were hammering at some enormous wine casks. A crowd of sailors pushed past, singing a wild song at the tops of their voices in a language Joe didn't recognize. He untied a length of string from his waist and fastened it around Boy's neck as a lead. The dog didn't have a collar. Collars were dear.

Mr Harvey bent to say something to Joe, but amidst the uproar of the docks, the boy couldn't make out what it was. In the end Mr Harvey simply pointed the way and Joe followed with the dog.

Along the quay, bales, baskets, sacks and barrels were stacked row on row, and cranes swung overhead depositing more cargo. Everywhere crowds of men were loading and unloading, shifting goods onto wagons while heavy dray horses waited patiently in their traces. Joe and Boy followed Mr Harvey past ship after ship, and every few yards the pungent aroma that hung over the quay changed from tobacco to rum to coffee to the sharp tang of sawn timber. Boy shook his head and sneezed and barked in surprise. The unfamiliar smells seemed to drive him wild.

They stopped at last by a rickety-looking gangway. 'Wait here for a moment, Joseph,' said Mr Harvey. 'I will just ensure that all is in readiness.'

He made his way slowly and carefully up the gangplank to a tall three-masted steamer. The great paddles at its side were still but a thin column of black smoke rose from its funnel into the hazy sky.

Joe squatted down on the dock to wait, Boy beside him. He looked at the ship's bright flags fluttering in the breeze. He stared out across the dock, but the haze hid most of the other ships from view. The sharp rattle of a chain startled him as a crane suddenly released its load and an enormous iron bin clanged down onto the dock beside him.

Joe stood up and peered into the open container. It was full of animal horns, all jumbled and piled in together. He didn't know what sort of creatures had died to fill the bin, but it must have been hundreds of them. As he watched, another container, also filled to the brim, came swinging off the ship and down onto the quayside.

A stack of huge bales, some jet black, others silvery grey, caught his attention and he walked further along the wharf to see what they were. The first bale was soft to the touch – softer than anything he had ever felt. They were animal skins of some kind. He moved on to the next bale and ran his hand over the fur, brushing it gently backward and forward, enjoying the sensation. Then the fur moved under his hand.

The boy let out a sharp cry of surprise and the dog at his side pricked his ears and edged forward, nose twitching at the strange, sickening smell that rose from the bale. It was the smell of rotting meat. The pelt Joe had his hand on heaved again, as if the animal it had once been were coming back to life or as if something else was living underneath its skin.

Then Joe saw them. Out of the holes where the animal's eyes

had once been, seething through the great pile of skins, thousands upon thousands of fat, white maggots twisted and crawled.

A sharp voice startled him. 'Oi! Keep that mutt out of it!' A crewman was shouting from the deck of the ship. Joe jerked round, dragging the dog with him.

As he turned, he saw a woman sitting on one of the bales, eyes cast down. She had a couple of bundles beside her and a row of old, rusty cooking pots at her feet. The woman glanced up suddenly and met his gaze. Her eyes were red-rimmed and they stared at him without blinking. She didn't speak. After a minute Joe felt he had to say something.

'Soft, aren't they?' he managed.

The woman looked at him as if she didn't understand. Perhaps she was foreign. He pointed at the bale of furs she was sitting on. 'They're very soft,' he repeated. 'I ain't never felt nothin' like 'em.'

'Rotten on the inside though,' she said suddenly. Her voice was hoarse and very quiet. She put her hand up to her mouth and coughed into a dirty-looking handkerchief. Joe wasn't sure if he'd heard her right.

'Rotten?'

'Underneath. Half the skins ain't cured proper. That's why they're crawlin'.' Suddenly she was struggling to her feet and reaching out towards Joe. 'What you want round 'ere, boy?' she demanded.

Joe took an involuntary step backwards. 'I'm meetin' someone off the ship,' he stammered.

'Off that ship?' She pointed to the three-master Mr Harvey had boarded. 'I wouldn't.' She never seemed to blink and her eyes stared through him. 'Ain't nothin' good comin' off of that ship, boy. Nothin'!'

'What do you mean?' Joe demanded. 'What do you know about it?'

But the woman had lost interest in him. She slumped back down on the bale of furs and her eyes glazed over, staring vacantly at her rusted cooking pots.

Joe went back towards the ship, wishing he'd never left it. The rotting cargo and the old woman had unsettled him, left him feeling there was something ominous about the tall ship with the flags fluttering gaily at its mastheads. He squatted down on the dock again to wait for Mr Harvey. The dog lay down next to him, put his head between his paws and fell asleep, oblivious to the racket of unloading that continued all around them.

After a few minutes a couple of sailors came slouching down the gangplank, laughing as they came. 'What a game!' one was saying. 'I'd shoot meself in the head for a berth like that.'

'He's a soldier-boy,' protested the other man. 'Got that wound fightin' for Queen and country.'

'Soldier-boy, be damned!' cursed the other man. 'He's a wild man bin out in the forest. Wouldn't never have lived through a fever like that otherwise. Anyways' – the man tapped a long finger against the side of his nose – 'there's more than one way to get a bullet in yer.' The two sailors laughed again at the tops of their voices and strolled on down the dock.

There was no knowing who they'd been talking about. Any number of sick passengers might be coming back to England on the ship. But Joe was somehow quite sure they were discussing the man he'd come to meet – the man Mr Harvey had told him was his father. Did these sailors know something about James Mundy that Mr Harvey didn't? Or hadn't Mr Harvey told him everything? There'd been a moment in that book-lined study when Joe had been sure the gentleman was keeping something from him.

'Joseph!'

Mr Harvey was standing at the top of the gangplank. Beside him two men in striped jerseys were holding a stretcher, piled high with the same kind of animal pelts Joe had been touching just a few moments earlier. Why were they unloading this lot by hand?

He stood up hurriedly, glancing back at the dock for the woman, but there was no sign of her. The bundles and cooking pots were gone as if she had never been there. Mr Harvey's voice came again.

'Joseph!'

The sailors had reached the quay and set their load down next to Joe. The boy waited for Mr Harvey, who was still talking to a man in uniform on the deck of the ship. Perhaps there had been some delay. Perhaps James Mundy wasn't on this ship after all. Perhaps ... He glanced down at the bundle of furs at his feet. They were thick and soft, some black and shining, others a ghostly grey like the bales on the quayside. But the smell that came off them was different – an odd mixture of animal hide and human sweat.

He reached down to touch their softness. Then he stepped back with a cry and Boy, who had been edging forward too to investigate the skins, leaped away with a startled bark, straining at his leash. Like the bale of rotting hides on the quayside, the pile of furs had moved. Something was alive underneath them.

At one end of the stretcher, almost hidden amongst the blackest of the animal hides, a pair of eyes glinted open. At first Joe couldn't make out anything else. It was as if the mountain of furs itself had grown eyes. Then he realized the shadows around the eyes were made not of animal hide but human hair. Thick, black, greasy locks, shot with grey, hung low over the brow and a heavy growth of coarser hair completely obliterated the lower half of what must be a face. Only the eyes were visible – dark, shining, blank.

With a shiver of surprise Joe realized he was looking at a man.

Of course, this must be the man called James Mundy, the soldier who was meant to be his father. The eyes showed no recognition. They didn't even show interest. They were fixed and empty and they meant nothing to Joe. He didn't know what he'd expected. His father had left England three months before he was born – Joe knew that much – so how could they recognize each other? But this man – this creature – couldn't be his father, could he?

He felt Mr Harvey's hand on his shoulder. 'Well now, Joseph,' the man was saying. 'Introduce yourself. Private

Mundy will take time to recover from his voyage, but I believe he understands what you say.'

But Joe just stood staring at the wild-looking man, unable to say a thing. Pulling hard on the length of string that Joe still held in one hand, Boy was whining and whimpering, struggling to get further from the stretcher. It was the dog that startled Joe out of his silence.

'Leave off, Boy! Stop it!' He turned to look for Mr Harvey. 'He don't like the smell of the skins, sir. That's what it is.'

'Yes,' agreed Mr Harvey. 'I expect that's it.'

Chapter 16

The Knife

Alec watched impatiently through the window of the dining room. He'd begged his father to cancel lessons for the morning and let him meet the RMS *Endeavour* at the docks too, but he'd known what the answer would be. After the excursion to Addison's he'd got three days in the Reformatory and now he wasn't allowed outside the house without his tutor. The only satisfaction was that yet again he was being punished for dirtying a set of clothes. What would his father have said if he'd known how, according to Bates, he'd lain unconscious in the footman's pantry for four hours before the effects of the 'medicine' wore off?

He'd watched his mother often enough, measuring the stuff out drop by drop. He saw every night what it did to her, as she sat at the dinner table swaying and mumbling and never eating. He'd wanted to know what it was like from the inside – to feel the way she felt – and it had frightened him. He'd lost the phial in the bar and he wasn't sorry. What had the man called it? The black drop? And what did he say about his mother? Alec didn't want to think about that. He could feel his blood boil inside him at the memory and he wanted to lash out again at the man, to send him sprawling across the floor.

There was still no sign of a cab in the street and Johnny had gone out after morning lessons. Alec took a silver letter-opener off the mantelpiece, and made as if to stab the portrait of Colonel Harvey. Then he ducked under the gleaming dining table and began to carve his initials into the wood.

It was tough work. The mahogany of the table was harder than the window frame in the tower room. Another couple of weeks up there just might see him levering the lock out altogether.

He'd carved the first line of a letter 'A' into the underside of the table before he realized putting his own name might not be such a good idea. He was trying to make up his mind whether to turn it into a 'B' for Briggs or a 'J' for Johnson when he heard the swift clip-clop of a horse outside. Alec was back at the window in time to see a hansom pull up and his father and Joe get out.

He noticed the way his father put one hand on Joe's shoulder, guiding him through the front gate, and he felt the same twinge of jealousy as he had that morning when the pair drove away. It wasn't Joe's fault. He was welcome to his slice of luck – if it was lucky to have a father shipped across the Atlantic to tell you what to do. But why did his father always have that gleam in his eye when he was dealing with the crossing sweeper, whereas all Alec got was the long face and the sniff through the nose? It was the same with the Fatherless Children and the Orphans' Committee and all the rest of the charitable works his father loved to spend time on. They got the gleam in the eye and the family got the long face – all except for dear little Flicky, of course. Where was the poison dolly, anyway?

As if in answer to his question Felicity came dashing out of the front door with her nursemaid, Alice, in pursuit. She ran straight to her father, throwing her arms around his waist and straining to see what was happening as a slow-moving ambulance drew up behind the hansom.

Alec watched through the window as the driver of the ambulance opened the back and Bates helped drag the stretcher out. There was a figure on it, covered from head to foot in thick furs. Was Joe's father underneath there somewhere? He couldn't imagine his own father covered in furs like that.

He hurried out into the hall, but they didn't come in that way. Through the baize-covered door he could hear raised voices in the basement and doors opening and closing. Of course, they were taking him through there. Bates's pantry had been turned into a sick room, much to the footman's disgust, and Alec wasn't even going to get a glimpse of the man unless . . . He pushed open the door and crept down the stairs.

The stretcher and the two men carrying it seemed to fill the entire passage. Behind it his father was giving orders to the sick-nurse in her white cap and apron. She'd been taken on specially to look after the patient. Bates had gone on about a nurse's wages until Alec had told the man to shut up. Joe stood in the passage to one side, wide-eyed. Mrs Briggs had her head poking out of the kitchen and both the housemaids were fussing around getting in the way.

'Alexander!' Naturally his father spotted him at once. 'I believe we have enough assistance here. You are likely to impede our efforts. Kindly retire to the school room.'

Alec went back upstairs, but he didn't 'retire to the school room'. Instead he crouched under the table in the dining room, waiting for things to quieten down. He had decided to make his 'A' for Alexander into 'J' for Joe.

After a while he heard his father talking to Bates in the hall-way. Then the front door opened and closed. Mr Harvey was going to the office. Alec waited a little longer. The house grew silent. Now was the moment.

He slipped out of the dining room, down the stairs to the basement and along the passage. Outside the door to what had been Bates's pantry he waited with his hand on the doorknob, pressing his ear to the woodwork. There was no sound from inside. The sick-nurse might be in there. Joe might be in there. But what could they do? His father had gone out and of course there was no sign of his mother. She'd be stretched out on her bed as usual. Alec knew now why she lay so still.

He opened the door softly. The room smelled of camphor and animals. Bates's day bed had been pushed against the far wall and almost all the other furniture removed. The walls had all been specially whitewashed. There was no sign of Joe or the sick-nurse.

The man's face stood out like a dark stain on the white pillow, the shaggy, matted hair spread out in a tangle. Alec went closer. The man's eyes were closed. Great beads of perspiration gathered on his forehead and ran down into the corners of his eyes. His breathing sounded laboured. Amongst all the hair his cheeks were sunken and hollow and his eyes had dark rings under them. Alec tried to see some resemblance to Joe in the sickly, battered features – people said he himself looked like his father – but this man didn't resemble any human creature Alec had ever seen.

The animal skins were piled over him. Alec recognized moose hides from pictures his tutor had shown him and otter fur like the hood of his mother's winter cape. But despite the furs and the warmth of the room the man shivered so violently that the whole bed shook, and even as he slept or lay unconscious – Alec couldn't tell which – his right hand gripped the skins as if fearing someone would take them from him.

Alec bent closer still. It wasn't just a stack of skins covering the man. Now he could see how the hides had been stitched together into an enormous coat with beaver and otter pelts around the edges, heads and claws still attached. He reached out to touch the softness of the fur, but the proximity of the man's hand made him draw back. It was a massive fist – more than twice as big as his own – bony knuckles prominent through skin that looked like leather. From the crook of the thumb to the wrist ran a livid red scar with rough stitch marks clearly visible all the way along.

The man stirred uneasily in the bed, groaning out something that could have been words, and Alec took a step backwards. He didn't want those dark-ringed eyes to open and see him there. He stared at the ham-like fist, imagining it gripping his arm or smashing into his face.

At the foot of the bed, propped against the wall, stood a bag made from animal hide and edged with fur like the coat. Alec glanced back at the bed: the man was still. He looked at the door: no sign of anyone coming. He bent quickly and undid the laces that held the bag shut, wrinkling his nose at the pungent smell of untreated leather.

He pulled out a pair of soft, kid leather gloves, trimmed with fur and decorated with beads and animal teeth. He turned them over, sniffed at them. He could see how the teeth which ran in a line along the backs of the gloves would rip into the flesh of an enemy. He slipped them on. They were far too large for his hands, but he flexed his fingers into fists anyway, hitting out wildly, imagining himself striking down a brace of savage tribesmen.

The figure on the bed muttered softly. Alec put the gloves down and reached into the bag again. His fingers closed on something soft and silky. It was a length of thick, dark hair, decorated with feathers and still attached to a small circle of skin, which had been painted red on the underside. Alec examined the strange object, running his fingers through the dark hair. It looked human, but how had it been attached to an animal skin and why?

Then he realized: it hadn't been attached. It had grown there. He was holding a human scalp in his hand, cut from the head of a dead enemy. It was too wonderful to believe, like stepping into the pages of a storybook. He dropped the gruesome trophy and felt inside the bag once more, half expecting his fingers to be seized by some vicious, sharp-toothed animal lurking there.

'Ow!'

He jerked his hand out. Something inside the bag really had jabbed into his questing fingers and Alec hadn't been able to stop himself from crying out.

He looked round fearfully, but the figure in the bed showed no signs of consciousness. He examined his hand in the dim light from the shaded window. The ball of his thumb was bleeding where something sharp had dug into the skin. He put it to his mouth and sucked hard, tasting the salt of his own blood. Then he reached into the bag again, more carefully this time.

It was a knife, perhaps a foot long. The blade was encased in a leather sheath. The handle was long and curved and made from animal horn. Instead of a pommel the end had been sharpened to a needle point: it was that which had cut him.

Alec wrapped his fingers around the handle. It felt warm to the touch. Then he drew off the leather sheath. The blade was serrated on one edge, smooth and razor-sharp on the other with a pointed tip. He ran his finger over the blade, carefully avoiding the edge. It wasn't smooth like the handle, but ridged and irregular. Alec's uncle, the one who'd been in the army, had swords and daggers from all over the world, but he didn't have anything like this in his glass cases. Perhaps James Mundy had made the dagger himself, but Alec didn't think he'd got it from the army.

Alec examined the blade. It reflected dully in the subdued light of the sick room, but it wasn't made of metal and it was too light for stone. Some kind of bone maybe. And there was writing. Low down on the handle, where strips of leather hide held it fast to the blade, something had been scratched roughly into the horn. The boy held it up to the light and mouthed the letters silently – 'T-r-a . . .' It said: *Trapper*.

He picked up the bag. The letters 'JM' were stitched neatly under the drawstring – James Mundy. The gloves had nothing on them. Yes, they did. 'T-r . . . Trapper' again! Who or what was Trapper?

Alec was turning the bag upside down to tip out whatever else was inside when the door swung smartly open. He just had time to stuff the contents back into the bag before the sick-nurse came in.

'What you doin' there, you little scamp?' The woman had a strong country accent.

'I am addressed as Master Alexander,' said Alec loudly, standing up and confronting the woman. He was taller than her which made him feel better.

'You ain't addressed no-how by me, you rascal. Now be off with you.' Alec opened his mouth to speak. 'Out! Afore I calls the master.'

Alec's shoulders slumped and he walked sulkily out of the room. Did the rest of the contents of the bag say 'JM' or 'Trapper'? He might never find out. But there was something odd about it.

Heavy footsteps sounded on the stairs coming down from

the hall. It could be Bates. It could be his father come back early from the bank: if he caught him down here there'd be trouble.

At the end of the passage was a cupboard where the house-maids kept mops and pails. Alec had found it one afternoon escaping from Mr Johnson and his Latin verbs. He ducked swiftly in there now, pulling the door shut behind him. Almost at once he heard his father's voice.

'Now, you must not stay with him long, Joseph. The main thing your father needs at the moment is rest. You have no objection to giving up your room for a time, have you, Bates?'

'No, sir. Only too pleased if it's your wish.'

In the darkness of the cupboard Alec imagined the sour look on Bates's face. He knew exactly how 'pleased' the footman was about the latest 'charity case', as he called James Mundy.

'Before you go in though, Joseph,' Mr Harvey went on, 'I have a proposition for you which I would like you to consider carefully. I dare say, Bates, that you would be glad of assistance with some of your more mundane duties. The cleaning of the knives and boots perhaps—?'

'Well, not really, sir—'

But Mr Harvey didn't allow the man to finish. 'What I am proposing, Joseph, is that you abandon your life on the streets, and enter my employment on a formal basis.'

There was an explosion of coughing from Bates, and Alec smiled to himself. The footman would be trying to hide his feelings in front of his employer, but Alec knew the last person Bates wanted working for him was the sweeper boy.

Mr Harvey waited for the coughing to die down, and went on steadily. 'My charitable works, as I said, have all been outside the home until the present. Now we have an old soldier who needs assistance under our roof and I have no doubt that Mrs Briggs could devise a place in the house for you to sleep, Joseph, which would be more attractive than your current lodgings in—'

'Crooked-back Lane,' finished Joe. 'Couldn't be worse nohow.'

'So what do you say, Joseph? Take your time if you want. No need to answer at once.'

Joe's voice came back straight away. 'I can answer right away, sir, beggin' yer pardon, sir.'

'I'll bet you can, you lucky young—'

'Bates!' Mr Harvey's warning voice stopped the footman.

'What I was goin' to say, sir,' Joe went on, 'is how it sounds a bit shut in, like.'

'Shut in?' Mr Harvey queried.

'I'm used to outdoor work, see, sir.'

'I see.'

Mr Harvey sounded disappointed. Alec felt a twinge of disappointment too. '*I'm his friend*,' Joe had told that stupid barmaid in Addison's. With Joe living in the house it would have been like having a real friend. But mixed with the disappointment was something else – something more like relief. There was a part of Alec that didn't want Joe coming any closer to his father.

'But what I would like, beggin' yer pardon, sir' – Joe's voice was eager now – 'is to work in the park with Mr Barlow, sir. He didn't hold with me at first. But he's grown accustomed. And I could sleep in the shed, sir.'

'In the shed?'

'Yes, sir. Fine shed with new hinges and a roof what keeps the rain out.'

'It does not sound a particularly attractive prospect, Joseph.'

'Oh, it'd suit me fine, sir. Better than I ever imagined, sir—'

'Well,' Mr Harvey interrupted, and Alec could hear the smile on his long face – the smile that was usually reserved for the poison dolly, 'if that is what you genuinely desire, Joseph—'

'It is, sir!'

'Then I dare say I can persuade the committee to accept my recommendation.'

'Oh, and Boy.'

'I beg your pardon.'

'The dog, sir. He'd have to sleep there too, sir. He don't take up much space.'

'And Boy, Joseph. We will see what we can do.'

'Mr Harvey, sir.' In the cramped cupboard Alec stirred uneasily at the sound of the country accent. It was the sick-nurse. 'I'm truly sorry to have to complain so soon, sir, but your son has been in the sick room messin' with the patient's things, and I can't be responsible—'

'Thank you, nurse.' Alec knew that cool, clipped voice. It meant his father was really angry. 'I will attend to the matter.'

Then he went on more slowly: 'It is strange, is it not, Bates, that to bring a lost soldier halfway around the world seems to be easier than to keep a boy with every advantage on the straight and narrow way?'

'Yes, sir.' The footman sounded awkward, embarrassed that Mr Harvey should talk to him about his son, especially in front of Joe and the nurse.

But the next minute Mr Harvey was back to his usual brisk and businesslike manner. 'You can rest assured, nurse, neither you nor the patient will be troubled again.'

Footsteps receded down the corridor and Alec huddled a little lower amongst the mops and buckets. He couldn't avoid his father for ever, but for now he was safe. He thought of Joe moving into the little shed in the middle of the square. It sounded a whole lot better than this great, echoing house with its gleaming mahogany and its Reformatory. He felt another twinge of envy go through him.

Chapter 17
A WILD MAN

The ranks of bright-red geraniums that Joe and Barlow had planted back in April stood up tall in the warm, summer sunshine. On a bench under a young plane tree Alec sat without his jacket on, an expression of unutterable boredom on his face, while Mr Johnson read aloud from a book of poetry. Out of the corner of his eye he watched Joe leading a small white pony, harnessed to a gleaming new lawnmower. Jeremy Barlow strolled along at the rear, guiding the contraption with one hand. The dog trotted at Joe's heels.

By the gate where the grass had already been cut Felicity was playing with a group of little girls, watched by Alice and a row of other uniformed nursemaids. Alice threw a shuttlecock and the girls took it in turns to swing a tiny racket as hard as they could. Mostly they missed. Occasionally they connected with squeals of delight and the shuttlecock flew into the bushes for one of the nursemaids to retrieve.

Alec eyed his sister balefully. 'When you see the splash of Jeremy Barlow's plants amongst the grass, Johnny,' he said, 'does it not put you in mind of a great pool of blood?'

Mr Johnson looked up sharply from his book. 'I have asked you not to address me in that manner, Master Alexander. My given name is Theobald, as you are quite well aware.'

Alec looked shocked. 'I couldn't possibly call you that, Johnny: it wouldn't be respectful.' Mr Johnson sighed heavily. 'You think I'm bad, don't you, Johnny?' Alec went on with a sunny smile.

'I think you present a challenge, Master Alexander,' said the tutor carefully.

'No you don't. You think I'm bad. Why don't you say so?'

'Perhaps,' said Mr Johnson, closing his book, 'poetry is over-stimulating to the young mind in early summer. Perhaps we should—'

'Call it a day!' exclaimed Alec, jumping up. 'Excellent idea, Johnny – er – Theobald.'

'That was not what I was about to say,' began the tutor.

But Mr Johnson didn't get the chance to tell Alec what he was about to say, because at that moment Felicity hit the shuttlecock high into the air and, as it was coming down once again into the bushes, a big hand shot out and caught it in a flash. The whole thing was so fast that for a moment Alec wasn't sure what had happened.

The nursemaid, Alice, spun round, looking to see where the shuttlecock had gone, and screamed at the top of her lungs. Felicity stood rooted to the spot, eyes wide in terror. Joe stopped and stared, and the pony stopped with him, and Barlow cursed. Alec took a step forward, his heart beating fast.

Clad from head to foot in his animal-skin coat, hair hanging to his shoulders, James Mundy looked like a creature that had stepped straight out of the wild and into the immaculately kept gardens of Lomesbury Square. He put his hands together quickly as Felicity still stood motionless. Then he held them open in front of the child's face. They were empty. The shuttlecock had disappeared.

Alec cried aloud with delight and moved towards the towering figure. He wanted to step into the storybook world James Mundy came from; he wanted to hold the dagger again and the scalp in his bag and see the long, livid scar on the man's hand. He wanted to touch the animal-skin coat, feel its softness.

Joe was ahead of him.

The shuttlecock had reappeared in Mundy's enormous fist. He was trying to give the toy back to Felicity, but the girl was still rigid, too terrified to hold out her hand. Alice was like a statue too, one arm stretched out towards the little girl. It was Joe who took the feathered ball out of the big man's hand and pressed it into Felicity's palm. The little girl started as if she were waking up and looked at Joe. Then she burst into tears and buried her head in Alice's skirts.

Behind the man the scowling figure of Bates took a pace forward. Bates was tall, but beside this fur-clad giant he looked like a midget. Alec could see the footman's fists clench, ready to fight. The boy didn't give him a chance against James Mundy, even if the man had just come out of a six-week fever.

But there was no fight. In fact Mundy took an unsteady step sideways and for a moment he seemed to need the support of

his sick-nurse. Alice and the other nursemaids collected their charges rapidly and hurried away across the park towards the gate.

'He's only allowed out for half an hour, mind,' said the sick-nurse sternly. 'Reckon he can manage without you now, Mr Bates,' she added, 'can't you, Mr Mundy?'

Bates's scowl deepened and he headed back towards the house without a word. Mundy didn't speak either and he didn't watch the footman leave. He was looking at Joe.

The boy held out his hand uncertainly, not sure how to address the man. He'd sat by his bed while Mundy lay sick all these last weeks, but he'd never been sure the man had known he was there and they had never spoken.

'How d'yer do, Mr Mundy?'

Mundy took Joe's hand without smiling. The palm felt as hard as tanned leather.

'How d'ye do, boy. I'm thinkin' you'd be Joe.' His voice was slow and quiet as a whisper.

'And you'd be – my father?'

The man didn't answer at once. His eyes narrowed, focusing on the boy as if he were trying to see into him. Joe could see a glitter like a little shard of ice deep inside those eyes. In the sick room he'd thought it was fever, but the strange light was still there. There were lines under and around the eyes that suggested pain or maybe cruelty: perhaps the mouth would have shown which, but a heavy growth of beard still covered the lower part of the man's face. When he spoke at last, his voice was so soft Joe had to lean forward to hear him.

'Seems like it.'

Joe let go of the man's hand. He looked around at the people watching. The sick-nurse had her arms folded and was tapping one foot as if she'd rather be somewhere else. Alec was there, eyes burning. There was a moment when Joe wondered what the other boy was thinking as he stared so intently at Mundy. Jeremy Barlow was seeing to the horse. The dog had disappeared. Someone had to say something!

'Got a room here,' said Joe finally. 'You want to see it?'

A flicker of surprise showed on Mundy's face. Then the creases around his eyes deepened. He was smiling.

'Sure,' he said. 'Why not?'

Mundy shrugged off the sick-nurse's supporting arm, and allowed Joe to lead him across the grass towards Barlow's shed.

'Ain't never had a place of me own before.'

Joe held the door open. He'd used a length of garden twine to hang a set of old curtains across the middle of the shed, dividing it into two rooms. Suddenly he felt an eagerness he couldn't explain to show this man what he'd done, how he'd made Barlow's shed comfortable, turned it into a home.

'Mrs Briggs give me the curtains. I found a whole box of twine in the ground out back,' he went on. 'There's all sorts of stuff buried. Still good string though. See?'

Mundy didn't say anything. His eyes ran over the tools hanging on their hooks on the wall. He examined the string. He looked carefully at the work Joe had done and his hand tested the curtain.

'That's where I sleep,' said Joe. 'You can pull the curtain back if you want.'

Mundy slid the faded curtains back. A shrill, furious barking erupted into the silence and Boy rushed at the man.

'Stop it!' Joe shouted at him. 'Stop your racket, Boy!'

The dog took not the slightest notice. All his attention was on Mundy. The hair along his back stood on end as he charged forward, barking and nipping at the big man's boots and then shrinking away into the corner by Joe's mattress, cowering and whining.

As quick as he had caught Felicity's shuttlecock, Mundy stooped and scooped the dog up in one hand. Boy seemed to shrink even smaller in the big man's grasp, struggling desperately, eyes wide with terror. Mundy put his other hand around the dog's muzzle and lifted the animal up until he was looking straight into Boy's eyes. The man's lips parted, baring his teeth, but he wasn't smiling. He bent close and whispered in the dog's ear, too quick and quiet for Joe to hear.

When the man set him down on the floor again, Boy lay stretched out, completely still and silent. His eyes were fixed, unblinking, on the bearded man and a trembling ran along the length of his body. Joe began to stammer an apology, but Mundy stopped him.

'He aims to warn or protect. That's what dogs do.'

'What did you do to him?'

'Told him who I am.' He looked down at the dog and Boy lowered his head sharply, apparently unable to meet the man's gaze.

'And who are you?'

The man looked at him quickly. 'I'm James Mundy, boy. And it seems like I'm all you got.'

'They told you, did they?' Joe stammered awkwardly. 'She died. My mother. Lizzie. She got the tramp fever in the spike – you know? The workhouse? It were bad that year, I reckon.'

'Yeah' – the man nodded slowly – 'they told me. And Mike and Jimmy.'

'Matt.'

'What?'

'Matt and Jimmy. Me brothers.'

'What did I say?'

'You said "Mike".'

'No, I didn't.' The man's voice suddenly had a hard edge. 'Reckon I know my own boys' names, don't I?'

The dog whimpered uneasily on the floor, but he didn't raise his head. Joe didn't know what to say. Mundy had been very ill. If he forgot things or got names wrong it was hardly surprising.

'Matt and Jimmy got the cholera too, sir,' he said nervously. 'They died and all.'

'Don't call me that.'

'What?'

'Don't call me "sir". Sounds like the army.'

'Sorry.'

Mundy looked at him. 'Bin around a lot of death, boy,' he said quietly. 'Too much, mebbe. Wears a man down.'

Joe searched for something else to say. 'That's my bed,' he managed at last, indicating the canvas mattress on the carefully swept floor. 'Horsehair, not shavings. No bugs or nothin'.'

He showed Mundy the suit of Alec's old clothes he'd hung on the wall. 'Too good to wear, mind. Just there for show.' He pointed out a couple of tatty music-hall posters he'd found lying in the street and nailed up above his bed. In the wooden ceiling directly over the mattress he'd hung an old horseshoe dug up from behind the shed.

Mundy looked at everything with the same serious expression, his eyes narrowed in concentration. Joe couldn't guess what he was thinking. He led him out to the back where young potato plants had come pushing up through the ground. Barlow was letting him tend them.

'I'll have me own spuds soon,' said Joe delightedly. 'Whole load of odds and ends in the ground too.' Ranged along the side of the shed were three more horseshoes, a hob-nailed boot and a rusted smoothing iron. Joe sorted through the broken crockery he'd dug out of the earth, holding up pieces where a pattern still showed. 'Ain't worth nothin',' he said. 'But they'll look good on the wall, I reckon. When I've cleaned 'em up a bit.'

Mundy still didn't comment. But he examined everything he was shown, sometimes nodding his head, occasionally baring his teeth in the same odd grimace he'd shown Boy. You couldn't call it a smile.

When he'd shown him everything, Joe led the man back inside and drew his curtain closed. He liked to feel he was in a part of the room that was just his. He sat on the floor and Mundy sat on the mattress, breathing heavily as if he were tired from walking again for the first time in a long while.

Joe couldn't think of anything else to say. The man was his father, but he didn't know how to act with a father. He didn't even know what to call him. He didn't like to be called 'sir' like Mr Harvey, but he couldn't go on calling him Mr Mundy.

'What should I call you?' Joe asked at last.

'Bin called most things one time or another,' said the man slowly. 'Call me what ya like.'

'I don't think I can call you Father,' said Joe. 'I ain't never had no father.'

'Call me Jimmy,' said the man. 'That's my name.'

'OK.' Joe smiled.

There was silence for a moment. 'What d'yer think about the place, then, Jimmy?' All of a sudden it seemed important to know what James Mundy thought about the room he'd worked so hard on. 'I ain't never had nowhere that was just mine. Pretty swell, eh?'

'Place is no good.'

'What?'

'Place is no good.'

Joe looked at the man. He liked the way he took what he said seriously, as if he was an equal, a man, not just a kid off the street. But why did he say the room was no good? Before he could ask, Mundy spoke.

'Can't defend it.'

'Defend it?'

'You need defence and you need a back door.'

'I don't need to defend it,' said Joe. 'Not in Lomesbury Square.'

'Don'tcha?' Mundy looked at him narrowly. 'Man never knows when he'll need to defend what he's got.'

Joe opened his mouth to argue, but Mundy's face suddenly stiffened and his eyes flickered sideways. In an utter silence that seemed impossible for such a big man he lifted himself to his feet, took a single stride and thrust one arm through the curtain. There was a sound of scuffling feet and Mundy's hand reappeared, holding Alec easily by the throat.

The man spat quickly on the floor and ground the spittle in with his boot. 'Dog's no good either,' he said. 'Don't hear folks listenin' in.'

He put Alec down. The boy looked simultaneously shocked and delighted.

'I was not listening. I have come to visit my friend. That's all.'

Joe looked at the other boy uneasily. After the afternoon at Addison's he'd promised himself not to have any more to do with Alec Harvey. The Harveys had given him steady work and a place to live and now they'd given him a family when he never thought he'd have one of his own, and Alec was a danger to all of it. Joe was quite sure of that.

'Jimmy's wound still pains him, Alec. You shouldn't oughta come creepin' up on him like that.'

'Pardon me, I'm sure,' said Alec, kicking moodily at the floor.

Mundy sat down heavily on the horsehair mattress. The

effort seemed to have tired him again. Joe sensed what an immense struggle he had been through to survive at all. 'You can lie down if you want to,' he told the man.

Mundy looked at him. There was no softness in his face but one eyebrow lifted quizzically. 'You like havin' a father, boy?' he asked slowly.

'I – I dunno.'

'You say you got more of that hemp twine?'

'I got a whole box of it.'

'Bring it me.'

Joe fetched the string from the other part of the shed. He didn't know why the man wanted it but he found he liked doing things for him.

When he came back, Alec was quizzing Mundy enthusiastically. How had he joined the army? Who had he fought with? Where had he lived? Watching him bent close to the man as if he wanted to memorize every line on his face, Joe found it hard to believe this was the same person who had lain stretched out in Addison's sawdust as if he were dead. James Mundy had brought yet another side out of this strange boy who could seem so totally different from one day to the next.

'But your accent,' Alec was saying. 'You sound as if you've lived in north America all your life.'

Mundy took three balls of twine out of the box and with quick, deft movements began to plait them together. He seemed to have forgotten what Alec had said. At length he spoke again, his fingers still flying backwards and forwards, creating a strong rope out of the thin string.

'You'd be Alexander Harvey?'

He looked Alec in the eye. His fingers went on with their work, even though the rest of him seemed completely concentrated on Alec.

'I like Alec better,' said the boy, trying to meet the man's gaze. 'Call me Alec. What did you mean by a back door? I heard you saying it: "You need defence and you need a back door."' Alec imitated Mundy's slow drawl, but the man didn't seem to notice.

'Back door,' he said slowly. 'Means a way out. If they catch ya.'

'If who catches you?'

But Mundy went on as if the boy hadn't spoken. 'Only one door here. And one gate in the fence outside. One way in. One way out. Ain't no good.'

'I'd never noticed,' said Alec. 'Did you learn that in the army? Or are you—? Were you ever—?' He took a breath. 'You look like a wild man. I've read about them.'

Again Joe saw Mundy's lips curl back from his teeth in something that wasn't quite a smile. The man looked straight at Alec and for a moment the quick hands stopped working on the string.

'There's a little wild in every creature, boy. Man, woman and child. Even that dog there. Some got it more'n others. That's all.'

Mundy's eyes went back to his work. Something about the way he sat hunched over said quite clearly he didn't want to talk any more. The dog crept closer on his belly until he was lying next to Alec and Joe on the floor, and the two boys watched as a great length of thin, flexible rope began to coil towards them. Alec reached out and scratched Boy behind the ear. The dog trembled as he always did when someone touched him, but he didn't move away.

'It appears I owe this animal a debt of gratitude after our less than successful visit to Addison's Superior Tavern.' Alec spoke quietly, his words intended only for Joe. 'And you too, Master Joe. However, it seems I am never to be allowed out of the house without Johnny Johnson again. He is standing guard outside now, you know.'

'Is he?' said Joe. 'Serves yer right.' He tried to sound angry, but in spite of everything he felt glad to have the other boy sitting there next to him. *I have come to visit my friend.* That's what he'd said. And Joe liked the sound of the words. Now he had two visitors in his own place.

'Yes,' agreed Alec. 'Serves me right.'

For almost an hour the two boys sat side by side and watched the strange man in the animal-skin coat. They tried asking what he was doing. 'Wait and see,' was all Mundy would say.

After a while he reached under his enormous coat and pulled out a long knife with a horn handle. Alec stiffened. It was the wicked-looking weapon he'd found in the man's bag, the one that had sliced into his hand.

Mundy drew the knife out of its sheath and cut a length of the rope he'd made, looping an end around a nail on the wall. Then he put the knife down next to him, and his fingers began to move swiftly and deftly again, twisting and knotting the rope over and over again. Gradually an intricate web started to form under his swiftly moving fingers.

And as he worked Mundy told them stories of his life in the wilderness of New Brunswick, of long marches through snow-bound country and battles with tribesmen where men had scalped the dead on both sides. Alec thought of the trophy he had found in the man's bag. Had Joe's father used the very knife that lay there in front of him to cut that scalp from the head of a man? Alec wanted to reach out and hold the knife again, to test its sharpness against his own skin, but he couldn't summon the nerve.

The stories went on and on, painting pictures of faraway places where the rivers were so full of fish you could grab them out with your bare hands and the land was so empty of people you could travel for weeks without meeting another living soul.

'I would give everything I own and everything I am ever going to own just to live that way for a day,' said Alec, his eyes shining.

'That's a lot to give, boy,' said the man. 'What d'you think you'd be gettin' in exchange?'

'Adventure,' breathed Alec.

'And you, Joe?' The man eyed Joe narrowly, fingers still working. 'You want adventure?'

'I dunno,' said Joe uncertainly. 'I like it here. I got me own room and all.'

Suddenly Alec seized one end of the web of knots and held

it up. 'It's a hammock!' he cried. 'You are a genius, Jimmy. Will you make one for me?'

'You ain't my boy,' said Mundy simply.

Alec's face darkened. It was true. He would never sleep in a shed or run wild in the streets of Pound's Field or catch salmon with his bare hands from a raging river. He was Jonathan Harvey's boy: son of a banker, and expected to be a banker himself one day. It was the sweeper boy who had a father who could fashion a hammock out of old string and who had fought in the army and who owned a knife like . . . The knife! That's what he'd been itching to know.

'Who's Trapper?' asked Alec suddenly.

There was scarcely a flicker to show that the man had even heard the question. His fingers didn't pause in their work. Alec saw the eyes narrow momentarily. That was all, but it was enough. There was something about the name the man didn't like.

'Where'd ya hear that name?' Mundy's voice was level, but Alec could hear an edge behind it.

'It's on your knife.'

'This 'un?' Mundy picked up the knife quickly and looked along its blade at Alec. 'You got good eyes if you can see that, boy.'

Alec scrambled to his feet, glaring down at the big man. He was caught out. Of course he couldn't see the name from where he was. Mundy knew now he'd been looking at his things. Well, so what? He went on fast, the words tumbling out now as his imagination began to weave stories to match Mundy's: 'You were a fur-trapper, weren't you, not a soldier. That's why it says Trapper. Or you knew someone named Trapper and that was his knife. Did you steal it? Or kill him for it? Is that what happened?'

'Alec!' Joe stood up, facing the other boy. 'He's bin ill. You leave him be.'

'Hey!' The man didn't raise his voice, but there was a note of command Joe hadn't heard before. The two boys were silent and the dog flattened himself against the floor. 'That's OK, Joe. The boy's curious. That's all. And he's got quite an imagination. But there's no mystery to it. I traded the knife in the army. Ain't never heard of no Trapper.'

Chapter 18

NORTH OF LOMESBURY

It was hot, so somewhere in the murky sky the sun had to be shining. But a wind from the south had stirred up a great cloud of city dust that blotted out the heavens and choked the London streets, even the neatly kept streets of Lomesbury.

Joe ran with a rag tied around his face. Boy kept pace at his side. Beyond Lomesbury Square to the north they passed two streets of big houses much like Alec's, then a row that was finished but unoccupied, and after that the ground started to rise slightly and open out.

Mundy ran ahead at a steady jog trot that ate up the ground, as if he knew exactly where he was going amidst this chaos of unfinished streets and ditches and houses with no roofs. He didn't seem to notice the choking dust or the heat of the day. Mr Harvey had been right about his personal physician, or maybe it was just a couple of months of Mrs Briggs's cooking, but scarcely more than four weeks since he'd tottered out into the park for the first time the man looked as strong as a horse.

At the top of the rise he stopped by an enormous pile of

bricks, stacked up like a staircase that led to nowhere. Joe caught up with him, wiping his sweating face, coughing with the dust. The dog stayed a short way off, keeping an uneasy eye on Mundy. Alec was behind them somewhere, and behind him the tutor, Mr Johnson – if he hadn't lost his way completely. Mundy ran as if unaware there was anyone with him, but he was looking down at Joe now. He didn't smile, but his gaze was level and steady. His eye didn't run over Joe's tousled mop of hair or his clothes which no longer looked new. Mundy looked him in the eye. Joe liked that.

'People too near together already,' grunted the big man. 'Dunno why they wanna build more of these ugly boxes.'

It was Sunday afternoon so there was no one working on the new houses. Half a dozen ragged children were clambering over the bricks. They eyed Joe suspiciously, moving closer, muttering to each other, pointing at Boy, but when they caught sight of the big man they ran without looking back.

'Tomato plants.' Mundy was at the side of the unmade roadway, examining a patch of spindly green plants that had forced their shoots out of the ground amongst the building work. 'Earth's still there underneath all – this.' He made a wide gesture, taking in the stack of bricks, the unfinished houses and the land beyond that was cleared and staked out ready for more building.

Joe sat down on the bricks. 'How come we're runnin', Jimmy?'

'This ain't runnin', boy. This is a Sunday stroll.'

Joe laughed. 'Where we goin'?' Mundy's gaze wandered

away northwards. His eyes narrowed, peering through the dust, but he didn't answer. Joe changed the subject. 'Reckon you'll like it in Mr Harvey's office, Jimmy?'

'It's work.'

Mundy's voice was neutral. The doctor had pronounced him recovered, and Mr Harvey had arranged for him to start work in the bank on Lombard Street in two weeks' time. Joe wasn't sure exactly what Mundy would be doing.

'Sounds—' Joe stopped. He wasn't used to expressing opinions, but Mundy always listened to him, always seemed to take what he said seriously. 'Sounds kinda shut in.'

This time Mundy looked at him. There was a hint of surprise in his face. 'You don't like to be shut in, Joe?'

'I'm used to outdoor work,' said Joe.

'Me too,' said Mundy, nodding his head thoughtfully. 'Me too. You tired?'

'No,' said Joe at once, struggling to his feet. 'I ain't never tired. I'm a good runner, I am.'

'Yep,' said Mundy. 'You're a good runner. But we'll set a whiles longer.'

He put his hand on Joe's shoulder, pushing him back down to a sitting position. The hand felt heavy and warm. Mundy was dressed in London clothes now, but there was still an animal smell coming off him, as if the scent of the skins he had worn so long couldn't be washed away. Joe was glad the smell was still there.

'Mr Harvey done a lot for the both of us, ain't he, Jimmy?' Joe wasn't thinking only of the job. Mr Harvey had found

Mundy a place to live too now, in a decent lodging house not far from Lomesbury. 'Why d'you reckon he done it then? I couldn't never figure it out.'

'Rich folks got their reasons,' said Mundy.

'I'll come and visit some time,' Joe went on. Then, when Mundy didn't say anything, he added, 'If that's all right.'

'Lodgings ain't no good.'

'Can't defend it?' Joe meant it as a joke, remembering what the man had said about his room in Barlow's shed. But when Mundy looked at him, his face was deadly serious.

'That's right.'

'Stay with me, if you want,' said Joe eagerly. 'Plenty of room. You could make another hammock.'

Mundy looked at him thoughtfully. 'Don't wanna crowd you, boy.'

He made it sound as if Joe would be doing him a favour. The boy tried to stop the grin from spreading across his face. Somehow he felt he shouldn't show the man how pleased he was. 'Wouldn't be no crowd, Jimmy,' he said. 'Shed's great. No bugs. No tramps. But it's a bit quiet, yer know? In the night. Bit too quiet for me.'

Alec reached the crest of the hill, gasping and choking on the filthy air. All the previous evening he had begged and pleaded, but his father had refused to let him come on the outing. It was only when Johnny Johnson had joined in the discussion that Mr Harvey had changed his mind.

'I believe the excursion might be both instructive and enjoyable, Mr Harvey,' the tutor had said. 'And perhaps the company of an old soldier might have beneficial effects on Master Alexander.'

That had done it. Alec didn't know why he hadn't thought of it himself. The army was the reason his father had shipped the man halfway across the world, set him up in the house, paid for months of doctoring. Once Mister Harvey got a charity idea in his head, there was no shaking it.

'I believe you are right,' his father had said. 'There is good in the man, Mr Johnson. He will repay our kindness by his future life. Mark my words!'

Of course Johnny simply wanted to go on the outing himself: he was as fascinated by James Mundy as Alec was. But his father didn't know that.

The sight of Mundy sitting there so easily on the stack of bricks with his hand on Joe's shoulder sent a familiar stab through Alec. Mundy never put his hand on Alec's shoulder like that. He didn't look at him the way he looked at Joe. He didn't talk to him the same way. Alec sat with the pair in Barlow's shed and walked with them in the park, but a lot of the time the big man didn't even seem to notice he was there.

It was only when he probed about his past that the boy could get much of a response at all. That was what had got him into the habit of questioning Mundy every chance he got – that and the look which flitted across the man's face each time he asked him who Trapper was. This big man with his quick hands and narrow eyes had lied about where he got his knife and he wasn't quite what he said he was. Alec was sure of that now.

The boy swallowed his anger and plastered a smile across his face. 'It seems that your father is cured, Master Joe,' he called out.

'Seems like it,' agreed Joe, looking up at the big man.

'Your wound doesn't bother you any more, Mr Mundy?' Since that day in the shed when Mundy had told him, 'You ain't my boy,' Alec had never tried calling him Jimmy again. 'You never told us how you got it.'

'Got what?'

'Your wound.'

'No.' Mundy looked steadily at Alec and his lips drew back from his teeth in that expression that wasn't quite a smile. 'I guess I never did.'

'Ah, there you are! You set a challenging pace, Mr Mundy.' Panting and mopping his brow, Mr Johnson had finally caught up with them. Alec laughed, making no attempt to hide his scorn. The tutor was wearing a thick tweed hiking suit and a peculiar broad-brimmed hat that made him look ready for an expedition to the Sahara Desert rather than the northern fringes of London. On his back he carried an enormous knapsack. 'This dust is quite appalling. Something really ought to be done.'

Mundy looked at him. Then he climbed halfway up the stack of bricks and shaded his eyes against the dust cloud. Alec followed his gaze towards the distant horizon. Through the haze he glimpsed a low line of hills beyond the great city. Was that where they were going?

As if in answer, Mundy spoke without looking round. 'Ain't far now. I can smell it.'

'You can smell what?' Johnson began. But he didn't get an answer, because Mundy was suddenly off again at the same jog trot, both boys struggling to keep up, Johnson labouring along behind.

They ran on past more new houses, more building plots, more signs of the City spreading ever further and further northwards. Alec strained every muscle to stay level with Joe. He wasn't going to be left behind again.

Gradually the air began to clear. The sun shone out overhead and the wind that had stirred up the dust on the London streets turned to a gentle summer breeze. They caught up with Mundy at the bottom of a hill by a little wooden bridge. The man was crouched very still in the shade of some trees, staring out across the stream.

The two boys squatted next to him. Across the bridge was a broad patch of rough grass dotted with bright-red poppies and beyond that a field with a crop growing. Further on there was a copse of trees and the line of another road with more newly built houses. But here was a patch that the builders hadn't disturbed yet. At the edge of the rough ground along the line of the hedgerow Joe caught a movement in the grass.

'Somethin' there,' he said, pointing.

The dog was standing stiff on his four legs next to Joe, trembling and staring straight ahead. He'd seen something too, or smelled it. Joe stayed low and reached down to hold Boy by the scruff of the neck. But Alec stood up at once, stepping onto the bridge.

'Look!' he shouted.

There was a flash of white and four or five rabbits disappeared instantly into the hedgerow.

'Now we'll have to set a while,' said Mundy evenly.

Alec waved his arm furiously in the direction the rabbits had gone. 'I scared them, didn't I?' He suddenly adopted his father's voice: '"Can you not do something right, Alexander?"'

'Don't signify,' said Mundy. 'They'll be back.'

Alec sat on the ground, keeping his distance from Mundy and Joe. He couldn't run as fast as Joe and now he'd made a fool of himself. Why had he come? Somewhere inside he knew Joe and his father would rather have been alone. Maybe that was the reason he'd been so determined to come with them.

They sat silent for a while. There was no sign of Johnson. Then Mundy rose in a half-crouch, stepped quietly into the shade of the trees, and in an instant he seemed to just fade into the undergrowth.

Joe glanced over at Alec. The other boy was still scowling and scuffing at the ground. All he'd done was scare a few rabbits. It made no sense to be so angry. But then plenty of what Alec did made no sense – like the way he'd acted in Addison's or accusing Mundy of stealing from a man named Trapper or even of killing him. Why did he say a thing like that?

Gentry – Joe put it all down to that – you couldn't expect to understand what gentry did, so why worry about it? And anyway there was something about the boy he couldn't help liking. You never knew what he was going to do or say next. Alec might be difficult, but he was never dull.

The dog whimpered quietly and Joe looked up with a start. He hadn't heard the man approach, but Mundy was suddenly squatting next to him again. He had a long, straight stick in one hand. In his other he held a knife, the same bone-handled dagger that had started Alec going on about Trapper.

Mundy began whittling at the stick. He worked quickly and silently, wood-shavings piling up on the ground between his feet. From time to time he tested the bend in the stick. Joe and Alec both knew better now than to question what he was doing. The man would tell them when he was ready and not before. Finally both ends had been shaped to a tapering blunt end. Now Joe couldn't restrain himself.

'How you goin' to get 'em with that?' he demanded. 'Ain't sharp enough.'

The man didn't say anything at once. He cut a notch in each end of the stick, then he fixed his gaze on Joe. Alec had crept closer to watch what the man was doing.

'Fetch me some sticks,' he said. 'Straight and dry. Half as long as this 'un.'

Joe got up at once, glad to be doing something even if he didn't know why. 'How many d'yer need?'

'Four or five.'

Joe headed off amongst the trees. Alec stayed where he was, watching the man. From his pocket Mundy drew a length of the hemp twine he'd used to make Joe's hammock. He fitted it into the notch at one end of his stick and tied it securely. Out of the corner of his eye Alec saw one of the rabbits emerge from the hedgerow again and begin nibbling at the green grass shoots.

'You are making a bow and arrow,' he said suddenly.

Mundy ignored him and began fitting the string to the other end of his bow, bending the stick carefully until the twine fitted into the notch. He slipped his knife back into the sheath which hung at his belt and pulled the string back to his ear a couple of times, testing the bow.

'Did you learn to do that in the army?' pursued Alec.

Still no response.

'You were not in the army all your sojourn in foreign parts, were you, Mr Mundy?'

The man just looked straight ahead. Two of the rabbits had reappeared from the hedgerow and were eating the grass not twenty yards away.

'How long were you in north America for?'

'Just about as long as your lifetime, Master Harvey.' Mundy still wasn't looking at him, but at least he'd got him to talk.

'Was it an arrow wound you had?'

'Bullet,' said Mundy shortly.

'Do the savages have rifles then?'

'Savages?'

'Well, if it wasn't savages who shot you, then who was it?' Mundy looked at him now. Alec struggled to meet his eye. 'Who's Trapper?' he asked.

Mundy's eyes were suddenly hard, flashing. His hand went to his belt where the knife hung and his fist closed tight around the bone handle. Alec went rigid, unable to move. Then just as suddenly the expression on the man's face softened, and his hand relaxed easily away from the knife, as another voice spoke.

'Master Alexander!' Mr Johnson was standing over them, his face dripping sweat. Mundy must have heard or seen him coming. 'First you go running on and leave me to search for you high and low. Then, when I find you, you are addressing Mr Harvey's . . .' The tutor hesitated. 'Mr Harvey's friend with impertinent questions.'

'Boy didn't mean no harm,' said Mundy easily. The moment had passed. He was his usual calm self again. 'Boys like tales of killin', don't they, Master Harvey?'

Alec scowled. He knew word would get back to his father now and it would mean more trouble. Then he laughed. 'Rabbits are gone again. That's your fault this time, Johnny.'

'Rabbits?' Johnson shaded his eyes uncertainly. 'Well,' he said, setting down his heavy knapsack, 'we can always fall back on my supplies. I have a decent bottle of wine in here, Mr Mundy, together with a cold fowl, several loaves of bread and – well, a fair proportion of the contents of Mrs Briggs's larder, I believe.' He laughed.

'You eat, Mr Johnson,' said Mundy. 'Reckon I'll wait a whiles more. Ain't tasted fresh meat in a while.'

'Oh,' said Johnson. 'Well, then I'll wait with you.'

Joe came back through the trees with a bundle of sticks, putting them down at Mundy's feet. 'Don't know if these are right,' he said uncertainly.

Mundy sorted rapidly through the sticks, throwing half to one side. Then he worked through the ones he'd kept, sighting along their length, discarding several more.

'These'll do,' he grunted at last. 'You done well, Joe.'

Joe ducked his head. 'Thanks, Jimmy.'

He sat down, glancing at Johnson and Alec. Alec was scowling down at his shoes. Johnson looked faintly pained as he always did when he saw Joe. But the look didn't bother the boy this time. An unfamiliar sensation burned hot in his chest. Mundy had told him to search for sticks – he didn't know what for – but he'd found some of the right kind. *You done well, Joe.* It was something about the way Mundy used his name that Joe liked.

He watched the man sharpen the sticks carefully with his knife and cut a notch in the blunt end. The hands were so quick and skilful. He thought of the hammock he slept in, slung across the far corner of Barlow's shed. Jimmy had made that for him, but he'd only watched him do it. This time he'd helped. He felt connected to those big but surprisingly agile hands and the extraordinary things that seemed to spring like magic from them.

The four sat quietly beneath the trees, waiting for the rabbits to reappear, for what seemed to Alec a long time. Mr Johnson pulled a book out of his knapsack. Joe asked Mundy about the bow he'd made, about what kind of wood to use and how to make sure the arrows would fly straight. Mundy answered his questions patiently, the way he never answered Alec.

'So,' Alec interrupted: he'd had enough of being ignored. 'Did you say it was the East Norfolk or the East Suffolk Regiment you were with in Canada, Mr Mundy?'

The man looked long and hard at Alec. 'Didn't say,

as I recall. Don't care to remember them days too much.'

'Really?' said Alec, his voice full of exaggerated surprise. 'But you've told Joe and me such a lot of interesting stories, Mr Mundy. Only you never say anything about the army. Or about Trapper,' he added innocently. Again Alec saw the hardening of the eyes and the hand that strayed to the bone handle of the knife. But he didn't feel afraid now. The man would never do anything with Johnny and Joe there.

'Must be a hard life as a soldier,' said Alec.

'Hard enough, I reckon,' Mundy responded non-committally.

'And what a shame you couldn't take your family with you, Mr Mundy. Doesn't the army ever allow soldiers to take wives and children overseas?'

'Reckon not,' said Mundy.

Mr Johnson looked up from his book. 'Oh, I don't think that is quite correct, Mr Mundy. Dependants may accompany members of the armed forces serving abroad. However, perhaps your family fell outside the quota or limit that is placed on their number.'

'Reckon so,' said Mundy.

'You don't remember?' asked Alec.

'It were a long time ago, Alec.' Suddenly Joe felt the need to come to his father's assistance. ''Fore I was born, remember.'

'What a lot of letters you must have written home though,' Alec went on. Johnson had stopped reading now and was watching the boy closely. 'And your wife must have written to you. Do you still have any of those letters, Mr

Mundy? I imagine they would be a comfort to you now.'

'Ain't much for readin' and writin',' said Mundy.

'Alexander' – Mr Johnson's voice was stern – 'this is hardly an appropriate line of conversation. Now, why don't we talk about something else?'

He looked over to Mundy. Joe looked too. The man was very still. His eyes looked closed. Had he fallen asleep? Joe was reaching out a hand to touch him when Mundy suddenly twisted sideways, fitted an arrow quickly to the string of his bow and in a single movement loosed it off into the long grass.

Alec was first to his feet – even before Boy – racing across the grass to where the rabbit lay twitching, an arrow neatly through its neck.

'It's dead!' he cried, holding the animal up. 'He's killed it!'

Thirty minutes later, skinned and gutted, the rabbit was cooking over a wood fire. Mundy cut a piece and passed it to Mr Johnson.

'I must say,' said the tutor, licking his fingers, 'that is extraordinarily good, Mr Mundy. I fear I would not have your skills if called upon to survive in the wilds.'

Mundy's eyebrow flickered. 'Mr Johnson,' he said slowly, 'I reckon you wander out into the wilds and you'd be eaten inside a minute.'

Mr Johnson smiled. 'I dare say you are right,' he said. 'However, Mr Mundy, I would venture that if you were to wander into a civilized drawing room you would be eaten in a minute too.'

Both boys looked anxiously at Mundy, wondering how the big man would react. But Mundy gave a great shout, halfway between laughter and the bark of an animal, that echoed in the woodland by the stream. 'Mr Johnson, I believe you're right.'

He threw the bone he'd been chewing to Boy and the dog leaped on it, making little high-pitched yelps of delight. After that he kept an eye fixed permanently on Mundy. He seemed to have forgotten his fear of the man.

Mr Johnson relaxed too and talked at length about the benefits of 'outdoor exercise', particularly for 'the growing boy'. Alec let the tutor's voice wash over him. He'd had plenty of practice at doing that in lessons. 'There are dangers,' he was saying, 'in the city life just as there are in the wilds, I believe. Our good lady, sadly a permanent invalid, is an example, I fear, Master Alexander.'

Alec hadn't been listening, but at the mention of his mother's name he was suddenly alert. What business was it of Johnny Johnson to be saying things about his mother, who couldn't help it if she was ill? But before he could say anything Mundy spoke.

'That lady ain't no invalid, Mr Johnson,' he said slowly. 'She's addicted to laudanum unless I'm mightily mistaken.'

Laudanum? Joe stiffened. So the man in Addison's had been right. He'd called it the black drop – opium. But it was the same thing. That was the stuff Alec carried in his little glass phial, the stuff he'd used on the robin in the park and then put in a glass and drunk himself.

Joe turned to the other boy to see what he would say, but

Alec was already on his feet. His mouth opened and closed but no sound came out. He was shaking and his eyes were full of tears, and his fists clenched and unclenched at his sides as if he were searching for something to grasp hold of.

'Master Alexander – Alec—'

Joe had never heard the tutor call the boy that. He felt sorry for him. It was obvious. That meant it must be true. Mrs Harvey was an opium addict.

Suddenly Alec lunged forward, scattering sparks from the smouldering fire. The dog leaped back barking. Mundy was on his feet, but Alec was too quick for him. He had the bow in his hand, an arrow already fitted in place, the string pulled back as far as he could draw it. He was pointing straight at Mundy's chest.

'You don't – you don't—' he stammered. 'I'm going to kill you. I'm going to kill you and skin you like a rabbit and—'

Mundy didn't move. His eyes didn't blink. He held Alec's furious gaze. Joe could hear his own heart pounding in his ears. Alec was going to shoot the arrow. He was going to kill his father – the man who had come thousands of miles across the seas to be with him again.

'Alec, it ain't his fault!' Joe reached out towards the boy, but Alec stepped sideways, keeping the arrow trained on the big man, moving closer, straining the bowstring back to his ear.

Still Mundy's gaze didn't flicker. His eyes seemed to bore into Alec's. The two were no more than three paces apart now. Surely the man would make a grab for the bow. Joe was sure he must. Those hands were so quick he could have it out of Alec's hand before he could loose the arrow, couldn't he? But still Mundy didn't move.

Then with a cry of despair Alec spun round and shot the arrow off into the gathering darkness. And while the string was still vibrating, Mundy had twisted the weapon out of the boy's grasp with one hand and with the other he had hold of Alec by the throat. For a moment he held the boy almost off the ground. Then he let him go and Alec collapsed, shaking with silent sobs.

Chapter 19
THE CAGED ANIMAL

It was dark. Joe lay wrapped in a blanket in his hammock and listened to the silence. The shed had been his home for three months now, but it was still a pleasant surprise to wake up here. He'd never had a clean place all to himself – no fights, no tramps pushing in looking for a bed in the middle of the night, no bugs crawling and biting. And now with Mundy sleeping just across the floor . . .

Joe lifted himself to check if the man was still asleep. Even in the darkness of the shed he could see how the other hammock hung loose and empty. Mundy was gone.

He slipped easily to the floor, feeling in the dark for his boots. There was no movement in the corner where Boy always slept. The dog was gone too. It made sense. Since Mundy had thrown him that rabbit bone, Boy never let the man out of his sight if he could help it. What was strange was that Joe hadn't heard either of them leave.

He fastened his boots and pushed the door open. Outside there was a hint of dawn. Then there was a tremendous crash and the entire ceiling seemed to collapse on top of him. Joe fell to the ground, stunned, unable to make sense of what was happening. Fear forced him to his feet. He staggered forward. The floor gave way under him.

He couldn't go forward or back. His right foot was jammed tight between the boards of the porch. He opened his mouth to cry out, and a name came instinctively to his lips: 'Jimmy!' But before the sound was out of his mouth he felt a heavy, familiar hand and Mundy was beside him.

'Easy, boy. You ain't hurt.'

Joe felt the pain in his ankle and he wasn't so sure. 'What happened?' he demanded. 'Where's the dog?'

'Dog's here.'

As he looked down for Boy, Joe could see what had happened. The nails had been removed from one of the boards in the porch, so that when he stepped on it his foot had gone straight through. And the ceiling hadn't fallen on him. It was half a dozen of Barlow's tools that had been rigged up to come crashing down when the door opened.

'What's goin' on, Jimmy?'

'I'll show ya.' The man led him carefully across the porch. Half the boards had been loosened so the whole floor was one big trap. 'Watch ya step, here. You'll have to show Barlow where I've dug.'

In the faint light of dawn Joe could make out four neat piles of earth amongst the young shrubs he and Barlow had planted in front of the shed. Deeper shadows showed the pits Mundy had made.

'I'll put thin board across the top and dirt later. Anybody

treads there—' Mundy made a gesture to suggest falling.

'What's it for, Jimmy? Barlow ain't gonna like it.'

'Pits are permanent,' said the big man. 'Everything else I'll fix when it gets light. If they're coming for ya, this is the time – just before dawn.' Mundy was as calm and matter-of-fact as ever. He didn't sound afraid. It was just one of those things you had to live with, like the cold in winter and the dust in summer.

'Who?' insisted Joe. 'Who's coming for yer?'

'Don't never know that.'

The light was building fast now. A bird started to sing somewhere in the park. It made Joe think of Alec and his trap. And now Mundy was building traps. It made no sense. They were in Lomesbury – just about the safest place Joe had ever been in his life. And Mundy had lived for years in wild places where there were bears and savage tribes and all sorts. Then something else suddenly occurred to the boy.

'How come the dog didn't bark? When all that stuff come crashin' down and I fell and all?'

Mundy was on his hands and knees, fixing the boards back in place on the porch. He didn't use a hammer: he just pressed the nails back in with his great thumb. 'Told him not to,' he said simply.

'You can't tell a dog not to bark.'

'I can,' said the man. He stood up. 'Got to get ready now. Diggin' pits is easy. Tying a necktie is tough work. You'd best lend a hand.'

That was when Joe remembered. It was the start of a new week. That meant it was Mundy's first day working. He hurried back into the shed, looking for the sharply pressed black suit they had laid out the night before. He liked the idea of helping the man get ready for his new life.

'Reckon we're gonna be late. Don't look good on yer first mornin'.'

Joe raised his voice against the din of the city street, but Mundy gave no sign that he'd heard. As the buildings had grown taller and the crowds of people thicker, the big man had grown more and more silent. Squashed tight now in the centre of a bench which ran the length of the omnibus's top deck, he looked like all the other clerks making their way into the city – almost. The shaggy hair was cropped short and plastered down with oil. The enormous beard had been trimmed to a pair of bushy whiskers. But without all the hair Mundy's face looked even more lined and sunken and his eyes still seemed to stare far off at a frozen horizon, even here in the centre of London.

Joe noticed the man on Mundy's other side glance uneasily at the big man. He obviously wasn't used to sharing the top deck of the omnibus with someone who looked like James Mundy. It wasn't just the face and the eyes. The clothes didn't look right either. They'd done their best in the shed that morning, but Mundy seemed to bulge out of his suit. The bowler hat perched uneasily on his head and the white cravat, which Joe had tied in a thick bow at his neck, looked too tight to be comfortable.

As if to confirm what Joe was thinking, Mundy flexed his

shoulders and ran a finger round the inside of his neckwear. Then he put his hands back on his knees. The boy could see the knuckles whiten as he gripped tight and then released. Grip and release. He looked at the grim face in profile. It was expressionless, but there was a tremendous tension in the man he'd never seen before. If only they could get moving again.

The boy leaned forward in his seat, peering ahead. An enormous wagon piled high with bales and bundles had come to a dead stop in front of them. Further up the road amidst a sea of carts and cabs and carriages Joe glimpsed a policeman waving his arms hopelessly, trying to direct traffic. Behind them stood a shining glass hearse, drawn by a pair of black horses with ostrich plumes on their heads and heavy blinkers on their eyes. Amidst the racket of drivers cursing and pedestrians pushing their way through the throng, the gleaming animals stood as still and quiet as statues. Only their long black tails twitched from side to side to show they were alive at all.

The eight horses pulling the bus took another couple of steps forward. Then they stopped. Then another couple of steps. Then stop again. Suddenly, as if he could bear it no longer, Mundy sprang to his feet, elbowing the man next to him, treading on feet. Cries of protest from the other passengers mixed with the racket from the street. Crouched at Joe's feet, the dog leaped up at once.

Mundy pushed to the back of the bus and climbed quickly down the iron ladder. Joe followed with Boy tucked under one arm, but as soon as they were on the ground the animal wriggled out of his grasp and scampered after Mundy. The big man had set off, marching down the crowded pavement as if the people weren't there, apparently expecting them to get out of his way. Joe hurried after him, waiting to see the man break into the tireless jog trot that had taken them north from Lomesbury Square a fortnight back. But the crowds were too tightly packed.

In front of a towering building with stone columns as thick as tree trunks, Joe hesitated amongst the mass of people. He'd lost sight of Mundy. Flower girls were selling button-holes here and boot-blacks shouting for custom. 'Shoeshine! Shoeshine!' A boy who could have been half Joe's age dodged amongst the traffic on all fours, scraping up horse droppings. 'Flamers! Best a-goin'!' A barefoot kid selling matches pestered the passers-by without success. Joe spotted several crossing sweepers working the crowded street. He wondered who you had to fight to hold onto a pitch like this.

He caught the sound of Boy yapping above the general hubbub. Joe might have lost Mundy but the dog hadn't. He was up at the corner, scampering backwards and forwards and barking. The man must have gone that way.

Around the corner the street was quieter, but the buildings were just as close together and the narrow road made them look even taller. Joe was just in time to see Mundy disappear into a high stone doorway. The dog stopped on the pavement outside, looking back for Joe. The boy stood where he was, glancing uneasily up and down the street. Well-dressed ladies and gentlemen went in and out of the grand buildings. Nobody looked anything like him. But then again there'd been no one in Lomesbury Square who looked like him that first frosty morning back in March, had there?

'If the dog's got the nerve for it, then I reckon I have,' Joe muttered aloud. He took a deep breath, squared his shoulders and walked down the street to where Boy was sitting on the pavement, scratching with one hind leg.

'What d'you want here, sonny?'

The man outside the bank wore a red coat rather like Freddie at Addison's. But this was an older man and Joe knew at once he wasn't as fierce as he sounded.

'Is this West, Woodford and Harvey?' asked Joe, remembering the name of the bank.

The man raised an eyebrow. 'You got money deposited here, young sir? Or a bone or two maybe?' He eyed Boy, who was still scratching.

'My father's a . . .' What was it? 'My father's an assistant cashier here. I want . . .' Joe's voice tailed off. What did he want? When he'd finished dressing that morning, Mundy had asked Joe to come with him. *Good to have family with me.* That's what he'd said. Family . . . The sound of the word was strange in the boy's ear – strange but good. But now that he was here, Joe didn't know what he wanted. 'I want to see him workin',' he blurted out awkwardly.

The man smiled. 'What about the dog? He want to see what an assistant cashier does and all?'

'He'll stay here, if I tell him,' said Joe.

'Go on then,' said the man. 'Only don't get in no one's way. And don't help yourself to any gold.'

Joe's eyes bulged. Then he realized the man was joking. 'Right,' he managed with a weak smile, and stepped through the high doorway into the bank.

It wasn't just the doorman that reminded Joe of Addison's. Inside the place looked a bit like a gin palace too. There was a big gas light burning in the ceiling and half the room was cut off by a long, semi-circular counter not unlike a bar. But the ladies and gentlemen standing at the counter didn't look like Addison's customers and they weren't ordering gin and peppermint or a pennyworth of rum-scrub. The well-dressed young men behind the counter waiting to serve them didn't look like barmen either, and if Joe wasn't mistaken, those piles of paper on the counter were money. Then he spotted his father.

Mundy was at the far end of the long counter, the last in a line of clerks, all half-hidden behind strong metal bars. The other clerks, who mostly looked about half the big man's age, had their heads down and were busily scratching away in heavy ledgers on the desk in front of them. Mundy's quill pen looked tiny clutched in his enormous fist and his hand moved slowly and laboriously over the paper.

Mr Harvey stood behind him, one hand on the big man's shoulder. He said something and pointed to the page where Mundy had been writing and the man looked up meekly, uncertainly.

For a moment, before he went back to his work, Mundy's eyes rested on Joe standing by the door, though the boy wasn't sure if he saw him. The vertical line of the bars seemed to cut the man's face in two. In his suit and tie and with a quill pen in his hand he hardly looked like the same person whose quick hands had fashioned a hammock out of old string or a bow from a stick. Could this be the same creature who before dawn that morning had been building defences around the place where he and his son slept?

Joe had seen Mundy and Mr Harvey together before: in the sick room and then walking together in the park, deep in conversation about Canada and the future and the importance of what Mr Harvey always called 'a second chance'. But here it was different. Mr Harvey's black suit was almost identical to Mundy's. He had the same stiff collar and white cravat wrapped tight around his neck, but Mr Harvey looked like a man at home in his own world. Mundy looked – the thought sprang suddenly into Joe's mind – Mundy looked like an animal in a cage.

Chapter 20

CRIME AND PUNISHMENT

'Do you think he was in the army at all?'

Bates didn't answer straight away. He seemed to be thinking. Alec tapped his fingers irritably on the windowsill next to where he'd been working on the lock. He always slipped a rag over the damage to hide what he'd been doing if anyone else came into the room. He could see Barlow on his own down in the square. Joe had gone with Mundy to Lombard Street that morning.

'I seen a wound on his shoulder one time,' said Bates eventually.

'Knife? Bullet? Arrow?'

'Couldn't rightly say, Master Alec.'

'I thought he was supposed to have been wounded in the leg anyway.'

'Could have one there too.'

Alec thought about that. Felicity and Alice were down in the square as well, and the sight of his sister made the boy even more irritable . . . *each morning for a full month, until you learn to show respect for your elders, even though they may be of a lower class than yourself* . . . His father's words repeated over and over in his ears. And it was Mundy's fault. Johnny Johnson had been the one to talk, of course, after the business with the bow. But Alec blamed the big man. He blamed him for everything and he was going to get his own back. Before it had just been curiosity, wanting to know the truth about this man who obviously hadn't told them everything about his past. But now, one way or another, he was going to prove Joe's father was a liar or a thief or a murderer – or – or – something. But first he had to get out of this room.

'He's got a knife that doesn't belong to him, Bates,' he said, watching the footman's response. 'And a whole lot of other stuff too. I think the man's a thief at least. Do you think he might be a danger to the family?'

Bates's fists clenched at his side. 'What I think is: scum once, scum always,' he snarled. 'Yes, he's a danger to the family all right. And he'll show his true colours one day. Same as the gutter boy.'

Alec smiled inwardly. He didn't believe Joe was dangerous. Joe was still his friend, but he knew this was the way to get Bates to do what he wanted. Bates would do anything if he thought he was protecting the family. 'If I could just get into my father's study for a moment,' Alec went on, as if he was talking to himself. 'There must be something there we could use.'

'I can't let you out of here, Master Alec,' said Bates. 'And that's final.'

Alec cursed silently. 'I'm just asking you to do what is right for the family, Bates,' he said, putting a hand on the footman's arm.

'I'm a servant, Master Alec. I go letting you out of here and unlocking your father's study, and I'll be out on the street. Do you know what happens to servants that get dismissed without a character?'

'But can't you see you would be saving the family, Bates? Saving dear little Miss Felicity, perhaps.'

Alec pointed down into the square and Bates came over to the window to look. The poison dolly was playing with its shuttlecock as usual. Stupid thing never got any better at it. The memory of Mundy's bone-handled knife slicing through rabbit fur was suddenly very clear in Alec's mind, and the way the man had reached in and ripped out the animal's guts. Just for an instant the image of his sister replaced the rabbit, then Bates interrupted the fantasy.

'I don't like the man,' said Bates slowly. 'But when it comes to charity cases – well, let's say your father has his ideas, though I'm speaking out of turn to say so. Anyhow' – the footman sounded more certain now – 'Mundy's out of the house now. That's one good thing.'

'You mean you've got your room back.'

'I mean,' insisted Bates, 'that the family's safe from him.' Alec opened his mouth to speak but the footman wouldn't listen to any more. 'I'm leaving you now, Master Alec, 'fore I do something I'll regret. Mr Johnson'll be along to let you out come dinner time.'

And with that he was gone. Alec heard the key in the lock,

but he threw himself at the door anyway. It was as solid and immovable as it always was.

He went back to the window. He'd never really thought Bates was going to let him out, but it had been worth a try. He was going to have to do it the hard way. He took what was left of the broken knife out of his pocket, removed the rag that had been hiding the damage to the window frame and went on chiselling into the wood. The sight of Felicity on the grass stoked his anger and another splinter flew out. Then another. He had two more weeks to run of this particular sentence and he was going to get the brass lock out if he had to tear it out with his teeth.

Something had woken him. A sound. Joe could sense the night was almost over and Mundy would be outside now, crouched somewhere near the shed, watching, waiting. But it wouldn't be him who'd made the sound. Despite his size the man could move in absolute silence, and Joe had never heard him leave in the night. Something else . . .

The dog growled softly in the corner. Joe strained his ears, listening. Boy never growled at Mundy.

Then he heard it – a long, stifled moan, like a terrified animal. The sound was coming from outside.

Joe climbed silently out of his hammock and moved to the window, pulling back the sacking an inch. Too dark to see. He didn't use the door. Mundy's booby trap would still be in place at this time. The man had cut another low door in the boards at the back of the shed. You could lift out a section of the wall now and crawl through. He called it his 'back door'. Joe went that way.

Outside the noise came again – muffled but close.

The gas lamps were still burning in the square, but there was light in the eastern sky away over the house tops. The young trees in the park stood out black and the whole garden was a milky grey in the dawn. Joe trod carefully. The dog stayed close, still giving the same low growl. The sound was coming from the side of the shed.

As Joe rounded the corner of the building, a hand came out of the darkness and gripped him by the scruff of the neck. He struggled, wondering why Boy didn't bark. He twisted and ducked. He recognized the knife before he saw who was holding it – bone-handled, blade serrated on one side. Then the man spoke.

'Easy, boy. We got us some company.'

Now Joe saw them. Side by side on the ground, propped up against the shed, lay two figures. There was something familiar about them. Mundy opened the dark lantern he was holding and a shaft of light lit up their faces. Bound hand and foot and each with a rag stuffed in his mouth, Bob and Charlie glowered back at him. Mundy had been right. Someone had come, and they had come just when he said they would. Only they hadn't been after the big man. They'd been after him.

'Friends of yours, Joe?'

'Not exactly.'

'Thought not.'

There was an edge of menace in Mundy's voice. He walked

slowly over to the two prostrate figures and crouched down, bending to speak in Charlie's ear.

'Now I'm gonna take the rag out of your mouth, boy, and you ain't gonna say nothin' except answer my questions. You understand?'

Charlie didn't respond. His eyes were wide with terror. With a sudden movement the man slit open the front of his shirt from top to bottom. He held the dagger over Charlie's belly, which seemed to shrink away from the needle-sharp point.

'I asked: did you understand?'

This time Charlie nodded his head frantically. In the light of the lantern Joe could see sweat standing out on his brow.

'That's better.' Mundy never raised his voice. There wasn't a flicker of expression on his face. 'Now what's your business here?'

He pulled the rag out of Charlie's mouth, and at once words were tumbling out: 'Don't mean no harm, mister. Weren't my idea anyhow. Bob here said we got to—' He didn't get to the end of his sentence. Mundy stuffed the rag back deep into his throat and his knife pressed against Charlie's bare stomach. The boy's scream was muffled by the gag. Joe could see blood at the point of the dagger.

'Don't, Jimmy,' he called out. 'I know them.'

Mundy's knife drew back half an inch. It had only pricked the surface of the skin.

'So, you got one more chance.' His voice was a whisper. 'On account of my boy's soft heart. What's your business here?'

He pulled out the gag again, and Charlie took a rasping breath.

'We bin in quod three months on account of him.' He threw a frightened glance at Joe. 'Come out day before yesterday. We' – he looked at Bob, who was shaking his head furiously, but Charlie had obviously decided there was no point in trying to hide anything now – 'we figured he split on us to the crushers. We come' – his mouth was hard and angry now in spite of his fear – 'we come to get a bit of our own back. We didn't know he was – we didn't know—' Charlie squirmed on the ground, struggling to get further from the point of Mundy's knife.

'You didn't know he was my boy.' The hand with the knife went back. Mundy's face was set. Joe cried out again.

'Don't do it, Jimmy. You can't.' The man hesitated. Joe went on desperately, 'He ain't a rabbit for the pot.' Mundy's eyes didn't waver, but Joe could see his grip on the knife loosen just a little. 'They won't come back. You learned your lesson, ain'tcha, Charlie?'

The two boys nodded wildly. Mundy gave a quick snort of disgust and handed the knife to Joe.

'Cut 'em loose then, boy,' he spat. 'Just don't let me set eyes on 'em again.'

Joe cut the ropes on Bob and Charlie's hands and feet. The blade was so sharp it slipped through the cords as if they weren't there. The two boys scrambled to their feet, backing away. Then they sprinted off across the park with Boy yapping at their heels. Joe watched them go. He handed the knife back to Mundy with a shudder.

'You weren't really goin' to do it, were yer, Jimmy?'

The man stood up, wiping the blade of the knife, checking he hadn't got blood on the dark business suit he wore each day to the bank. The clothes and the bloody knife looked so strange together, for a moment Joe wondered if he was still asleep and had dreamed the whole thing. Mundy looked at him steadily.

'Sometimes it's you or them, Joe,' he said. 'You got to know if you want to survive or not.'

Two hours later Mundy was gone and Joe was sweeping up in the shed when Jeremy Barlow came through the door. He'd never said anything to Mundy about the traps or the piece cut out of the shed wall, but when the big man wasn't there it was a different story. He was grumbling to himself now as soon as he got inside.

'Ain't no way for a soldier to carry on. What's 'e scared of anyhow?'

Joe knew who he was talking about.

'He ain't scared of nothin'.'

He hung the broom back in its place on the wall. He never used it in the square any more. The park was his work now. Truth was there'd never really been enough muck or people on quiet Lomesbury Square to warrant a sweeper.

'Is that a fact?' Barlow stood with his hands on his hips and looked Joe squarely in the eye. 'So what's the traps for? And how come he's kippin' here 'stead of at his own gaff? He's got a place of his own, ain't he?'

'Maybe he wants to be with his – with his family,' said Joe.

'Meanin' you?'

'Yeah. Meanin' me. I'm his family, ain't I? We look out for each other – we do.'

'How touchin'!' sneered Barlow. 'Now I was talkin' to Frank Bates only yesterday, and he reckons—'

'I don't care what Mr Bates reckons,' Joe interrupted. 'He's got it in for me and Jimmy.'

'You don't care what nobody thinks, Master Joe. Is that right? You got your friends amongst the gentry and your odd-ball father and you think you're all right.'

'Didn't say that,' said Joe defensively. 'Don't mean you any-way, Mr Barlow. You—'

But Barlow didn't wait to hear what Joe had to say about him.

'You still workin' for me, boy? Or you too fancy now?'

'I'm still workin',' said Joe. 'What you want me to do, Mr Barlow?'

'I want you to go out back and grub up every one of them old potatoes. And then we're puttin' in the new shrubs what the gentry wanted.'

'But you said I could—'

Barlow put up his hand. His voice was firm but he wasn't scowling any more. 'Let me ask you somethin', boy,' he said. 'You ever bin hungry?'

Joe didn't have to think about that. 'Yeah,' he said.

'You ever bin out on the street with no place to stay and no chink in yer pocket?'

'Yeah. I bin that too.'

'Me and all.' Barlow looked him in the eye. 'Don't never

forget about it. The likes of you and me, we're always just that far from bein' out there again.' The old man held up his thumb and forefinger. There was dirt in the grain of his hands. 'Do your work. Please them as has the money on their side. Otherwise . . .'

Barlow made a gesture as if he were throwing away a scrap of paper. Joe opened his mouth to protest. But the old man wouldn't let him speak.

'Go and do like I told yer, Joe. And remember who you are. Otherwise things have a funny way of remindin' yer. Spuds has all got blight on 'em anyhow.'

Joe didn't argue any more. He took a spade off its hook on the wall and went out to the back of the shed. The green leaves of the potato plants that had come poking up through the ground stood up strongly. Joe spat on his hands and dug deep into the soil.

The first spadeful had half a dozen potatoes amongst the dirt. Joe bent to pick one up. It was soft to the touch and gave off a rancid smell. He dug under another plant. It was the same. And now that he looked at the leaves more closely, they all had brown patches at the centre. Barlow had been right. The whole crop had rotted under the ground.

Chapter 21

ESCAPE

The lock was on the floor at Alec's feet. It had just given way all of a sudden when he wasn't expecting it and now, after weeks and weeks of chipping tiny splinters, it was gone.

He'd lived this moment so often – the feel of the air on his face as he threw up the sash, the climb to the roof – but he didn't touch the window straight away. There was always a chance of someone seeing him from the square below. Besides Alec had a better plan now than the roof.

He picked up the knife again and worked his way round the room, cutting string from every box he could find. Then he crouched down in his hole amongst the boxes, where he read his *Starlight Sal* and *The Boy Burglar*, but he wasn't interested in penny dreadfuls today.

He'd watched Mundy do this. *You ain't my boy.* He could still hear the man as he'd plaited rope for Joe's hammock, the hammock Joe slept in now, slung across the corner of Barlow's shed. Mundy slept there too, though he was supposed to have his own lodgings somewhere. Well, Alec didn't have a

244

hammock, but he had yards of string and he was going to use his rope for something a lot more interesting than sleeping.

It seemed to take hours. Three times the whole thing came unravelled and he had to start again. But in the end he had a length of three-ply rope, maybe ten feet long. The only thing was, he had no idea how strong it might be.

Alec went over to the window. He tied a loop in the rope and slung it over the hasp of the broken lock, then he leaned back, testing the strength of the rope. The loop came away and he tumbled over backwards, banging his head hard against the floor. The pain only angered him, made him more determined. There had to be a better place to fasten the rope.

Finally, he dragged the grate out of the fireplace, wedged it between two piles of boxes and tied one end of the rope firmly to the fire bars. This time when he pulled, the rope held firm, but there was no way of testing whether it would take his full weight. He was going to have to chance it.

The window that had been locked so long slid up easily, as if it were opened every day of the week. Felicity and Alice and some other kids were down in the park but there was no sign of Barlow or Joe – probably taking a break in the shed. A wagon made its way slowly round the other side of the square, but the driver didn't look up. Alec dropped the loose end of his rope out of the window, craning forwards to see how far it reached.

Leaning right out he could see the window below him, but the rope stopped short of the window ledge. It was too short! He could plait another length and knot it to this one. There was more string. But that would take too long. It was past eleven. At midday Johnny would be there to let him out and the opportunity would be gone for the day, and now that he had got this far Alec couldn't wait another day. He hooked one leg out of the window, took hold of the rope in both hands and climbed onto the sill.

He'd imagined how the air would feel on his face, how the rough bricks would scrape his hands. But it wasn't like that. It was better. The colour of the trees in the square was brighter and the air smelled fresh and above his head the clouds rushed past in a sky that was bluer than he had ever seen. Alec felt his head swim and he looked down, away from those racing clouds.

The black iron spikes of the front railings of the house looked closer than they had through the closed window, as if they were reaching up to him, waiting. He'd imagined them too. He'd seen himself falling, falling, impaled on their sharpened spikes, dying slowly and agonizingly as his father looked on, horrified. But those spikes were somehow more real now, sharper, and his father wasn't there. He'd left early for the bank. And then Mundy had gone, all dressed up in his suit and tie and looking like an idiot, just like every day for the last week. Well now he was going to do something to change everything. He didn't know what yet. But something. Whatever it cost.

Alec took a firmer hold on the rope, and let his feet drop over the edge of the windowsill. The fibres of the rope creaked, stretching under the strain. He felt his hands slipping and he scrabbled desperately for a foothold. The rope was twisting as it stretched, and cutting into his hands, and he still couldn't get a decent grip. He should have put knots in it – something to hold onto. There was still time to go back and do it. He could still reach up with one hand and grasp the window ledge and lever himself back into the tower room – suddenly it didn't seem like a place of punishment any more: it seemed like a place of safety.

But Alec wasn't going back. Swinging wildly backwards and forwards, his right foot caught the top of the cornice-work above the window below. Now he had a foothold. He let the rope slip through his hands a little more.

At any moment he expected to hear a shout from below – Felicity's little piping squeak of a voice or a passer-by who had spotted him, but there was nothing. He had sweat in his eyes, but he couldn't let go of the rope to wipe it away.

Even with a foothold his whole upper body was beginning to shake now with the strain of supporting his full weight. There was a burning weakness in his left forearm, as if the muscle inside was losing its strength, tearing. He was going to have to move – up or down – it didn't matter which any more. But if he stayed where he was another second he would fall.

Again he let the rope slip through his fingers just a little. Again the twine made its creaking, ripping sound as if it might give way at any moment. He stretched with his right toe for another hold. It would have been easier going upwards where he could see where he was putting his hands and feet. It would have been easier without shoes – more feel for holds. Too late

to think about that. And going upwards was no good. That wouldn't take him where he wanted to be.

He reached down blindly with his foot again. There was nothing. The wall was smooth. It was too smooth. It wasn't wall he was feeling at all – it was glass. The sound was different as he tapped his foot against it. Too hard, and it would shatter, and then someone was sure to look up and see him, and then what? Better to fall than to have Johnny Johnson go to his father with the story of this 'latest outrage'.

He felt lower down with his right foot. Why was there glass? Was the window shut? If it was, that was the end. He was going to fall. In fact, he was going to fall anyway. The weakness was spreading up his arms to his shoulders now. His fingers were cramped on the rope – cramped and without strength. He couldn't hold on another moment.

Alec's left foot slipped off the cornice and he closed his eyes, waiting to feel the air rush past him and then the sharp impact of the black railings. Instead his foot felt solid resistance below. Then his other foot was in the same place. He was standing on something firm and – and then the whole wall seemed to move suddenly and sharply downwards. The rope slipped through his fingers. He really was falling. And then he was face-down on the deep-piled carpet in his father's study.

He had been standing on the half-open window. His weight had made the window slide down, and he had fallen forwards into the room, not backwards. He was safe.

Alec lay still on the floor, waiting for his heart to stop hammering and the feeling to return to his arms. He had never been in this room alone before. He had never been here without hearing a lecture from his father. The silence was overwhelming.

Then the clock on the mantelpiece struck the half-hour. In thirty minutes he had to have climbed up the outside of the house without being seen and be back in the tower room for Johnny to find. There was no time to lose.

Alec got painfully to his feet. The whole process of climbing down from the window above couldn't have taken more than half a minute, but every muscle in his body was in agony. He went to the door and tried the handle. It was locked, of course, but he wanted to be sure. Then he went to the desk and sat in his father's padded leather seat.

The desk was an enormous thing, made of dark wood so highly polished you could literally see your reflection in it. It had a roll top that slid up and drawers down both sides. Alec didn't try any of them: he knew they would be locked.

In the top of the desk a key with a long, gold tassel unfastened the roll-top mechanism. Alec turned the key, and opened the desk. Inside was an array of tiny drawers and cubbyholes. An inkwell stood ready by the blotter along with half a dozen quill pens, cut and ready to use. Meticulously lined up in their usual place on the right-hand side of the blotter were two mechanical pencils with ends shaped like elephants. They had fascinated Alec since he was five years old, but he'd never been allowed to touch them. He didn't stop to look at them now.

He reached into the central cubbyhole, feeling with his

fingers. When his father did this he always told Alec to look away, but the boy knew how the mechanism worked. There was a catch back here somewhere, and if you – yes, there it was. Alec pulled on the hidden spring and a tiny drawer above the cubbyhole flew open. Inside was a selection of keys. Now it was just a matter of finding the right one.

Down the left-hand side of the desk were four drawers, but on the other side was what looked like a single drawer and below that a cupboard. Alec knew the door and sides of the cupboard were lead-lined. It was a safe.

He glanced over at the carriage clock on the mantelpiece. He had twenty-eight minutes. He started trying keys. The third one opened the safe.

The boy rifled quickly through the papers inside. There were rolled-up parchments in legal language, which he ignored. There was a collection of letters carefully tied at the corner with black ribbon. He read at random: '... *and it is therefore with regret that we are asking you to remove your son from the school with immediate effect* ...' It was about him!

Alec leafed through the letters. They were in chronological order – of course: how else would his father keep correspondence? – and they told the story of Alec's one year and one term at boarding school. They held him until the clock struck the quarter hour. Then he stuffed them back into the safe. He was wasting time.

There was a cash box full of paper money. He put it back as it was. There were the deeds to the house. There were letters from doctors about his mother, tied up in ribbon too. Alec held them in his hand for a moment. He sniffed at the thick, cream-tinted paper, imagining he could detect the faint scent of rose petals which always pervaded her bedroom and everything she wore or owned. But he didn't read the letters. Addicted to laudanum. That's what James Mundy had said. The man in Addison's had said the same thing, except he'd called it opium. Alec shook his head angrily and put the letters to one side. He was still wasting time.

Then he found it – a single sheet of flimsy paper with a regimental stamp at the top, each word upright and clear like a line of soldiers on parade. Alec scanned through the conventional opening. The officer was replying to his father's enquiry. Yes, he had information about a man he believed to be Private James Mundy, '*but the information may not be entirely pleasing to you or to the man's son,*' the letter went on. '*The man currently in danger of his life in our military hospital here in Fredericton, New Brunswick, carries military identification naming him as Private James Mundy of the 20th Regiment of Foot, the East Devon. He was found close to death in wild terrain on the other side of the Petitcodiac River. However, said Private Mundy was listed as absent without leave three years ago, and his battalion returned to England without him. Desertion from Her Majesty's forces would normally earn Private Mundy a lengthy term in a military prison, but given the long passage of time since the offence, his extremely poor state of health and a previously exemplary record, I am authorized to release him hereby into the charge of Jonathan Harvey Esquire of London. I should add that my impression in this case is that Private Mundy's absence without leave was out of character and followed an incident in which he may have been unjustly sentenced to eighteen months in the guard house. This makes him, in the regiment's view, deserving of a second chance. It should be added, on the other hand, that I can give you no account of his way of life in the last three years. Yours faithfully . . .'*

The letter hung limply in Alec's hand. A thrill of excitement went through him. A deserter! Joe's father was a deserter! And – he re-read the last two lines – no one knew what he'd been up to for the last three years. It was better than he could have imagined.

The clock said ten minutes to twelve. He couldn't take the letter with him or his father would know someone had broken into the desk. He slipped it back with the other papers and locked the safe, and as the key turned once again in the lock, the outline of a plan was forming in Alec's mind. His father had kept this a secret from Joe, and almost certainly he had kept it from the bank too. There was a way to use this. And it was more than a way to take revenge on Mundy, or to rob a sweeper boy of the father he thought he'd found. It just might be a way to wipe that look of chill disapproval off his father's face for ever, to make the man call him enterprising and intelligent and courageous like he'd called Joe.

Alec put the key back in its secret compartment. Then he took a sheet of writing paper from one of the cubbyholes in the desk, picked up a quill pen, dipped it in ink and began to write swiftly. He addressed his letter to the Chief Cashier, West, Woodford & Harvey Ltd, Lombard Street.

'Sir,' he wrote, '*It is with regret that I write to you on a delicate matter. It has come to my notice that the bank has lately employed one James Mundy in a position of trust. I feel it my duty to warn you . . .*'

Alec wrote with one eye on the clock. He finished with three minutes exactly to spare. At the bottom he signed his letter: '*From a well-wisher.*'

Chapter 22

A Crack in the Wall

'A what letter?'

'Anonymous,' Alec repeated. 'It means no one knows who sent it.'

'Well who did send it?' demanded Joe.

'How should I know? All I know is what it said. He's a deserter.'

'I don't believe it,' said Joe at once.

'No,' said Alec quickly. 'Nor do I. But apparently the chief cashier at West, Woodford and Harvey does.'

Joe sat down on the floor in the corner of the shed where the dog usually slept. Boy got up, looking surprised. Then he came slowly back and lay down next to Joe, gazing up into his face.

Alec stayed by the door, watching. He felt no guilt about Mundy. The man had got him locked up and he'd got his own back. That was all. But with Joe it was different. He'd expected to enjoy telling the sweeper boy his father was an army deserter and had been fired from his job, but when it came to it he hadn't.

Suddenly Joe was looking over at him, his eyes very intent. 'How come you know so much about it?'

For a moment Alec couldn't think of an answer. He felt the blood drain out of his face. Then he knew what to say.

'I heard them talking.'

'Who? At the bank?'

'No. At the house. He came back after – well, after it happened. Mister Harvey brought Jimmy back to the house.' Alec was on top of the situation again now. Part of this was true anyway. His father and Mundy had suddenly reappeared in Lomesbury Square that morning, but Alec had known what it was about without eavesdropping. One look at their faces in the hallway and it was clear his letter had arrived and done the trick. 'Mister Harvey's in a jolly awkward spot too,' he went on, trying to keep the satisfaction out of his voice, 'because apparently he knew all along and he didn't tell anyone at the bank.'

'He knew all along?'

'Seems like it.'

'And he didn't tell me? I don't believe any of it.'

'Perhaps he wanted to spare you the knowledge.' Alec's voice was heavy with forced sympathy. He sat down next to Joe on the floor, one hand reaching out to stroke Boy's back. The dog got up and moved away.

'I got to see him. Right now.' Joe was on his feet

'He's not at the house. There's nothing you can do, Joe.'

'Yes, there is. I can tell him I don't believe it. Where is he then?'

Alec knew the answer to that one. 'He went to Addison's.' He smiled inwardly at the memory of his father standing at the front door calling after the man: '*Don't turn to alcohol, Mr*

Mundy. It is a solution to nothing.' And Mundy had just walked away. The look on his father's face as for once in his life somebody didn't take a blind bit of notice of him! Just that moment made the whole thing worthwhile. 'They won't let you in, though,' he added. 'Not after—'

'Not after your performance,' said Joe bitterly. 'I expect you're right. But I reckon I know another way into that stinkin' gin shop, and I'm goin' to fetch him home.'

There was a fierceness in Joe's voice Alec had never heard before. He'd always looked and sounded so impressed and cowed by everything to do with the Harveys. But what had happened to Mundy had made him forget all that. And he wouldn't even believe the man was a deserter. Nothing about the scene was going the way Alec had planned.

He hurried across the park after Joe. The boy simply brushed past Barlow as if the old man wasn't there and strode off up the road with a look of grim determination on his face. Alec had no idea what he was planning to do. If Freddie was outside Addison's, Joe wouldn't even get past the door, and if he did, he'd be thrown out before he took a breath.

But Joe didn't go round to the front of the public house. He stopped on the side street before Upper Road, looking around to check who was watching. Twenty yards behind him Alec stopped and took a quick look around too. There was no one else in sight. When he looked back, the dog was still standing on the pavement, but Joe had disappeared.

Had he gone round the corner? There hadn't been time. Alec had only looked away for a moment. And why hadn't the dog followed him? He hurried over to where Joe had been standing.

He'd never noticed it before but there was a broad crack in the wall where the new Lomesbury bricks had pulled away from the old side wall of Addison's. The dog was sniffing and scratching at the opening, as if he couldn't quite get up the nerve to go through. Joe must have gone that way.

Alec edged sideways into the crack. He was bigger than Joe. He let all the breath out of his body and strained every muscle. No good. He struggled out of the opening, tore off his jacket and tried again. He could hear the cotton of his white shirt ripping as he tried to force his way through. He twisted his neck sideways, stretching one hand through the opening, feeling for a hold. His fingers closed on something solid. He pulled. He felt himself move but no more than an inch.

Suddenly he had a vision of himself stuck there between the bricks. It was starting to rain. Perhaps the damp would make the wall shift again and he would be crushed to death by the massive weight of masonry. A rising panic gave Alec an extra burst of strength. The brickwork tore at the skin of his chest. Then suddenly he was through.

He found himself standing in a narrow, rubbish-strewn alley between the back wall of Addison's yard and the garden wall of the first house on Lomesbury Square – soot-crusted bricks to the right, new red bricks to the left, and hardly more than a shoulder's width between them. There was no sign of Joe.

He looked up. There wasn't a hand- or foothold anywhere to be seen and the wall had to be ten feet high – more on the

Lomesbury side. But Joe had come through the gap and he wasn't here now, so there must be a way to climb it.

The two walls were so close together you could barely turn round. Maybe that was it . . . Alec braced his back against the new bricks and his feet against the old. Inch by painful inch he began to wriggle his way up the wall.

If there'd been anyone in the back parlour of Addison's they'd have spotted Joe for sure. But the place was empty as the boy slid up an unfastened window and hooked one leg over the sill. This room was for the gentry and there were deep leather armchairs and tables, but it stank of tobacco and gin just like the rest of the place. Joe went straight to the door that connected with the public bar and opened it a crack. He could hear Mundy at once, his voice loud and slurred.

'. . . folks call 'em savages, just like you say. But I've met men in black suits and top hats I'd call just as savage as any Indian.'

Voices were raised in agreement. 'He's right there!' 'You said it, mister!'

Joe peered through the crack in the door. Mundy was standing near the bar with a glass in his hand, and everyone else in the room was either grouped around him or facing in his direction to listen.

'Tell us another,' a man in the corner called out. 'I like a good story, I do.'

'Yeah,' another voice joined in. 'Tell us about the wild men, mister.'

'I'll tell you about wild.' Mundy's voice was raised in a way

Joe had never heard before. Usually he spoke so quiet and level you had to strain to hear him. It was the gin talking: Joe knew that. 'I seen men killed for nothin' more than a few beaver pelts and I done my share of it too.' He downed the contents of the glass. 'You dunno what's inside of you. No one does. Not until you bin hunted and starved and lived the life of an animal. A man'll do anythin' – anythin' he has to.'

'Terrifyin', ain't it, boys?' The man in the corner stood up, staggering slightly. ''Cept I reckon he made the whole bloomin' thing up.'

There was laughter and suddenly the mood in the room had changed. All eyes had been on Mundy, captured by his tales of life in the wilds. Now they were jeering and scoffing along with the man in the corner.

'Do you believe him, Joe?'

Joe wheeled round to find Alec crouched next to him by the door. He hadn't even heard the boy approach.

'The only thing is,' Alec went on, his voice a whisper: 'he says he was hunted like an animal. Now how come a soldier gets hunted like that? Eh, Master Joe?'

'What you talkin' about?'

Joe's response was angry and would have been loud enough for half the room to hear, but at that moment a sudden uproar drowned his words. The drunken man who had been jeering at Mundy from the corner had walked over to the big man and taken a wild swing at him. Mundy caught the fist, spun the man around and kicked him across the room, scattering the other onlookers.

The crowd had been laughing but suddenly they weren't laughing any more. Freddie appeared in the doorway, but he made no move to stop what was happening. He stood watching, arms folded and a half-smile on his face, as the crowd closed in on Mundy.

Joe screamed at the top of his lungs, 'Leave 'im! Let 'im be! He's my father!'

But his voice was blotted out by a great shout from the crowd: Mundy had pulled the bone-handled knife from his waistband. Joe saw knives appear in several hands. There were too many for him. Even with that knife he was going to be beaten to a pulp or worse. Then suddenly a slight figure leaped up onto the bar.

'Hey there, my fine fellows! Now which of you lucky louts is going to buy me a drink?'

It was Alec.

At the sight of the boy Freddie's face darkened. 'Little Lord Muck!' He pushed into the room, shouldering the other men to one side. The crowd forgot Mundy instantly. This was an easier game than tackling a big man with a nasty-looking knife. The doorman got to within grabbing distance of Alec and made a lunge for the boy.

'Gotcha!'

But he hadn't.

Alec jumped off the bar, ducked under a couple of outstretched arms and sprang up onto a barrel on the far side of the room. Joe saw his chance. Mundy was still standing, knees flexed ready to fight, but no one was looking his way now. Joe sprinted across and grabbed him by the arm.

'Come on, Jimmy!'

The man swung his arm round in an arc, the blade flashing in the gaslight, but in the split second that he recognized Joe, he changed the direction of the knife. Joe felt the blade graze his hair.

'Joe!'

'The door, Jimmy! Go on!'

Joe was shouting and pointing, and the man seemed to understand at last. He pushed a couple of men aside and headed for the door. When Joe looked back, Alec was still up on the bar right at the far end of the room. Mundy was at the door.

Joe cupped his hands to his mouth. 'He's gettin' away!'

It was enough to stop the pursuit of Alec just for a moment. Every eye turned to see Mundy disappear through the front door, but the crowd didn't follow him. This boy with the posh voice had been annoying them too long. It was time to teach him a lesson he'd never forget. But in the moment's pause Alec leaped off the bar and was through to the back parlour before anyone could stop him. Freddie had his shoulder to the door in an instant, but Alec had shot the bolt inside.

'We got 'im now!' yelled the doorman. 'Ain't no way out of the yard. Come on – give me an 'and!'

Freddie slammed his shoulder into the flimsy timber and the doorframe trembled. Joe smiled. Alec would already be over the wall at the back and safely away.

Chapter 23
ALEC'S PLAN

For a long time the only sound in the shed was the summer rain hammering on the tin roof. Mundy slumped in Barlow's broken cane chair, eyes fixed on the floor. Alec and Joe squatted by the door, breathing heavily, watching the big man. The dog lay still, watching him too. There had been no pursuit. The customers at Addison's might have given Alec a beating on their own territory, but they wouldn't follow him into Lomesbury Square. Lomesbury was gentry, and the crushers looked after the gentry – everyone knew that.

Joe studied Alec's face. They wouldn't have got out without him distracting the crowd. But why had he done it? He didn't like Mundy and he'd been pleased when the man lost his job. That was obvious. So why suddenly help him?

Alec didn't know the answer himself – except that it hadn't been part of his plan for the man to get torn to pieces by a drunken mob. He still wasn't sure what exactly he had been hoping for by writing the anonymous letter. But that certainly hadn't been it.

Joe turned back to Mundy. His voice was tentative, uncertain. 'You lost yer job, Jimmy?'

The man didn't move, but his eyes flickered sideways. He looked stone-cold sober now. 'Seems like it,' he murmured through gritted teeth. 'Someone bin runnin' their mouth.' His eyes went to Alec. The boy forced himself to look steadily back at the man. Mundy's gaze went back to the floor. 'Harvey said it weren't him. But somebody done it.'

'Done what?' Alec's voice was all innocence. Mundy didn't answer directly. He seemed to be thinking aloud.

'Now I got me no money and no way to get none.'

'Mr Harvey'll help yer find another job, Jimmy.' Joe tried to sound encouraging. The anger in the big man's voice frightened him. He went on, stammering as he tried to find the words. 'I – I heard tell – Alec here was sayin'—'

'Sayin' what?'

Mundy's eyes bored into Alec as if he could see straight into his soul. This time the boy couldn't look at him. He got up and went to stand by the window, anywhere just to be a little further away from that knife and those huge fists. 'I told Joe what I heard you and my father speaking of this morning,' he said hurriedly. 'That's all.'

'I don't believe it, Jimmy. You ain't no deserter, are yer?'

Mundy's face softened. 'You got faith in me, ain'tcha, boy?' There was a trace of wonder in his voice.

'Course I have.'

'We're family. No matter how long I bin gone' – he hesitated – 'and no matter what I done.'

Joe's face split into a quick grin. 'Yeah. We're family.'

Then Mundy let out a heavy sigh. ''Cept it's true, Joe. I run from the army.'

'You did?'

Alec watched Joe intently. It was coming. The boy was about to find out the truth about this hero of a father who dressed in animal skins and could shoot rabbits and make hammocks. Any moment now and he wouldn't look quite so much of a hero.

'I felt—' Mundy's eyes went up to the ceiling as if he were searching for the right words. 'I felt—'

'You felt shut in, like,' Joe finished for him.

Mundy looked surprised. 'Sum'n' like that. There was a fight and somebody said I done a thing I didn't. I ain't so sure I remember no more.'

'Same as me,' Joe went on quickly. 'Ma sent me to the tailor's shop like Matt and Jimmy. Shut in, it was. And "Do this – do that" all day. So I run. Like you. Shouldn't oughta have done it.'

'Me neither, boy.' Again Mundy sighed heavily. 'Shouldn't oughta have done a lot of things.'

His body suddenly coiled and he sprang out of the chair and the timber of the shed shook as he paced heavily up and down, slamming one fist into the other.

''Cept now there ain't no goin' back.' He seemed to be talking to himself again now. 'No way forward and no way back. Ya know what a bear does when he's trapped, Joe?' Mundy pulled the knife out of his belt again and looked at it long and

265

hard. 'He fights.' The man stared around him, as if he were looking for someone to fight.

Alec stirred uneasily by the door. 'The problem is, Jimmy, that if word of your – er – difficulties with the army has reached one employer, it might reach another. Perhaps Mister Harvey will give you money to return to north America.'

'No!' Joe took a step forward as if Mundy might leave that moment.

'Ain't no risk, Joe. Harvey said he wouldn't give me money for my passage. Said he feared I might "go back to my old ways".' Alec laughed at the man's imitation of his father. But Mundy's quick glance silenced him. 'I'm a hunter,' he snapped. 'Only there ain't nothin' to hunt around these parts.'

'I know something you can hunt,' said Alec. The words had just sprung to his lips: almost as if he hadn't meant to speak. 'She'll think the whole thing's a game.'

'Who'll think what's a game?' Mundy's eyes narrowed.

'Felicity.' Alec hurried on, and as he spoke something was becoming clear in his mind. Perhaps he had always been planning this far ahead, as soon as he started picking holes in Mundy's story, as soon as he saw the name Trapper on the man's belongings. And even now as the plan spilled out of him he realized with a shock that there was still no answer to the question: 'Who's Trapper?' That would have to wait: there was too much else to think about now. 'You need money, right?' he was saying. 'Who's got money? Mister Harvey. And there's one thing that will make him part with it – a lot of it. The poison dolly. Dear little Flicky.'

Joe's eyes bulged. 'Felicity? What you talkin'—?' he began. But Mundy interrupted.

'Let the boy say his piece.'

Alec went on quickly, the whole plan crystallizing in his mind as he spoke. There were details to be worked out, but this was it – this was the way he was going to make his father call him, Alexander Harvey, enterprising and intelligent.

'You pretend to kidnap Felicity.' Alec ignored Joe's attempt to interrupt. 'Then you get a ransom from my father and release the girl to me unharmed. I bring her home. You'll have money for a passage across the Atlantic – with Joe,' he added, glancing at the other boy, 'and everyone's happy. What do you think?'

Mundy said nothing. His face was inscrutable.

'This is a joke, right?' said Joe. 'Your family's brought Jimmy halfway across the world, they had me eatin' at their table, got us both work and we pay them back by kidnappin' their daughter?'

'You are just another do-gooding project, Joe,' said Alec. 'Like the Asylum for Fatherless Boys and the Orphans' Committee. It doesn't mean anything. It's like you might throw a stray dog a scrap of bread. That's all.'

Joe looked at Boy. It was exactly how the dog came to be lying there curled up in a corner of the shed: Joe had thrown him a piece of bread one dark night and the animal had never left him since. Were he and Mundy really no more than a pair of stray dogs to Mr Jonathan Harvey? His eyes went to Mundy.

'He's right about that much,' said the man bitterly. 'They

don't really care for the likes of you and me, Joe. Poor folk got to get what they can for theirselves. Takin' money from rich folks ain't wrong. Not always.'

Was that right? Joe's eyes closed for a moment as he tried to puzzle out what the man was saying to him. This was his father, but he'd heard something like it before from someone else. Who? *Ain't wrong to take money from rich folk, Joe.* It was what Bob had said about robbing the house. That made Joe's mind up.

'I ain't havin' nothin' to do with no kidnap,' said Joe flatly.

Alec looked at him for a moment. Then he burst out laughing. 'It was a joke, Master Joe.' He slapped the other boy on the back. 'I may not like the little brat much, but do you really think I'd kidnap my own sister? Even if she was in on it?'

Joe didn't know what to think. He looked at Mundy. The man gave a snort and went back to his chair. It seemed like he hadn't taken Alec seriously. Perhaps it had been just another of the boy's jokes. Joe broke the long silence.

'I got to get back to work. Barlow's goin' to have plenty to say about this mornin'.' He faced Mundy. 'I'll see yer later, Jimmy.' The man didn't answer. He seemed lost in thought again. 'We'll work somethin' out. You'll see. I got a bit saved. We won't starve.'

As Joe closed the door behind him, Alec's eyes met Mundy's.

'She'd think it was a game?' The big man's voice was as calm and level as ever.

'She might. She might not.' Alec smiled. 'But I can get a

268

drop of something that will quieten her down so it won't matter. What do you say, Jimmy?'

Mundy looked away. Alec couldn't tell what he was thinking. But when the man looked back at him his lips were set firm. Alec's heart thumped in his chest. Mundy was going to do it!

'You know the nursemaid, Alice?' Alec asked quickly. Mundy grunted. 'Well, it seems she has a gentleman follower. I have watched her from the window, and most days around midday she tries to make sure she and little Flicky are out in the park . . .'

Mundy's eyes were half-closed. Alec watched him as he outlined his plan. The man looked exactly the way he had the moment before he loosed the arrow that day – the arrow that had flown straight and true and pierced clean through the rabbit's neck.

Chapter 24

KIDNAP

There'd been no rain that morning – not yet anyway – but the clouds hung low and dark over Lomesbury Square as Joe worked through the flower bed, digging weeds. He and Barlow had seeded the ground here back in the spring in the shape of a giant Union Jack, and sure enough the flowers had come up red, white and blue. But all through the summer wild grasses and old vegetable plants had kept springing up just as they did all over the square and you couldn't see the pattern properly any more. With his small feet it was easier for Joe to pick the weeds out from amongst the flowers than it was for Barlow.

The old man had gone to buy his dinner at a stall on Upper Road as he usually did. He and Joe rarely stopped work at the same time. 'Always make it look like you're busy.' That was Barlow's advice on working for the gentry.

There was a rumble of thunder in the distance. Over on the grass Boy growled softly and Joe glanced up from his weeding. The air was hot and still. A storm was coming: the dog could smell it.

The children who had been playing over by the new fountain had gone home. They'd trampled through a circular flower bed: Joe would have to do what he could to repair the damage later. Only Felicity Harvey was still there, hitting her shuttlecock as far as she could and then shouting for Alice to retrieve it. Joe mopped his brow and watched the little girl for a moment. Then he saw Alice coming towards him.

'Do me a favour, will yer, Joe?'

Joe knew what was coming and he didn't like it. Every other day Alice was asking him the same favour: 'Just for a minute, while I go and see my friend. She won't be no trouble.' It was the same story today.

'Mr Bates wouldn't like it,' said the boy moodily.

'You won't tell 'im, will yer?' Alice sounded scared.

'No.' If he did, the footman was more likely to blame him than Alice.

The young woman hurried over to the gate, glancing nervously up at the house, as if she feared someone might be watching. Joe looked that way too, but there was no one to be seen. Felicity took a mighty swing with her racket and landed the shuttlecock in amongst the flowers where Joe was working.

'Give it, Joe!' the little girl shouted at the top of her voice, running towards him across the grass. Somehow Joe always felt uneasy dealing with Felicity. She was only a kid, but she was the Harveys' kid: he was never even sure what to call her. 'Miss Felicity' sounded stupid.

'Mind the flowers,' he warned.

'That's OK, little Flicky. I'll get it for ya.'

Joe hadn't heard him coming. One minute the big man wasn't there and the next he was right beside him. He'd shed his black city suit and put on the old animal-skin coat again. It looked stifling in the summer heat.

'Have a toffee.' Mundy pulled a single brown sweet out of the pocket of his coat and held it out to the little girl. Felicity's eyes widened. She grabbed the toffee without a word and stuffed it into her mouth. 'Sorry, Joe,' the man added casually. 'I only got the one.'

Felicity sat down on the grass, her face a picture of content-ment as she sucked on the sweet. There was another low rumble of thunder. Joe hoped Alice got back before the rain started. Then Mundy spoke again.

'You think bad of me, Joe, for walkin' out on your mother – and the army too?'

'No,' Joe answered instinctively, without thinking. It was the only time Mundy had mentioned his mother or the rest of his family since the day they first sat talking in the shed. 'I'm not sure,' he added more slowly. 'You said the army wouldn't let you take us.'

'Maybe I didn't ask too hard.' It was a kind of apology. He looked Joe in the eye. 'Things ain't always black or white, right or wrong, boy.' There was a weariness in his voice Joe couldn't remember hearing before. He stepped carefully through the flowers to stand next to the man. Boy got up from where he had been sitting and joined them. Mundy looked down at them both, his face strained, serious. 'You'll stick by me, Joe, won'tcha? No matter what?'

'Course I will. Things'll get better, Jimmy. You could maybe work here with me and Barlow for a while, and then—' Joe left the sentence unfinished. He could tell Mundy wasn't listening. His eyes were very far away.

'Sometimes you gotta do sum'n' seems wrong' – he was speaking so quietly now Joe could barely hear him – 'only it leads to sum'n' good. You understand me, boy?'

'I dunno.'

Joe felt the first drop of rain splash heavily on his hand. Then another. He looked round for Felicity. He was going to have to take the girl back to the house himself and if Bates caught him he'd get the blame: that was sure. Where was the kid anyway? Then he saw her.

Felicity was lying on her side on the grass. Her mouth was half open. Her eyes were closed. Joe moved quickly towards her, a sick sensation in his gut, but Mundy was quicker. The thunder rattled overhead, louder now.

'She's all right, Joe. She's just sleepin'. That's all.'

'Sleepin'? Whatcha mean? What you done to her?'

Joe's eyes searched the square desperately. There was still no sign of Alice. The blank windows of the Harveys' home and the whole long line of terraced houses that surrounded the square stared down at what was happening as the rain began to fall harder, but no one came. He turned back to Mundy. The man stooped and lifted the little girl easily, and she disappeared into the folds of his great shaggy coat as if she'd been swallowed.

'No harm will come to her, Joe. Harvey'll pay good money

to have her back, and you and me – we'll be free to go as we please.'

'Alec said it was a joke!'

'He give me two bottles of the stuff, Joe.'

'You drugged the toffee?' The disgust in the boy's voice was too strong to miss. He saw Mundy wince, but his arms still held the girl tightly out of sight.

'You said you'd stick by your father. No matter what,' said the big man. 'You gonna give me up now, Joe?'

A gust of wind and suddenly the rain was lashing down in great sheets, flattening the bright flowers Joe had been tending, tossing the young trees this way and that. The boy had to shout to make himself heard. 'You gotta let her go. We could say it was an accident.'

'Can't be done, boy. It's a hangin' offence already. You gonna hang your own father?'

Shielding his eyes against the rain, Joe looked back at the house. He had only to run and fetch Bates and the girl would be safe in a moment. It was the right thing to do. He knew that. But a hanging offence! He looked at Mundy, standing soaked and dripping. Was he really going to give up his father to the hangman? He felt as if he were being torn in half.

'I'll take you somewhere safe,' he said miserably. 'I can – I can make this all right. Somehow.'

'I'm headed north. Find a place to hide out.'

'No,' said Joe shortly. 'You gotta do what I say or I'm nosin' on yer. Hangin' or no hangin'.'

'Whatever you say, Joe.'

The rain was coming down so hard it was difficult to see what was happening in the park any more. Alec threw open the window and squinted through the downpour as a flash of lightning lit up the square, followed almost at once by a terrific clap of thunder which made the window rattle.

He'd made sure he got into trouble that morning so he could watch from the tower, and he'd seen it all. He'd watched breathless as Mundy handed Felicity the drugged sweet. He'd seen her keel over exactly like the robin he and Joe had trapped that day in the square. The only part he hadn't reckoned on was Joe himself.

Mundy was going now: he was through the gate and heading for the main road. But where had Joe gone? Was he going to wreck the whole thing? Alec wiped his hand across his face as the rain blew into his eyes. Had Joe come to the house? Was he downstairs right this minute raising the alarm? Then he saw him coming from the direction of the shed. He had something in his hand. It was – it was the bow and arrows Mundy had shot the rabbits with. He was taking it with him. He was following Mundy. He was going to be a part of the kidnap too. Just for a moment Alec's excitement evaporated and he shivered as the rain soaked through his jacket.

He hadn't meant Joe to get involved. When the poison dolly woke up she'd get a fright and that was fine, and then the good part would come when he, Alec, went to the rescue. Exactly how that would work he wasn't quite sure yet, but it would work: he was certain of that. And then his father would have to call him enterprising and intelligent and courageous.

But Joe . . . Joe was as guilty as Mundy now, and if Mundy was caught, he'd drag Joe down with him.

Alec shook the feeling of guilt away. It was the boy's own fault. He didn't have to get involved. He'd stopped now anyway. What was he doing? Perhaps he'd had a change of heart. Perhaps he wasn't going to follow Mundy after all.

The rain came even harder and it was like watching through a thick, white curtain. Joe was shouting something. He was shouting to someone. No, he was shouting to the dog, calling Boy to follow him, and above the sound of the rain Alec could hear the animal barking furiously and see him back away from Joe across the grass. Boy wouldn't go. He wouldn't follow Joe. Alec had never seen him behave that way before.

Joe spun round and was gone. He was running after Mundy. And the dog stood in the middle of the park, looking in the direction the man and boy had gone with the little girl, barking furiously in the drenching rain.

Chapter 25

CROSSING THE LINE

He was crying! His father was crying! Tears flowed down that long face. They hung from his nose. They gathered in his mutton-chop whiskers and soaked the front of his waistcoat. And great sobs shook his whole body, so that the letter trembled and fluttered in his hand as if a wind were blowing through the room.

Alec stood by the door, ignored by everyone, and stared. This was Mister Harvey, the man who listened to accounts of his son's wrongdoings from Johnny Johnson and meted out punishment without emotion. And now it was as if Mister Harvey had disappeared and been replaced by another man who looked just like him but who wept like a child.

At the other end of the long, empty dining table his mother sat, swaying slightly, with a tumbler of water in front of her. As Alec watched, she let six drops fall from a slim glass phial into the water. He'd spied on her in her room as she swallowed the mixture, but never, never had she sat like this where everyone could see and taken the poison in front of them. Bates, Johnny, his father, they were all in the room. It was like an admission of something they had all tried to deny so long. Mundy was right. Freddie, the doorman, was right. His mother was an opium addict. And it was he, Alec, who had brought it into the open.

The boy gazed around the room, thrilled and appalled by what he had done. It was getting dark outside, but the curtains were wide open still and there had been no talk of food that evening. Johnny was in his usual place, but his eyes were riveted to the single sheet of paper, which even at that moment fell from Mister Harvey's trembling hand. Bates stooped smartly to pick it up and Alec could see the footman scanning the few words on it.

Alec knew them by heart. He had used his left hand to write the ransom demand in painfully slow capital letters, and then 'found' it in the shed in the square as everyone searched for his sister through the long afternoon. 'I HAVE YOUR DAUGHTER,' it read. 'IF YOU CONTACT THE POLICE, YOU WILL NEVER SEE HER AGAIN. FURTHER INSTRUCTIONS ABOUT PAYMENT WILL FOLLOW.' it was signed: 'JAMES MUNDY'.

Bates had brought Alice in now. She was standing, weeping miserably, on the hearthrug in front of his father, but he seemed unable to look at the girl. He was doubled over in his chair as if a terrible pain were tearing at his insides. Alec stared in fascination at a little bald patch he'd never seen before on the top of his father's head. That clipped brown hair with its distinguished streaks of grey had begun to fall out, all in an afternoon. Alec wondered whether if would have happened if *he*'d been kidnapped.

His father made a feeble gesture to Bates, and the footman

stepped forward self-importantly. 'It is understood you were consorting with a man when the young mistress was taken. What have you got to say for yourself?'

Alice couldn't seem to answer. Her mouth opened and closed like a dying fish. Alec bit his lip to keep from laughing. The silence went on and on. Then his father made a furious gesture as if to obliterate the girl from the face of the earth and she was hurried out of the door. The boy could hear Bates ordering her to pack her bags and be gone that night.

One by one the servants were brought in and questioned, but no one had seen anything. Briggsy had been in her kitchen, the housemaids had been at their duties. Bates had been preparing to serve luncheon for Mrs Harvey. Johnny had been in the school room covering one of Alec's compositions with red ink. His father had been at the bank.

'And you, Alexander?' His father roused himself, turning a tear-stained face to Alec. The boy couldn't meet his eyes. He felt that guilt was written across his forehead for all to see, but his father was in no condition for reading anyone's thoughts. 'Did you see nothing?'

'I was in the Reformatory, Father,' said Alec. 'But I was reading *Lectures to Children* by Mr John Todd, as you told me. I saw nothing.'

Out of the corner of his eye Alec saw Bates look sharply in his direction. The boy pretended not to notice. Bates might be a loyal friend but he couldn't be trusted with this.

'Well, we know where he obtained the drug.' Mr Harvey rose unsteadily to his feet. Anger seemed to have stopped his tears. A glass phial, still half full of laudanum, had been found amongst the bushes in the park. 'Your poison, madam, has destroyed my daughter as well as yourself.'

Mrs Harvey didn't move. She was staring out, unblinking and unseeing, at the gathering darkness in the square. She could have been deaf for all the effect his words seemed to have on her.

Mr Harvey raised his arm, pointing an accusing finger down the length of the gleaming table. 'I hope you are satisfied.'

And then she turned, her whole body twisting slowly towards the man, as if her neck was too stiff to move. Her face was deadly pale and bathed in sweat. The pupils of her eyes were tiny pinpoints, blazing with hatred.

'I?' The voice was a hoarse whisper. 'Who brought that man into our home? Who insisted I invite the sweeper boy to dine with us? Who did that, Jonathan? Was that me? Was it?' Her voice rose to a scream and she plunged her hands into her hair, tearing at the array of combs and hairpins that held it in place.

The words shocked Mr Harvey back into his seat. He tried to respond, but his voice was uncharacteristically feeble: 'An old soldier . . . A man who had served in the same wild lands as Colonel Harvey . . .' His eye strayed for a moment to the portrait on the wall.

'Your father is dead, Jonathan. It's too late to please him now.'

'I – I don't know what you mean. I—'

'You could have put the man in a hospital somewhere. But no! You bring him into our home, get him lodgings and a job he wasn't qualified for—'

'Charity dictated that—'

'Charity!' Mrs Harvey spat the word back at him. 'You don't understand the word. When have you ever shown me any charity, Jonathan? Or your own son?' Alec cried out in protest as his mother gestured wildly in his direction, but she didn't hear him. 'Shutting him up like a prisoner in his own home. You think I don't know?'

Mr Harvey slammed his fist down on the table, making the candlesticks tremble. 'I have done my best by the boy, madam,' he shouted. 'I have done my best to be both mother and father to him and your daughter since you – you—'

'Since I what?' Mrs Harvey seized the glass phial in one hand. 'You think I take this stuff for the pain or because I can't live without it? I take it because I can't stand living in the same house as you, Jonathan Harvey, or your precious father!' She hurled the bottle straight across the room, but not at her husband. It smashed into the portrait of Colonel Richard Harvey, splitting the canvas and spraying the enormous painting.

Alec took a step forward. He couldn't bear this. His mother was slumped back in her chair now, hair hanging ragged about her shoulders, eyes fixed and staring. He ran to her side, holding her head against him, rocking her like a baby.

'It's all right, Mother,' he murmured softly, trying to push the great weight of her hair back into place. 'It'll be all right. I'll make it all right.'

'You?' His father's voice was contemptuous. 'What do you

propose to do?'

Alec swallowed the scorn in his father's voice. It hardened him, made him more sure than ever he had done the right thing. He stroked his mother's cheek automatically. He would show Mister Harvey now. He was the only one who knew what had happened to his precious little Flicky. He'd planned a rendezvous with Mundy where they'd hunted rabbits last month. Now that Joe had intervened they'd probably have gone somewhere else, and Alec had a fair idea where. Only he wasn't going to say anything. Oh, no! He was going to *do* something instead – something that would get everyone's attention.

Bates was talking now. 'I think I know how he got the – how he got Madam's medicine, sir,' he was saying. 'The sweeper boy, Joe. He was in and out of the house, and I seen him watching Mrs Harvey one day take her drops. It must have been him as stole it and gave it to Mundy.'

'You see!' Mrs Harvey roused herself briefly.

Mr Harvey ignored her. His voice was hollow. 'Dear God, that boy is a disappointment to me, Bates. Boy and father.' He gripped the footman by the shoulder. 'You were right about them both. You never liked them, did you? You're the only one of us with any sense left. We must go to Mundy's lodgings.'

'I've been there already, begging your pardon, sir,' said Bates, trying unsuccessfully to hide his satisfaction. 'As soon as Miss Felicity was found missing I knew who done it. But Mundy wasn't there. Landlady said she hadn't seen him in more than a month.'

'I know where he's been.' All eyes were suddenly on Alec.

Tonight he really did know more than anyone else about what had happened – not like the night when Joe had brought those two little toughs into the house. 'He's been sleeping in Joe's shed in the square. Where we found the note.'

'I'll go and search the place again,' said Bates at once. 'With your permission, that is,' he added hastily, looking at his employer. Mr Harvey waved a hand and subsided into his chair, looking exhausted. Bates hurried out of the room, and Alec slipped out after him.

He hovered in the hallway for a couple of minutes, giving the footman time to get over to the square: he didn't want to run into him outside. Then he eased the front door open. It was almost dark, but the air still felt warm and heavy, as if there could be another storm that night.

He skirted round the square, staying in the shadows. He passed the crack in the wall where he and Joe had broken into Addison's. Beneath his feet the neat rectangular paving slabs of Lomesbury gave way to the horse dung and stone chippings of Upper Road. The heavy rain had churned the surface into a quagmire and Alec's shiny black shoes were caked in filth before he had gone a dozen steps. He hurried past the gin shop, trying to stay out of the glare of the gas light.

Another couple of hundred yards and Upper Road became Lower Road. His father had brought him to the Asylum for Fatherless Boys here one evening, made him serve soup to the filthy women and their disgusting children, called it 'a character-building experience'. Alec had said something loud about the smell and got three days in the Reformatory. As he passed the side road he had an impulse to go and knock on the door under the gas light, to present himself at the soup kitchen, see what happened when they found Jonathan Harvey's boy out on the street. But he headed on down the main road. He had more important things to do.

Alec had never been down this far except in a cab. On foot you noticed the change more. Further on, Lower Road turned odd corners, meandered past dingy shops and dark alleyways. You'd hardly have known you were still in the same city as Lomesbury Square.

'Where you off to in such a hurry, young gentleman?' A woman had hold of his sleeve. Her hand felt the cloth of his jacket, testing the quality of the material. 'You come with me.' She drew him towards a darkened doorway. Alec saw the red gash of her lipstick, inhaled the sharp smell of gin. 'Come on, dearie. Don't be frightened.'

Alec pulled away sharply. Even this late the main road was crowded with people and traffic, and he stumbled into the path of other pedestrians. 'Look out, toff!' 'Hold onto your gold watch, little swell!'

A group of heavily built lads coming up the street jostled him into the road, laughing. 'Mind out, Lord Muck!'

Alec jumped back just in time as a wagon driver reined in his horse to avoid him. He fell heavily in the mud, the stinking mess clinging to his hands and clothes. He clambered to his feet, filthying his jacket still more as he tried to wipe the street muck off his hands. And for a moment he almost ran back where he'd come from, back to the safety of Lomesbury

Square, where the streets were wide and clean and no one pushed you off the pavement and he lived in a house bigger than most of these people had ever seen.

He backed up against the wall, eyeing the passers-by fearfully, waiting for the next insult, the next shove into the road. But no one seemed to be looking at him any more. He caught sight of his reflection in a shop window. He'd left the house so fast he wasn't wearing a hat and his suit was torn and filthy now. He no longer looked like the son of Jonathan Harvey of West, Woodford & Harvey Ltd. He looked like one of the street kids he'd watched from a cab as he drove briskly through the dirty streets of London with Johnny Johnson or his father. He looked like Joe.

Alec hurried on down the darkening street, guessing the direction, more excited than he had ever felt in his life. He knew where he was going. He might not know exactly how to get there, but he knew where Joe had gone. He thought of the sweeper boy boasting in the park the first time they talked. He'd said he was never going back, but with Mundy and the poison dolly to hide Alec was guessing he'd have changed his mind. Joe had taken them to Pound's Field, and Alec was going to find them.

Chapter 26
THE PLAGUE PITS

Coming down Flower Street, Joe's heart was beating fast. Somehow, however hard he tried to keep away, Pound's Field just kept dragging him back. It was like a nightmare when you couldn't wake up no matter how much you wanted to. But there was no choice – Joe was quite certain of that: these twisting, turning streets and alleys were the only place in London he knew well enough to hide Mundy in.

They passed Nimms's gin shop and the soap works, and there was the grating in the gutter that had been his way into the sewers for more than five years. It looked just the same: you could see nobody had sealed the cover down. The sewers would be treacherous after the heavy rain, but sure as shuffling some other kid was under their feet this very minute, searching the filth for something to sell. Someone else was the Ratboy of Pound's Field these days: Joe was just a ghost, come back to haunt a place where he'd once lived. The thought calmed him a little. If he was a ghost, then perhaps no one could see him.

Mundy walked behind. The man was as strong as a bull.

They'd come five miles without stopping, going roundabout routes, keeping off the main roads as far as possible, and he still had the girl out of sight under his coat. Didn't show a sign he was even carrying anything.

They passed the police station. Joe tried not to quicken his step, tried not to do anything to attract attention. People had looked at them as they passed – the big man in the strange coat and the boy with a bow and arrows – but no one had tried to stop them. Joe wasn't even sure why he had brought the bow. Somehow back in Lomesbury Square it had just felt right.

Just past the police station a massive railway arch straddled the junction of Flower Street and River Lane. This was the very spot where the cab had got stuck in traffic as he and Mr Harvey came to meet Mundy off the ship. That was almost exactly four months ago. It felt like a lifetime.

'Which way, Joe?'

'Straight on. Past the warehouses.'

Joe had thought long and hard about this as they headed south from Lomesbury. He was assuming the police would be after them – probably that night – but crushers didn't like Pound's Field and they wouldn't search the back alleys if they could help it, and certainly not in darkness. But that didn't mean just anywhere round here was safe. If they showed their faces in a flop house or a cookshop, Mother would know inside half an hour. What would happen then to a stranger or a little girl in a flowery pink dress was anybody's guess, but Joe knew what would happen to him. He'd be in the river by nightfall. But down past the warehouses was a place with no lodging houses, in fact no people at all, and here they just might be able to hide until he could persuade Mundy to let the girl go.

'She all right?' Joe kept his head down, looking for a break in the traffic.

Mundy looked quickly inside his coat. 'Sleepin' like a baby.'

They cut quickly across the busy street and then straight on down a narrow cobblestoned alley, the blank, windowless backs of new warehouses towering on either side. Joe knew where the alley led but he'd never been down this way. Back when he was working the sewers there'd been no point. There were no drains down here and no pickings for a tosher. Besides the place had a bad reputation.

The alley ended abruptly at a ramshackle barrier of timber and masonry. Old bedsteads and scraps of broken furniture had been piled high on top of the remains of several collapsed and demolished buildings. Someone had painted a sign on a piece of wood and nailed it roughly to a post at the very summit.

' "Plague pits",' read Mundy in the gathering gloom. 'What's that mean?'

'Don't mean nothin',' said Joe. 'Come on.'

Right in the shadow of the last new warehouse the heap of rubbish was a little lower. A section of what had once been a wall lay at a crazy angle, making a path almost to the top of the barrier. Joe led the way, scrambling up the sloping brickwork and then picking his route carefully over jagged timbers and piles of junk. Behind him he heard Mundy curse. He was heavier and his burden slowed him down. Joe looked back to see the man dragging one leg out of a hole. Mundy met his eye.

'It's good, boy. We can defend this. Now we just need us a back door.'

Joe sighed.

On the other side of the barricade the cobblestones stopped and the dirt road opened out a little. Up ahead against the darkening sky the outlines of some old warehouses and a crowd of ships' masts showed they had almost reached the river. Joe could hear the shouts of the labourers on St Saviour's Docks and the cries of boatmen out on the water. But here there was no one – no movement, no sound, just a mist that crept up the lane from the Thames and a sweet, sickly smell that hung heavy in the still evening air.

To the right stood a row of tumbledown, one-storey shacks with the roofs fallen in. To the left was another low building with a sloping roof and glass windows – all broken.

'Should be safe here tonight, Jimmy,' he said. 'Ain't no one comes down this way.'

'How come?'

Joe didn't answer.

The door of the first shack wouldn't budge. The next one was the same. Mundy was on the other side of the lane, trying the bigger house. Then a high, terrified scream pierced the silence.

Mundy had got the door open. He was standing on the threshold, his back blocking the doorway. Joe pushed past. The effects of the drug had worn off and Felicity had woken up. She was pressed against the rough stonework by the door, as if she were trying to disappear through the wall. Her eyes were wide and staring and her mouth hung open from the scream. Joe followed her gaze.

A long bar cut the room in two. The roof above gaped open to the sky. The place was a gin shop. Or it had been once. The mirrors behind the bar were smashed and most of the liquor barrels had been staved in, but one table and an ancient chair still stood upright in front of the bar, and propped in the chair, as if sleep or something worse had overcome him there one night long, long ago, was the skeleton of a man.

A tattered blue jacket and trousers clung to the bones. A dusty glass and bottle stood on the table. The empty eye-sockets stared at them.

Mundy was the first to recover his wits. Ignoring the corpse, he pushed open a door at the back of the room and immediately recoiled, holding his hand across his mouth, coughing.

'There's more,' he said. 'Sickness here, I reckon. Must be plague. That's why they closed off the road.'

The shock had stopped Joe for a moment. Now he went to the little girl and stood uncertainly, not knowing how to quieten her.

'It's all right.' It was all he could think of to say. 'He's dead.'

Felicity opened her mouth to scream again and Mundy made a move towards her.

'Don't let her do that,' he said sharply.

Joe took hold of the girl by the shoulders as gently as he could. He had no idea how to deal with the child.

'There there,' he murmured, glancing awkwardly at Mundy. 'Joe's here. You're all right.'

Felicity buried her head in her hands and fell against him, sobbing desperately. Joe patted her tentatively on the back with one hand. 'What do I do, Jimmy? Ain't had no dealings with young 'uns.'

Mundy took the dead man's dusty glass off the table, wiped it briefly on his sleeve and vaulted over the bar. He turned the tap on one of the unbroken barrels and, to Joe's surprise, a clear liquid flowed into the glass. Then the man dug into the pocket of his enormous animal-skin coat and produced a small glass phial.

'No, Jimmy!' Joe's voice was urgent.

'It's better,' said Mundy, measuring drops into the glass.

'She don't want no more of that stuff, Jimmy. She'll be all right. Won'tcha, Flicky?' Joe tried to lift the girl's face to him. 'You won't make no noise, will yer?'

The girl looked at him. Her frightened eyes flickered side-ways as the big man swung his legs across the bar and came quickly towards them, holding the glass. Then she looked back at Joe and gave a little shake of her head. 'I'll be quiet.' Her voice was scarcely more than a whisper, but she'd stopped sobbing.

'See,' said Joe triumphantly. 'She's a brave 'un, she is.'

He clasped an arm round the little girl. She coughed as the air was knocked out of her and Joe loosened his grip a little. Perhaps he'd squeezed a shade too hard. He patted her on the back in a way that was meant to be encouraging. Boy would have understood that. Maybe little girls were the same. What had happened to the wretched dog anyway? Why wouldn't he come? Wouldn't even follow Mundy, and the animal worshipped him.

'Can't stay here.' Mundy was rummaging in cupboards behind the bar. Then he went into the back room and came out with a lantern and a can of oil.

Before they left, Joe took a quick look through the door at the back. There were two beds in the room. Another skeleton lay stretched out on one, an arm thrown out to the side. There was a second, smaller body on the other bed with two little bundles clasped against it. They looked like rags. Joe didn't go any closer. He'd seen enough.

Mundy led the way now as the lane began to slope towards the river. Joe stumbled along behind, holding Felicity up as best he could. There was still light in the sky, but here old warehouses pressed close on either side, blotting out the view of the river, making the lane almost dark. Above him Joe could see wide loading doors like black holes in the crumbling brickwork. They made him think of the blank eye-sockets of the skeletons they'd just seen. No wonder people stayed away from the area. It crossed the boy's mind that he'd made a mistake coming here, but it was too late to think of another plan now and maybe they wouldn't have to stay longer than one night.

Mundy stopped. A heavy iron hook hung down at street level on a long rope, still waiting for cargo to be loaded and hoisted to the upper floors of the warehouse. The man handed the lamp and oil to Joe and leaned on the rope, lightly at first, then applying more weight. The rope creaked and shuddered. There was a groaning, cracking sound high overhead.

'Look out!' Joe pulled Felicity back against the wall as the hoist tore loose from the brickwork forty feet above and came crashing down into the alley in a blinding cloud of dust.

'Jimmy?'

There was no reply. Joe held Felicity against him and peered into the dust. The little girl was shaking but she had made no sound. Had Mundy been crushed under the falling timber? If he had, Joe could take Felicity Harvey back to her family tonight, and then – and then – and then what? He had no idea. For months every thought about the future had had James Mundy in it. But Joe didn't know any more if that was a good thing or a bad. Should he take his chance and run now with the girl whether Mundy was coming back or not?

He called again: 'Jimmy? You there?'

A hulking figure loomed out of the murk, coughing and choking into his hand.

'Keep goin', Joe,' he said brusquely. 'Be a better place some-wheres near.'

A dozen yards further down the lane Mundy kicked open the rotting door of a building and stepped warily inside. Joe followed. Enough light filtered through the upper windows to show that the warehouse was a ruin. There were four reasonably solid walls and most of the roof was still there, but the upper storey had collapsed, filling the floor with shattered timbers. Mundy grunted, backing quickly out and heading on down the silent lane.

The next door was the same, only this time the roof was completely gone and the building was open to the dim sky. The clouds overhead were a solid, unmoving mass, threatening more rain. Seagulls nesting in the broken walls squawked angrily at the intruders. They moved on.

A few yards further and an old ladder led up to a loading door on their right. There was a pulley system over the door, just like the one that had collapsed outside the first warehouse, and a long rope hung down. Attached to the end was a heavy rope cradle for lifting cargo. Mundy bent down, running his hands over the cords, sniffing at the pungent smell of tar. Then he examined the ladder. He put a heavy boot on the first rung and it snapped instantly under his weight. He grunted with apparent satisfaction and left the ladder where it was.

Joe held Felicity's hand awkwardly and peered up at the dark warehouse wall. A narrow plank bridge spanned the street high over their heads. It made him dizzy just to look at it. Men must have crossed from one warehouse to the other on that bridge, probably with heavy loads. He wouldn't have liked to try it himself.

When he looked down, Mundy was emerging from the building opposite. 'Stairway gone in there,' he said. 'That's good.' Joe couldn't imagine why it was good.

The man pushed open a door just behind the rotten ladder and peered inside. 'This is it.' His voice echoed eerily from within the building. 'This is the one. We can defend this.'

Joe left Felicity for a moment by the door and took a look himself. There was still an upper storey to the building, though the boy could see holes in the timbers over his head. On the far wall an open stairway led up, but whether it would support their weight was anybody's guess. If Mundy was planning to go that way, then it was up to him, Joe, to try it first. He was lighter. He turned back for Felicity. The girl was gone.

Without a word Mundy pushed past him in pursuit. By the time Joe reached the door he was already coming back, the girl hanging limp under one arm, not struggling. Mundy set her down next to Joe.

'Either we give her another dose or you hold her. Which?'

'I'll hold her.' Loose in Pound's Field Felicity would be worse off than she was with him and Mundy. He reached out to the girl, trying to sound reassuring. 'You got to stay with me. I'll see you're all right.' She shrank from him, looking anxiously to Mundy. In her eyes there was fear and hatred for both of them. And why not? What did he look like but one half of a kidnap plot?

Mundy was testing the hoist – more carefully than the last one. Finally he seemed satisfied, easing his full weight onto the cradle. The ropes creaked and groaned. But they held.

'Wait here,' he said. 'Keep a hold of the girl.'

Through the open door of the warehouse Joe watched the man climb the timber staircase inch by inch on hands and knees. He was spreading the weight and going slow to reduce vibration, but the old timbers shook under the load and dust began to fall as if the rickety structure were close to collapse.

'Come back, Jimmy,' he called to the man. 'You're too heavy. Let me.'

Mundy didn't answer. He was more than halfway up now –

twenty feet from the floor at least. A fall from there could be fatal.

Joe held his breath. Out in the lane when the rope gave way, a part of him had been hoping Mundy wouldn't reappear. But as he watched him now, crawling up the broken staircase on all fours, he knew he wanted this man to survive more than anything else in the world. Mundy had made a bad choice. He'd been desperate and he'd done a wrong thing. Joe knew that. But this was his father. He'd been brought up to believe he was dead and he couldn't wish him dead now, or wish him gone, or wish he'd never seen him. Like the man had said himself: they were family.

Joe breathed again. Mundy was at the top. He leaned down through the hole in the floor. 'Outside, Joe. Wait with the girl.' Then he kicked out with both feet at the top of the stairway. More dust fell. Mundy kicked again, stamping with all his strength on the top tread. Nothing happened. He stamped again. And all at once, with a mighty, tearing sound, the entire stairway gave way, crashing onto the open floor below. Joe leaped back in shock. If the man was ever coming down again, he wasn't coming that way.

By the time he got out into the lane Joe could see what Mundy was planning. He was at the wide upper door of the warehouse, leaning out with one hand on the rope which hung down into the street.

'In the cradle, Joe,' he called down. 'Put her in the cradle.'

Felicity shrank back, eyes wide in terror.

'She won't do it, Jimmy. What about the ladder?'

'Not the ladder,' came the quick reply. 'It won't hold ya.'

'I'll have to bring her then.'

'All right. Get in.'

This time she came to him and together they climbed into the heavy rope cradle. The cords were so thick and had been soaked so long in tar they were still strong even after years hanging unused in the damp London air.

'You can't lift us both,' he called up to Mundy. But looking up he could see the man had another plan.

High overhead the rope passed through a pulley. Mundy was fastening heavy bags – sandbags maybe – to his end of the rope. He loosed them over the side and with a sudden jerk the net rose swiftly and effortlessly into the air, the bags acting as a counterweight. Almost before Joe could catch his breath, he and Felicity were being half helped, half lifted out of the cradle and into the upper loft of the warehouse.

'Good!' Mundy's face was set grimly. 'Now we need defence and a back door.'

Chapter 27

MOTHER

'I am looking for the docks.'

'Which docks?'

'I am not sure.'

The man threw back his head and laughed.

'Runnin' away to sea, are yer, sonny? Does Mummy know you're out this late?'

'My mother has nothing whatever to do with it!'

'Oh, don't she? Talk posh, don'tcha?' The man took hold of the collar of Alec's jacket. 'Even if yer duds is none too clean.'

Alec pulled away sharply and hurried on, taking a dimly lit side street at random. It was dark now. Somehow he hadn't quite been able to make himself ask the way to Pound's Field and he'd been wandering for hours, aiming in the general direction of the river without ever quite reaching it. The way was so confusing. The roads kept turning back on themselves or the street was suddenly blocked by a high brick wall or the towering arch of a railway viaduct.

This lane was quiet with high walls on both sides. Under a

gas lamp Alec stopped to examine a street sign. 'Sweetwater Lane'. Hah! It didn't smell any too sweet.

The shadowy road seemed deserted, but up ahead under the next lamp he could see something that looked like a bundle of rags lying on the ground. As he drew closer Alec realized it was a figure, sitting or squatting in the dirt. He couldn't tell if it was a man, a woman or a child, but whoever it was, he was going to have to ask them for directions.

It was a woman. She was huddled on the ground where a tiny passage led off between the houses. A tattered shawl was draped over her head. Alec saw her stir at the sound of his footsteps – 'Tapes and laces. Who needs 'em? Best tapes and laces.' She was selling something. There was a tray of rags in front of her. 'Best tapes and laces.' The voice was a steady drone.

'Excuse me.' The drone stopped, and the woman squinted up into Alec's face. 'I'm sorry,' he said, 'I do not have any money so I cannot buy your wares, but I am looking for Pound's Field.' The woman stared vacantly at him as if she didn't understand. 'I want to get to Pound's Field,' said Alec very distinctly. His voice sounded strange in his own ears, echoing from the soot-blackened bricks.

'Are you mad?' She had said something, but Alec wasn't sure what. Now she suddenly reached out a bony hand and gripped him by the leg. 'Where's your home, little boy?' she croaked. 'Where's your home?'

All through the long afternoon as he wandered the streets Alec hadn't been afraid. He was on an adventure. At last. He was going somewhere his father and Johnny Johnson and probably even Bates had never been, and somehow he was going to come back a hero. They'd be writing penny dreadfuls about him by Christmas – *Boy Detective* maybe or *Alec the Great*. But now, in spite of himself, he felt a chill of fear. The old woman's eyes were so intense, her voice so urgent. Her grip cut into his ankle.

'Get away!' she croaked, pushing him from her. 'Get away while you can, little man.'

As the old woman finished speaking, there was a whoop and a shout from the narrow passage behind her, and a big lad in a collarless shirt burst out of the darkness, almost tripping over the old woman, scattering the rags on her filthy tray.

Suddenly her voice was raucous and powerful. 'Oi! I'll do you down, little muck-snipe!'

'Shut your mouth, you old hay bag!' The big lad raised his hand as if he were about to strike the old woman. But at that moment he spotted Alec. His hand fell slowly to his side and an odd little smile twisted the corners of his mouth.

Four more boys came running out of the alley, laughing and colliding with each other as they skidded to a halt. At the sight of Alec they were silent, looking to the big lad for what to do next. He made a quick gesture – a circling movement with his right hand.

Two of the boys hesitated, as if unsure what they were supposed to do. There was something familiar about them, something Alec couldn't quite place. But he was sure he'd seen these two somewhere before.

The big lad snapped his fingers and pointed quickly – 'Bob!

Charlie!' – and the two boys moved behind Alec.

That was it! Bob and Charlie. They were the pair from outside Addison's, the ones Joe had led into a trap. Alec hadn't recognized them that night in the hallway of his home, but he knew who they were now. The question was: did they know who he was? He spun round quickly. He was surrounded, but the boys' eyes were hard and blank. They didn't know him.

The old woman's harsh cackle broke the silence. 'Lookin' for Pound's Field, are yer, sonny? Well, you found it. Yes, you found it all right now!' She looked up at the big lad and suddenly her voice was wheedling. 'I found him for yer, Billy. Tell Mother it was me as found 'im.'

'Did you say *Mother*?!' Alec didn't feel afraid now. Even as Bob and Charlie and the two other tough-looking boys circled around him and the big lad she'd called Billy rolled his shirt sleeves tighter, exposing the muscles on his arms, he felt good inside. Mother was the woman Joe had talked about – the fence – and Bob and Charlie were housebreakers who'd been inside Pentonville Prison. He was in Pound's Field. He wouldn't have been surprised if Starlight Sal herself had stepped out of the shadows to join them.

'What you grinnin' at, toff?' The big lad sounded genuinely amazed as Alec's face split into a broad grin.

'Let me understand this correctly,' he said. 'I am in the district known as Pound's Field? And the Mother of whom the aged hay bag just spoke is the local criminal panjandrum?'

'The local what?' Billy looked stunned.

'The Empress of Evil. "The old monster", as Joe would say.'

'Who?' Three voices spoke at once.

The name had just slipped out, and Alec wasn't surprised it had touched a nerve with Bob and Charlie. But it was the big lad's eyes that looked as if they were about to pop out of his face. 'Joe who?'

This boy named Billy knew someone called Joe, and now it all came back to Alec. *Can't never go back round Pound's Field. Left owin' money.* He could see Joe's pinched little face in the park in Lomesbury Square. *The old monster'd have me in the river soon as look at me.* That night in the darkened hallway Alec had wanted so much to be a part of the story of Joe and Bob and Charlie: now there was a way of making them and this big idiot of a lad into part of *his* story. If only his father could be there just for a moment to see how cleverly he was going to use this bunch of thugs to bring his precious little Flicky home again.

That was it. That was the way the story had to run. Mister Harvey had to be there. It was no good just rescuing the brat or paying off the ransom. His father had to see him do it.

'Joe Mundy,' said Alec. Then he thought again. 'Except that around here you might know him as Joe Rat.'

Billy's mouth clamped tight, and Alec could see the muscles of his jaw working. 'Joe Rat?' he grated. 'You know where Joe Rat is?'

'I might,' said Alec. 'Now, do I get the pleasure of meeting Mother?'

'Oh, yes.' Billy smiled slowly. 'If you know where Joe Rat is, then you get to meet Mother all right. 'Cept you may find it ain't such a pleasure. And he certainly won't!'

'Well! What a fine-looking lad, I must say!'

It was a woman's voice, soft and cooing, but with just a hint of steel. A strange, musty smell filtered through the blindfold tied tight around Alec's face, and out of the corner of one eye he could see light: they were inside now after the twisting, turning way Billy had brought him through the streets. He had fallen several times and his knees were scuffed and scraped. He felt hands on him.

'Beautiful cloth! That's a young gentleman's suit, Billy, my lad. You wouldn't recognize that, would you? But dirty!' The hand brushed hard and unexpectedly at his jacket, making Alec stagger. 'And torn!'

Alec winced with pain as the wounds on his knees were examined none too gently. But the voice was even more soothing if anything.

'Oh! Mother's sorry. Did the clumsy old thing hurt the young gentleman?' Then she suddenly rapped out a command. 'What you standin' there grinnin' at? Take the blindfold off, you great lump of lard!'

Alec blinked in the light as Billy pulled the blindfold roughly from his face. He was standing next to an enormous, dilapidated four-poster bed, looking into the face of a woman. She lay back, eyeing him without blinking. A little white mouse stuck its head out of the brightly coloured pink scarf draped around her neck. It seemed to stare at him too. Alec screwed up his eyes, wondering if he'd imagined it. When he looked again the mouse had disappeared. But the woman was still there.

He couldn't guess how old she was. The face was unlined, but that was only because it was so swollen with fat. Great folds of skin hung at her neck, and her eyes were tiny gleams of light, almost lost under drooping eyelids. Her head was wrapped in great swathes of fabric and the rest of her body was invisible beneath a mountain of filthy rags and shawls and blankets.

An image of his own slender mother with her long white fingers and faint, faraway smile floated before Alec's eyes for a moment. Then another white mouse scurried across the bedding and dived into the sleeve of the woman's enormous bed jacket. This time he definitely hadn't imagined it.

'You keep pets, do you, young gentleman?'

Alec swallowed hard and found his voice. 'No, ma'am.'

The woman threw her head back, laughing or coughing – Alec wasn't sure which. Then she spat into a dirty silk handkerchief which she handed to a man just behind the bed. Alec noticed him for the first time, and a second stone-faced character who flanked the woman on the other side.

'See what real breeding sounds like?!' The woman's harsh bark took in the two men at the head of the bed and Billy, who was hovering next to Alec along with Bob and Charlie. 'Why don't none of you call me ma'am? Eh?'

'Everyone calls you Mother, Mother,' said Billy, nervously.

'Hold your gas, dog's meat!' the woman snapped. Then her eyes went back to Alec, and the voice was soft and purring again. 'You're a well-brought-up young gentleman. But you can call me Mother like the rest of this rabble!'

The last word was flung out sideways. Alec saw Billy wince. Bob and Charlie looked frankly terrified. It was obvious the woman – Mother – had taken a shine to him. This was going to be easier than he'd imagined.

'I believe we can be of mutual benefit to each other,' he began.

'Mutual benefit!' Mother interrupted. She seemed to like the expression. 'Such a beautiful speaking voice . . .'

'Yes.' Alec wasn't sure what to say to that. He hurried on, using the old woman's name awkwardly. 'The fact is – Mother – I'm in Pound's Field to rescue my sister. A man has kidnapped her and—'

'Kidnapped?' Mother's voice was all innocent amazement.

'Yes. Now this man and his accomplice—'

Again Mother interrupted. 'Accomplice!' The word came out in a prolonged hiss, as if she liked the sound. 'I don't know your name, young gentleman,' she said suddenly.

'Never mind my name,' said Alec. 'What I want—'

Mother suddenly stiffened in the bed. Her eyes were hard. 'What you want? What you want! Do you know where you are?'

Alec swallowed hard. His eyes shifted left and right. He could see a little smile on Billy's face. The two men behind the bed were expressionless. Bob and Charlie still looked scared. 'I'm sorry—' he began, but Mother spoke over him, brusque and businesslike.

306

'I asked what your name is.'

'Alexander Harvey.' Suddenly there didn't seem to be anything to do but answer this woman's questions.

'And your father. Who is he?'

'Jonathan Harvey.'

'Of?'

'Of Lomesbury Square. He's—' Alec broke off.

'He's what?'

The eyes bored into him. Alec hadn't wanted to say all this, but somehow he couldn't help himself. He felt Bob and Charlie's eyes on him. Now they knew who he was. Alec felt a long way from Lomesbury Square.

'He's a banker.'

'Ah!' Mother let out a long sigh and settled back amidst the cushions and rugs. 'A banker!'

From inside a little paper bag she drew out a morsel of cheese, and four or five white mice, noses twitching, darted out to be fed. She made a quick signal to the men behind the bed and they disappeared through a door at the back of the room. When Alec looked round, the three boys were gone too. He was alone with Mother.

'Now,' said Mother very softly and distinctly, 'come and sit a little closer to Mother, Alexander, and tell her all about it.'

For a moment Alec couldn't move. The heat of the room made him feel faint. He looked to the door. Billy would be out there with Bob and Charlie, and the other way were the big men Mother had sent out of the room and heaven knows how many more of them. There was no escape. And anyway, meeting this woman had been part of what he wanted in Pound's Field, hadn't it?

He took a step forward. Mother held out a trembling, pudgy hand towards him. He took another step. She patted the bedclothes next to her. He sat down, sinking into the mattress, hearing the bed creak under him as if it might collapse with the extra weight. He began to tell her about James Mundy and Felicity and the demand for ransom he had written and how he had hoped to prove himself a hero to his father.

'West, Woodford and Harvey Limited . . .' murmured Mother, when Alec had finished his story. 'West, Woodford and Harvey Limited . . .'

Just the sound of the Lombard Street bank's name seemed to fill her with a tremendous satisfaction, as if she already held in her trembling hands the vast wealth it suggested.

'You can collect the ransom,' said Alec eagerly. 'I don't care about that, provided I—'

'Ransom?' Mother was back to her tone of mock innocence. 'Mother doesn't involve herself in things like ransom, Alexander. That's against the law. However,' she went on, leaning close enough for Alec to see the dampness on her forehead and upper lip, 'Mother might return a beloved child to its anxious parents for' – she searched for the right word – 'a finder's fee, shall we say?'

'But I have to be there,' said Alec desperately. 'I have to stay here until Mister Harvey – until my father comes. And then I want – I want to—'

'You want to save your dear little sister?' suggested Mother.

'Yes!'

Mother's laugh ended in a violent fit of coughing. 'And so you shall, Alexander,' she managed at last, gasping for breath. 'And so you shall. Now' – her hand seized Alec's wrist so suddenly the boy cried out in surprise – 'this matter also involves a – a friend of mine, I believe.'

Before she could say anything else, Charlie's voice interrupted. He was standing in the doorway with Bob trying to pull him back. 'I know 'em both, Mother. I know this Lomesbury swell here. And I know Joe and all. Little noser split on us on a job and we—'

Mother's pale face seemed to swell and turn suddenly purple in front of Alec's eyes as if it were about to burst, and her hand gripped his wrist so hard he gasped in pain. A pair of white mice that had been feasting on the last of the cheese scurried across the bed and darted under the mountain of cushions that supported Mother's back. Bob and Charlie backed quickly out of the door again, but they weren't quick enough.

'Stand where you are!' The two boys stood still. 'Do I under-stand that you two bottle-headed bog trotters have been taking up space in Mother's Court for a month without telling me you know Joe Rat!'

'Sorry, Mother, we didn't realize—'

'See, we didn't know it was the same—'

Bob and Charlie were both talking at once, but Mother wasn't listening. She gave a jerk of her head, and Billy, who had appeared in the doorway behind Bob and Charlie, brought a fist smashing down on the back of both boys' heads, sending them sprawling to the ground. He reached down and grabbed them by the collar, but Mother raised a finger. She'd recovered her composure now.

'No, wait! They can take a little message for me to Mr Jonathan Harvey of West, Woodford and Harvey Limited.' She paused. 'And if they make a mess of it, you can chuck 'em both in the river.' Billy laughed. 'Now clear that mess out of Mother's parlour, William. The place is like a rubbish heap.'

Abruptly she seemed to forget all about Bob and Charlie. The grip on Alec's wrist loosened and she took his throbbing hand, massaging his fingers gently.

'Oh, now clumsy old Mother has hurt her new boy.' Alec found he was trembling uncontrollably. 'Don't be afraid of your Mother, Alexander. Sometimes she has to chastise her little family but it always hurts her more than it hurts anyone else. Now' – she drew him to her – 'come close. Come very close and tell me all you know about my dear little Joseph!'

Chapter 28

TRAPPER

'Reckon we're as safe as I can make us, Joe.' Mundy had been working on what he called 'defence' the whole day. He'd pulled up the rope with the counterweights that had lifted Joe and Felicity so easily. He'd been up a set of timber steps through the trap door over their heads, muttering about 'a back door', and he'd come back down an hour later with a look of grim satisfaction on his face. Then he'd taken out his bone-handled knife and used the serrated edge to saw neatly through the centre of the first three steps.

'Climb over them if you have to get out in a hurry,' he told Joe. 'Should slow down anyone chasin'.'

He'd removed more than half the floorboards on their level and used them to block the loading door where the rotten ladder led up from the lane. All that remained was a narrow gap at the top and a hole where they could spy out without being seen. With so many boards gone, the floor was like the porch of Barlow's shed, except that anyone trying to get to them wouldn't just put their foot through a hole if they weren't careful, they'd fall thirty feet to the ground below. The only solid area left was directly under the steps to the loft above. Felicity lay there huddled up on some empty grain sacks, whimpering softly.

Joe tried to soothe the little girl. It was late in the afternoon and they'd had nothing to eat last night or all that day. Mundy wouldn't let him out to buy food.

'I can keep out of sight, Jimmy. I'm good at that.'

'Can't risk it, boy.' Mundy had said the same words a dozen times. 'Another dose'll keep off the hunger.' He pulled out the phial of laudanum, but Joe put himself between the man and the little girl, and Mundy didn't try to move him. He stood and looked down at Joe. There was a softness in his voice when he spoke. 'You shouldn't be a part of this, Joe. I was wrong to let ya.'

'We're family, Jimmy.' Joe tried to sound cheerful. 'Like you said. Promised to stick by yer, didn't I?'

'I'll take ya down with me, boy. I feel it. You should leave.'

'Let me take her back, Jimmy. 'Fore Mother gets wind.' Joe had explained to Mundy about the woman who ran Pound's Field. 'Then you can hide out and I'll get money somehow and you can ship back where you come from and no harm done.'

'I made my choice, Joe. I gone wrong too many years back to change now.'

Mundy made his way between the missing boards to the other side of the loft. There were broad arches over there, looking vertically down onto a disused quay. Back when the warehouses had been in use, the wharf men must have lifted cargo straight out of the boats and up through there into the loft. Mundy hadn't bothered blocking the arches. There was no way up on that side.

'Keep watch just the same,' he said quietly, settling down with his back against the bricks.

A heavy silence descended. The little girl stopped whimpering and her breathing grew regular. Joe checked. She was asleep. He looked over at Mundy, hunched and still as a statue. Through the brick arch behind him the sky was dark and threatening, and the light was going in the loft although it was still afternoon.

'It ain't too late, Jimmy.' Joe's voice was an urgent whisper. He didn't want to waken Felicity again. The girl's face was like an accusation. 'You just took a wrong turn. That's all. You done a bad thing, but you're a good man really. I know you are.' Mundy's back stiffened at the words. He didn't look round to face Joe as he spoke.

'A man who walks out on his family ain't such a good man.'

'You didn't have no choice, Jimmy. Army wouldn't let you take us.'

Mundy sighed deeply. 'Men with families drew lots, Joe. Draw a marker and the wife and young 'uns come along. Draw a blank – they stay at home.'

'And you lost. You couldn't help that.'

'I won.'

'You won?'

'I gave my marker to another man. Took his blank. I could've taken your brothers and your mother and you growin' inside of her. If I'd have wanted to,' he said softly. 'I didn't want to.'

'You felt shut in, Jimmy. I know.'

Mundy looked at him. 'Come here, boy.'

'I got to stay with the girl, Jimmy. She—'

'Come here.' His voice was soft but there was a note of command in it. 'I gotta tell you sum'n'.'

Joe picked his way across the floor to Mundy. Even some of the remaining boards had been loosened. You had to check the nail holes to see if you were treading somewhere safe. Once it got dark they wouldn't be able to move from their corner and no one could get near them. There was no way into the place anyway except up a ladder that collapsed under your feet. Mundy had obviously left it there deliberately.

From the archway Joe could see over disused wharves and derelict buildings downriver towards the docks where Mundy had landed that morning four months back. An image of animal horns and hides crawling with maggots flickered across Joe's memory. And the old woman with her pots and pans – what was it she'd said? *Ain't nothin' good comin' off of that ship, boy.*

He looked at the man. 'What is it, Jimmy?'

Mundy glanced over at Felicity, but the little girl still seemed to be sleeping. He drew Joe down next to him.

'What I told ya just now, boy. That ain't the truth.'

'You drew a blank, did ya? Is that—?'

'That ain't it, Joe.' Mundy's eyes went down to the floor, not meeting the boy's questioning gaze. 'I'm gonna tell ya now, so you'll see how ya gotta leave me and the girl here and look out for yourself.'

Joe started to protest, but Mundy put a hand on his arm. Then he began to tell a story of two men, living wild in the back country beyond the Petitcodiac River, three thousand miles away across the great Atlantic Ocean. One of them was a deserter from the army named James Mundy, the other was a woodsman and a thief called Trapper.

'Trapper?' The name sent a chill through Joe. It seemed to bring Alec Harvey into the echoing loft with his endless '*Who's Trapper?*' Apparently he was about to find out.

'They lived for a time huntin' and trappin' game, these two. Tradin' with the Indians. Weren't hard to keep ahead of the army redcoats. They didn't search too long for one private soldier gone missin' anyhow. But then game got scarce and they turned to other ways.'

Mundy spoke very softly as he told his story of how the two men had taken to robbery, crossing the frozen river through the winter to steal from farmers' hen houses, then growing bolder and breaking into cabins at the edge of town.

'Then one bad day towards the end of winter we snuck into a woodsmen's camp before dawn.' Mundy's eyes went out towards the lowering sky across the river. It was the first time he'd said 'we'. Joe sensed he was getting to the point of his story. 'Got a bullet. Both of 'em. Bullet in the soldier's thigh. Bullet in Trapper's shoulder. Bled like stuck pigs in the woods.' The man reached into his waistband and produced the bone-handled knife, digging splinters from the wooden floor as if he were digging once again for lead in wounded flesh. 'Shoulda died, the pair of 'em. Woulda bin better.'

His voice was a harsh cry. Joe reached out his hand and placed it on the big, bony fist which held the knife. 'That was you – Dad.' His lips stumbled on the word. It was the first time he had ever used it. 'Weren't it?'

The man looked him full in the face for the first time since the story began, and Joe saw with a shock of surprise that there were tears in his cold eyes. 'That was me, Joe. 'Cept—'

'Except what?'

A voice rang out startlingly loud in the dimness. Mundy was on his feet in an instant, knife at the ready. Joe spun round. Alec was climbing over the boards that half blocked the entrance to the loft.

Felicity leaped up from the floor and ran to her brother, clinging to him, sobbing. It was pure luck she trod where there were still boards in the floor. Alec just stood there, wet from the rain that had begun to fall outside. He didn't put his arms around the girl or say anything. His eyes were on Joe.

'I think I like this place better than Barlow's shed, Master Joe,' he said cheerfully. 'Have you got room for one more?'

Mundy was across the room, checking quickly through the spy hole down into the lane below. 'Ladder should've broke,' he muttered.

'He's lighter than a man, Jimmy,' said Joe. 'You didn't reckon on a kid.' A rumble of thunder sounded far off across the river. A storm was coming from the south, just as it had this time yesterday as they fled to what Joe had hoped was safety in

Pound's Field. He questioned Alec urgently: 'Does Mother know about this place?'

'Who?'

'How d'ya find us, boy?' demanded Mundy. 'Who else is with ya?'

'No one is with me,' said Alec scornfully. 'You are a very nervous pair of kidnappers, I must say.' He held Felicity from him at arm's length. 'Big brother has come to rescue you, little Flicky,' he said sarcastically. 'What do you say?'

'I want to go home.'

'All in good time, little Flicky,' said Alec. 'All in good time. First these two gentlemen and I have financial matters to consider.'

'You got Mother in on this, ain'tcha, Alec?' Joe's voice was furious. 'She's the only one could've found us this quick.'

'What makes you think you are the only clever one, Joe Rat?' said Alec.

'Don't call me that!' snapped Joe.

Alec ignored him. 'I found you myself,' he said.

'I don't believe you,' said Joe. 'He's lying, Dad.' He went straight to Mundy, who was still cursing at himself for not realizing the ladder would hold the lighter weight of a boy. Rain was falling more heavily outside now. 'We gotta get out of here,' said Joe. 'Mother's in on this now. Got to be. And that spells trouble. Big trouble.'

But Mundy was shaking his head. 'Not "we", Joe. You got no call to follow me no more.' Joe tried to interrupt but Mundy wouldn't let him. 'I didn't get to finish my story,' he went on grimly. 'About them two bullet wounds. Take a look-see.'

He pulled off his heavy animal-skin coat and bared a brawny shoulder. A ragged, circular scar with another neat white line running across it was clearly visible on the man's upper right arm. Alec stepped quickly over the missing boards to look also. Even Felicity crept forward, fascinated by the ugly mark on the man's skin. Thunder pealed more loudly from the south.

'But you said the soldier got it in the leg,' said Joe.

'That's what I said,' agreed Mundy slowly. 'He cut into that with this knife.' He held up the bone-handled weapon. 'My knife.'

'Your knife?' It was Alec who spoke this time.

'Who cut into yer?' demanded Joe. 'What you sayin'?'

Suddenly there was a tremendous crash from outside, but it wasn't thunder. Joe was first to the spy hole. This time the ladder had given way. It lay in splinters on the ground thirty feet below and struggling back to his feet in the lane was the unmistakable figure of Bates. Boy was yapping excitedly round him: the wretched dog had led them straight to him. Down the lane Joe could see a dozen more figures and even through the driving rain he recognized two immediately. Bob and Charlie! He'd expected Mother's mug-hunters, but what were those two doing here?

Mundy had been telling him something. Something important. Something that changed everything. But Joe didn't think about that now. He made a dash for the corner of the room, leaping over the gaps in the floor as if they weren't there.

He picked up the bow and arrows the man had fashioned and was back at the opening in an instant.

'Miss Felicity Harvey!' Bates's voice boomed up from below. 'Are you there?'

Before anyone in the loft could move, Felicity hurled herself at the barricade of floorboards, scrabbling up towards the gap at the top and freedom. 'I'm here! I'm here! Joe took me! It was Joe!'

As the first flash of lightning lit up the sky, Joe caught the girl just before she threw herself into mid air. Another shout came from below above the hammering of the rain. 'Leave her, Joe Rat, or you'll hang with him!'

'Go, Jimmy!' Joe's voice was an urgent command. He fitted an arrow to the bow the way he had watched the man do it. 'I can hold 'em off.'

'Joe!' The man crouched on the floor beside him with the lantern in one hand and the knife in the other. He twisted the boy's face to make him look at the old scar on his shoulder, holding the light close enough to burn the flesh. 'You're not hearin' me, boy. James Mundy cut into me. Your father. He got the ball out. And then he did the same for himself and he bled out on the dirt floor and he died.'

'He died?' Joe looked into the man's staring eyes. He knew what it meant but he didn't want to say it.

'That's right. He died. And I took his papers and some of his things and when they found me they thought I was him.'

Alec's voice broke the silence: 'So you're Trapper! Of course! That's why you were scared of the name.'

The man ignored Alec. He put the knife and lantern on the floor and took hold of Joe by the shoulders. 'I ain't your pa, boy. Your pa died in the snow three thousand miles away. You don't owe me nothin', Joe.'

Chapter 29
THE RIVER

Joe let the bow fall from his hand as the thunder came again. 'You ain't my dad?' he said weakly. But the man didn't answer. He was on his feet, looking wildly around. His eyes fixed on the steps leading up to the next floor.

He had his foot on the fourth rung, above the ones he'd sawn through. Then suddenly he seemed to change his mind. Leaning down, he grabbed Felicity around her waist and began to climb, holding the girl easily under one arm.

He was almost through the trap door when Alec picked up the knife from where the man had left it and hurled it without aiming in the direction of the fleeing figure. It could have hit Felicity. It could have lodged in the rotting timber of the warehouse, but the knife stuck two inches deep into the calf of the escaping man.

He let out a scream of pain, pushing the little girl through the trap door above his head and reaching down to pluck the knife out of his leg. Alec stared stupidly as blood gushed from the wound. The man raised the dagger to throw it back at Alec. Transfixed by the sight of all that blood, the boy didn't move.

The man's eyes were wild, furious. Joe watched horrified, waiting for the wicked-looking weapon to arc through the air and lodge in the other boy's chest.

But it didn't happen. With another cry of rage, Mundy threw the dagger from him, sending it clattering onto the wooden floor, and disappeared through the trap door.

Alec was after him in an instant. The first step broke under his foot. So did the second. He stretched for the fourth rung and scrambled upwards.

At the top of the steps there was no sign of them. Alec looked quickly around. A wide arched window looked straight out over the wharf, but there was no way down there. On the far side of the loft a low wooden doorway was set into the wall.

Alec sprinted across the room and threw his shoulder against it. The door swung open, leaving him gripping frantically at the timbers of the doorframe to stop himself falling. He was forty feet above the lane. Far below he could see Bates with a rope coiled in one hand, poised to throw. In front of him a single plank, glistening wet and slippery, spanned the width of the lane to the building opposite. The rain hadn't had time to wash away a red splash of blood.

The man had gone this way. If he could do it, then Alec could. But had he done something to the bridge like he had to the steps? Alec guessed he hadn't had time. He took a breath and stepped out onto the wet plank, arms outstretched for balance, swaying precariously as the timber sagged under his weight. How had the man got across here carrying Felicity? Alec took another step. And another. He tried not to look down.

'Master Alec! Come back! I'm coming up!'

Bates's shout roused Joe. He hadn't even noticed as a rope snaked up from below, lassoing the end of the derrick that projected out over the lane. But now he could see the rope jerk and strain. Someone was climbing. He risked a look through the spy hole Mundy had left. No, he couldn't call him that any more. He couldn't call him Mundy or Jimmy. It had all been a lie. He didn't have any family, just like he'd always known he didn't. And maybe it was just as well, if this was the kind of trouble they brought you.

The lightning flashed bright overhead, and Joe looked straight into the face of Francis Bates. The man's teeth were gritted tight with the effort of climbing, but he let out a gasp when he saw the boy through the gap in the boards.

'Joe Rat!' he hissed as the thunder came.

Suddenly Joe's mind was clear. If Bates caught him, he was done for. The girl thought he was part of the kidnap. Even if the Harveys got her back, she wouldn't back him up. And if they didn't get her back . . . ? Would the law say he was old enough to hang? The rope that Bates was climbing jerked and groaned before his eyes as if in answer to his question.

He scrambled to his feet, picked up the knife from where it had fallen and threw himself at the broken steps. He was at the top before the footman got over the barricade into the loft.

Joe saw the door Alec had left open. He edged quickly across the slippery plank and then heaved at the wet timber, trying to send it spinning down into the lane below. But it was nailed fast. Then he saw Bates.

'Street trash!'

The footman was at the other end of the plank. Ten feet and a torrent of pouring rain separated them. Joe turned, desperately scanning the dimness ahead for any sign of where to go next. If the man had been over this way earlier, he could have booby-trapped the place just like the other loft. The floor might give way under him at any moment. But Alec must have come through here too and there was no sign he'd fallen.

Joe skirted round the edge of the loft, playing as safe as he could. There was a trap door open on the far side. Surely this must be the man's 'back door'.

It wasn't. There was no ladder.

Joe turned to see the tall figure of Bates framed in the doorway.

'Got you now, boy!'

The footman came straight towards him. He was twenty feet away. Ten feet. Joe took a step backwards and felt a brick wall. He closed his eyes, waiting for the man to grab him.

Instead there was a sharp cry. Joe opened his eyes. The footman's legs had gone straight through the floor. The place had been booby-trapped. Bates was levering at the timber with his arms, already beginning to struggle free. Joe looked around quickly. The only other way out of the loft was a narrow brick arch where lightning flashed across the darkened sky. He made for that.

In the opening he stared up at the wild sky and the rain and then straight down into the river. It was high tide or close to it and directly beneath him the water swirled brown and dirty against the old brickwork of the warehouse. Heavy timbers bolted into the outside wall showed where steps had once led down to a quay here. They had collapsed long ago, but just to his left Joe could see the remains of a rickety-looking walkway still clinging to the crumbling wall. This was the 'back door'.

The lightning flashed again and Joe saw him out on the walkway. Left leg hanging useless, Felicity still clutched struggling under one arm, the man Joe had called his father staggered on a swaying rope bridge above the swirling river. His black hair was plastered to his head. His enormous coat hung soaked and dripping. He was a wounded, hunted animal, still trying to drag its prey to safety. And Alec was behind him, almost within touching distance.

Alec looked down, dashing the rain out of his eyes. The shattered timbers of an old landing stage rose from the river water, pointing jagged fingers at him. Then they disappeared again with the swell of the tide. He looked ahead.

The man had stopped on the far side of the rope bridge, swaying as if he were close to collapse. Beyond the bridge the timber structure looked weaker. He was stuck. This was the moment. But where was his father? Mother had promised he'd be exactly five minutes behind Alec. Once Bob and Charlie got back with the money from Lomesbury the whole scheme had seemed to amuse her no end. The dog must have run on ahead and Bates had followed. The stupid footman had come close to ruining the whole thing. Where was his father? He had to see him do this.

As if in answer a cry came from below.

'Alexander!'

Directly beneath him the lane ended abruptly at the water's edge and through the slats of the bridge Alec could see his father and Johnson both holding lanterns. There were other people too, all looking up, shielding their eyes from the downpour, all watching him – Bob and Charlie, even Boy was there.

'Let them go! It is too dangerous!' his father's voice boomed out again.

'I can get her, Father! I'll show you!'

'You do not have to! Alec, you don't have to!'

The boy registered the name. Alec. His father never called him that. It felt good. Then he saw Joe coming towards him along the walkway through the rain.

The sweeper boy was going to take the glory. He was going to rescue the poison dolly and Mister Harvey would be treating him like a son again and he, Alec, would be back in the Reformatory, staring through the window at the rain. It wasn't going to happen.

He made a lunge for the huge figure in the shaggy coat. The man stumbled backwards and seemed to lose his balance. Alec couldn't see what had happened, but Joe spotted the thin length of twine stretched across the walkway. The man had fallen over one of his own tripwires. Still clutching Felicity, he threw out his free arm to steady himself. The sudden movement was too much for the rotten timbers of the walkway.

Joe saw one of the supports give way, falling down, down to the racing river. 'Jimmy!' he shouted out over the thunder. He didn't know what other name to say.

The man looked wildly round. For a moment his balance seemed to come back to him. Then the entire walkway beyond the rope bridge lurched abruptly sideways, dragging loose from the back of the warehouse, swaying out towards the river. Only a pair of tall pilings driven straight into the mud of the river bed were holding it up now.

'Jimmy, leave her!'

The man's movements suddenly looked very slow and deliberate as the lightning flashed across the sky and the thunder answered. He put the little girl down, carefully, tenderly, pushing her back towards the rope bridge, towards Alec and Joe and safety. Then there was a crack as loud as the thunder and one of the last pilings buckled.

Alec thrust his sister behind him: this wasn't the end of the story and she was in the way. The man was escaping. He was going to jump. As the whole length of walkway began to collapse into the river, the man made a great leap into the darkness and Alec followed. He saw the broken timbers reach out of the water towards him, like the black and pointed railings of Lomesbury Square.

A hand grasped his wrist.

'Alec!' It was Joe. 'Alec, hold on! Pull yourself up.'

But Alec was still reaching out into the dark, trying to follow where the man had gone.

'Alec!'

For a moment the two boys were looking into each other's eyes. The noise of the storm was so loud Joe could barely hear what the other boy said. It sounded like, 'Sorry.' Then Alec twisted in Joe's grip and his voice was suddenly shrill and loud. 'He's getting away, Joe! I'm going to catch him!'

Alec wrenched his hand from Joe's and kicked out desperately. His legs worked for a moment, as if they were trying to run through the air after the man in the animal-skin coat. Then the jagged staves of the old landing stage rose up into the storm again and Alec fell without a sound.

Joe looked away. There was nothing he could do for the other boy now.

'Street trash!'

Bates's voice cut loud and clear through the storm. The footman had reached the rope bridge. He had Felicity. The girl was safe anyhow. Now he was coming for Joe.

The boy peered into the darkness where the man he'd thought was his father had disappeared. He'd fallen just like Alec. There was no doubt about that at all. Joe was standing on the last few boards of the walkway: ahead was nothing but a blank wall and below was the dark and dirty river, boiling in the lashing rain. There was no way forward and no way back past the menacing figure of Bates. Joe made up his mind. If he had to follow the man into the river, then so be it, but Bates wasn't taking him the way he'd taken Bob and Charlie. He lifted the dagger with the bone handle.

As the lightning flashed again he saw Bates's eyes suddenly widen in fear. Then Joe brought the razor-sharp weapon slashing down, slicing through the frayed and rotted rope that held the bridge in place.

Bates gave a cry of surprise, bracing himself against the wall of the warehouse, clutching the little girl to him. But the section of walkway he was standing on didn't shift. Only the rope bridge fell, leaving a clear gap between him and Joe.

'Not this time, Mr Bates!' Joe called out against the storm.

'It's me or the river, Joe Rat,' came the footman's response. But Joe had other ideas.

He raised the knife high again and sent it flying out into the darkness, spinning over and over, catching the last of the lightning as it fell down and down and splashed into the swirling water where its owner had disappeared. Then he slipped off the edge of the walkway, hanging by his fingertips above the river, which seemed to rise every instant higher towards him.

He swung himself back and then forward, trying to build momentum. Looking down after Alec had fallen, he'd seen a shadow on the wall below. It could only be one thing. With a final swing he let go his hold.

Joe felt the damp air rush upwards against his face, and then he landed heavily on brick, pitching forward onto timber. He'd made it to the floor below. Now he had a chance.

Or he thought he did.

'Ratboy!'

The voice was horribly familiar. He'd escaped the footman and walked straight into the steel grip of his old enemy – Mother's favourite bully boy, Billy.

Chapter 30

MOTHER'S COURT

'Would you like to say a final fond farewell to your father, Joseph?'

'He weren't my father. He were a fake.'

The four figures carrying the open coffin hesitated in the middle of the new red carpet that ran the length of Mother's front parlour. A small dog with one torn ear stopped behind them as the heavy coffin lurched dangerously: the two at the front were much smaller than the heavily built men at the back. It barely came as a surprise to Joe that Bob and Charlie should be helping to carry the corpse of the man he'd known as James Mundy.

The crumbling four-poster bed where Mother had lain, massive and immovable, for as long as Joe could remember, was gone, and the old woman stood, more or less upright, at one end of the red carpet, supported by two bodyguards. The rags and rugs and shawls were gone too. She was wearing a vast hooped skirt that ballooned out to fill half the room and a hat with brightly coloured feathers that brushed the ceiling.

It wasn't easy to tell, but from the way she leaned back

against her two bodyguards Joe had the feeling that she wasn't actually standing at all. But if there was a chair or a stool under her, it was hidden beneath layers and layers of shimmering scarlet satin.

She made an impatient signal and the four coffin-bearers set their burden down on the floor with obvious relief, backing out towards the kitchen. 'Open the window, will you!' she snapped. 'I can't stand the smell of death.'

Charlie drew back the heavy velvet curtains which hung over the room's single window and pulled down the sash. The rain had stopped outside. The storm had blown away, and through the open window Joe could see a scattering of stars above the chimneypots of Pound's Field. Charlie winked and bared his teeth at Joe as he slipped out of the room. Joe made no response.

The dog lay down at the foot of the coffin and Mother wrinkled her nose in distaste – 'Mangy little cur!' – but she let Boy stay where he was. The dog's nose twitched furiously and a shiver ran down his flank as a pair of white mice scurried amidst the flounces and feathers of Mother's new clothes, but he didn't leave the coffin.

'You've noticed the new decor, Joseph.' Mother's voice was a gentle purr. 'A nasty boy in many ways, your friend Alexander—'

'Weren't my friend,' said Joe sullenly.

A lift of one eyebrow showed that Mother had noticed the interruption, but she went on as if she hadn't, taking a chocolate from a silver bowl at her side and chewing on it thoughtfully. 'A nasty boy, as I say, and he came to a nasty end too—' Laughter shook the old woman, making her two body-guards stagger, and ending, as Mother's laughter always did, in a hacking cough.

She tipped the remaining chocolates into her hand along with a mouse that had been hiding amongst them, and spat into the silver bowl. One of the bodyguards took the bowl and disappeared into the kitchen and another figure took his place. Joe hadn't recognized either of the first two men, but here was someone he knew – someone who knew him too. Billy's face broke into a wicked leer at the sight of Joe. Mother leaned back heavily against him.

'Your friend did have a certain – polish about him though,' she went on, 'and he inspired us to make a few changes.'

'Weren't my friend,' repeated Joe. 'He snitched on me.'

Something like a smile made Mother's eyes disappear to bright little pinpricks in the folds and jowls of her face.

'So he did, Joseph. So he did. But only in the way of business. The late Master Alexander had a very interesting little scheme of his own, but illegal, Joseph. Illegal!' Mother tut-tutted in mock horror. 'I decided to send intermediaries directly to Jonathan Harvey Esquire of West, Woodford and Harvey Limited' – she bowed her head reverently as she spoke the name of the bank – 'offering to recover his charming young daughter for a fee. A considerable fee!' Mother popped three chocolates in at once and went on with her mouth full. 'Naturally I kept the unfortunate Alexander with me as added insurance until my fee was delivered.'

'So you done pretty nicely every way round,' snapped Joe.

To be back here in this room and in Mother's power again made the boy feel sick to his stomach. But to have to listen to the old monster gloating over how clever she'd been was more than he could stand. 'Why don't you chuck me in the river and have done with it?' he demanded. 'Billy's just itchin' for it, ain'tcha, Billy boy?'

Billy made a move towards Joe, causing Mother to lurch alarmingly sideways.

'Stay where you are, you jackass!' she snarled. Billy resumed his position. 'My Joseph's come on in the world, haven't you, my dear? Quite forcefully spoken you've become, young Joseph, and a real villain too. Kidnapper, no less. Only you don't seem very grateful to your old Mother for keeping you out of the clutches of Jonathan Harvey Esquire, do you, Joseph? Or that ugly-looking footman, Bates. Perhaps I should give you to Billy here after all.'

'You do what yer like. I don't care no more,' said Joe.

There were plush-looking chairs all round the room, but Joe ignored them. He slumped down on the floor with his head between his knees.

'Awww! Now he's upset!' mocked Mother. Billy smirked and Mother rounded on him. 'That's your fault, William. Now say you're sorry to my Joseph.' Billy's face crumpled into a scowl and he grunted something Joe couldn't make out. Mother went on, 'Mother's made a very tidy return from the whole business, Joseph, and she's willing to forget the past – and allow you the opportunity to pay off the sum you still owe her. Now what do you say?'

'You what?' The words had simply exploded out of Billy's mouth. 'He done a runner. He owes money. He's—'

But Mother didn't let him finish. Her hand reached up and gripped Billy's face, twisting his mouth and nose. Billy let out a gasp of pain. 'Did I ask for your opinion, William?' Her voice was soft and level.

'No.' Billy's words were muffled by Mother's grip.

'I can't hear you, William.' She twisted harder.

'No!'

'I didn't think so. So hold your gas, dog's meat!'

She pushed him from her and Billy staggered away, holding his face. Mother turned calmly back to Joe as Bob and Charlie came smiling through the kitchen door to take Billy's place. When she leaned back again it took both of them to support her weight on that side. Joe noticed they'd stopped smiling.

'I believe you know my two new boys, Joseph. Robert and Charles. Strange how all the poor waifs in our great city come to gather in the safety of Mother's arms.'

Charlie staggered slightly with the effort of holding Mother up, but his eyes never left Joe. 'Seems like you ain't Just Joe after all, eh, boy? You're Joe Rat and a filthy snitch.'

'Now, boys, boys!' Mother sounded quite distressed. 'Little birds in their nests must agree. Can't have no ill feeling in the family. As I was saying, Joseph, what with your talents for taking up with the gentry and running off with their dear little children, you might make a very useful member of Mother's close family now. I'm sure Robert and Charles would agree.'

Joe listened but he couldn't believe what he was hearing. She was offering to make him a member of the gang – a full member this time – which meant money and safety from the crushers. His eyes took in the red carpet and curtains and the expensive furniture that now filled Mother's old front parlour. For a moment it reminded him of the candlelit room in the Harveys' home – real fancy but a bad smell underneath. Only here, instead of a footman in a powdered wig, there were Bob and Charlie scowling at him. And instead of the gleaming dining table, a plain wooden box stood in the middle of the floor with a dead man inside.

Joe got up and went over to the coffin. Boy hunched lower, watching him, emitting a low growl.

'What you at, mutt?' Joe looked down at the dog. 'You led 'em straight to us, didn'tcha?' The dog edged backwards, keeping his eyes fixed on Joe as the boy bent low over the coffin.

The man looked the same – almost. The black hair clung wetly around his face as it had in those last moments in the storm as the walkway collapsed under his feet. The hollow cheeks were the same too, though the skin was paler, with an odd, waxy sheen, and the strong jaw hung slack.

It was the eyes that were really different. Wide open and blank, they stared up at the ceiling. The little shards of ice no longer glittered deep inside. Those eyes didn't see frozen horizons or wide skies any more. A milky film covered them as if a curtain had been drawn. Joe put his hand on the man's face and felt the clammy chill of death. There was no back door out of that.

The boy drew the eyelids shut and turned to Mother. 'Where'd you find him?'

'Fished out of the river under Blackfriars Bridge, I believe,' said Mother casually. 'Might have made a nice find for a young tosher, Joseph, if a young tosher was at his work.'

'I ain't in that line no more,' said Joe.

'We know, Joseph,' said Mother silkily. 'We have noticed your absence.'

'Whatcha want with him anyway?' demanded Joe, ignoring this.

'Business, Joseph,' said Mother with a sigh. 'Always business. The surgeons at Whitechapel pay handsome for a corpse.'

'They cut him up?'

'"Dissect" is the word, I believe, Joseph,' said Mother impatiently. 'Now leaving this interesting discussion to one side, what do you have to say to Mother's very generous proposal?'

What did he have to say? *Get back where you belong.* That's what Bates had said outside the house in Lomesbury Square. And maybe Bates was right. Bob and Charlie had found their way to Pound's Field like half the villains in London. Maybe this was where he belonged too. Maybe he was a kidnapper and a thief, just like this drowned man he'd thought was his father. And now Mother was going to sell his body to the bone-cutters.

Joe looked down at the dead man. Either the river or Mother's mug-hunters had stripped him of his animal-skin coat and the rest of his clothes were in tatters. You could see the old scar on his arm – the one that proved he was a thief and an

336

impostor named Trapper, not James Mundy. There was an ugly gash on his calf too, where Alec had thrown the knife. That wound had weakened him. If it hadn't been for that he might have reached safety with his final desperate leap into the darkness.

Joe looked back at Mother. He knew what her offer was about now: she couldn't bear the fact that he'd got away from her, and she'd rather have him in her power again than have him dead. He'd be working for nothing again, just like always, paying off the money she said he owed her. But what other choice did he have? The words: 'All right. I'm in' were almost on his lips when he glanced one last time at the lifeless body of the man he now knew as Trapper. And then he spotted something else.

High up on the man's right thigh was another scar. It was almost exactly the same as the pale bullet wound in his arm – ragged and circular – except that even in death this wound was a livid brownish colour, and the scar that ran across it, where someone had dug out the bullet, was a jagged, raised line of skin. This was a much more recent wound than the one in the arm.

Two bullet wounds, the man had said. Joe could hear his quiet voice again, telling his story of the raid on the woodsmen's camp. *Bullet in the soldier's thigh. Bullet in Trapper's shoulder.* That's what he'd said. The words beat in Joe's brain over and over again. *Bullet in the soldier's thigh. Bullet in Trapper's shoulder.* This man had a bullet in his thigh. This man was the soldier.

Joe's gasp was a mix of disbelief and pain and happiness. 'Jimmy!' His eyes went to Mother, demanding an explanation. 'Why did he tell me he was a fake?'

'What?'

'In the warehouse. When they come for us. I'd have held them off. I had his bow and six arrows. He could have got clear away. He weren't a fake! He were real! Look!'

Joe pointed at the wound on James Mundy's thigh, but Mother showed no sign of moving from where she was. She let out a long, exasperated sigh. 'Does it matter, Joseph? After all—'

'Yes!' Joe interrupted her furiously. Mother's face stiffened. 'Yes, it matters. He was – he was family!'

'Perhaps,' said Mother with barely suppressed annoyance, 'he was trying to protect you. I believe it's something fathers do.'

'What?'

'If you thought he wasn't your father, then you wouldn't feel like you had to help him no more. Would you? You wouldn't start shooting arrows all over the place and getting in deeper than you already was. Perhaps he was a better father than he looked. All right,' she went on with a heavy sigh, 'I won't give him to the bone-cutters if you'd rather not. Now I can't say fairer than that, can I? They don't pay that well anyway,' she added to herself under her breath. Then she went on briskly: 'Now that's enough of Mr James Mundy or whoever he is. Are you coming back to Mother's little family, Joseph? I might add that if you refuse' – her voice was suddenly flinty; here was the

338

threat Joe had known was coming – 'I may be forced to inform Jonathan Harvey Esquire of your whereabouts. Without the protection of your dear old Mother, you'll be looking at a lengthy term in Pentonville Prison, which according to Robert and Charles here is a rather less than comfortable establishment. That is if they don't hang you for chucking young Alexander in the river!'

Her voice rose to a shout, but Joe wasn't listening. He was staring down into the dead face of James Mundy and he no longer knew what to think of this great bear of a man who had come across the ocean to be his father and then destroyed his life with one stupid and desperate act. The Harveys had done everything for him and he'd repaid them by kidnapping their child. Whether his name was Mundy or Trapper he was a bad man, just like he'd said himself.

But then why had he told that lie to stop Joe getting in deeper than he was? And why hadn't he thrown the knife back at Alec? Joe had seen the vicious weapon stick into the man's leg. He'd heard him scream with pain, pull the dagger out, hold it up to throw, but he hadn't done it. Why not? And he'd pushed Felicity Harvey to safety. He'd drugged the girl and taken her from her family, but at the last minute he'd pushed her to safety. The time it took to do that might have cost him his life. *Maybe he was a better father than he looked.* That's what Mother had said. But what did she know?

Joe looked at the woman as if for an answer. Without her protection he could be running for the rest of his life: from Mother, Bates, Mr Harvey, the police, everyone. She had a hand stretched out towards him. She was beckoning him to her. And that was when Joe made up his mind.

He put a hand lightly on James Mundy's wet hair. It was a gesture of farewell. Then he made a spring for the window.

'Stop him!'

Mother's voice rose in a shriek, and Bob and Charlie and the other bodyguard rushed at Joe. The old woman lurched backwards, the enormous hooped skirt flying up into the air. The two boys and the bodyguard hesitated between catching her and pursuing Joe. It gave Joe the chance he needed. He just had time to notice that the old monster had indeed been sitting on a high stool, as she fell flat on her back, legs in the air, and then he was through the window and sprinting for the entrance to Mother's Court.

The lookout under the archway was on his feet. Joe sidestepped the man easily and went flat out down Greenfield Passage. Mother could have a dozen mug-hunters after him inside a minute, including Billy, but Joe knew without looking behind him that the closest would be Bob and Charlie. They were new. They needed to impress. And they hated him.

It was almost a year since he'd last fled through the streets and alleys of Pound's Field, but every twist and turn was still printed on Joe's mind. He raced under the railway arch, checking quickly behind him, feeling a strange exhilaration at the familiarity of the chase. He could hear running footsteps – two sets only. He didn't know how fast Bob and Charlie were. Maybe faster than him. But what was more important was that they didn't know Pound's Field, and that meant this was going to be easy because in Pound's Field Joe had his own back door.

He skidded round the corner onto Flower Street, turned left across the road and into a pool of darkness in the space between the gas lights. Almost without breaking stride Joe had the loose grating out of the gutter and slipped feet first through the hole in the filthy street, pulling the grating back down after him.

He hung out of sight just beneath the roadway, hands gripped in the bars of the iron grating. The drain felt tighter than he remembered – he'd grown fat on Mrs Briggs's broken victuals.

In five years as a tosher he'd never noticed it, but now the sickening stench of the sewer hit him from below like a blow to the stomach and he gritted his teeth against his rising gorge.

On the roadway above he heard running feet. He heard them stop. He heard voices.

'Where'd 'e go?'

'Little ramper's disappeared into thin air!'

It was Bob and Charlie just like he'd known it would be. They'd be terrified of what Mother would do to them if they lost him. More than likely they'd hoof it out of Pound's Field altogether in a minute. He could nip out of the drain and disappear, and Billy and the gang wouldn't have any idea which way he'd gone. Joe had quit Pound's Field last time, but he hadn't gone far enough. That was his mistake. This time he'd put half the city between him and Mother and Mr Harvey – half the country if he had to. Then Joe felt something cold and wet on the fingers of his right hand.

The shock loosened his grip. He braced his feet desperately

against the sides of the drain, sending loose chippings cascading down into the sewer below. If he fell, Bob and Charlie would hear the noise and the hunt would be on again in a moment. Now he felt the same eerie sensation on his left hand where the knuckles were exposed above the grating. This time he managed to keep a tight hold on the bars. But what was it?

Joe craned his neck, trying to see what was happening above him. He came face to face with Boy. The dog must have followed the chase from Mother's Court. Now he had his head down to the grating, sniffing at Joe's hands. It was the animal's wet nose he'd felt.

Back in Mother's parlour Boy had growled at Joe and looked as if he hated the sight of him. He was going to break out barking any second. Joe knew it. He was going to give him away. He stared into the animal's eyes, willing him not to make a sound.

'Look out!' Bob's voice came clearly again from above. 'There's Billy comin'. If he finds out we lost him, it'll be you and me in the river.'

Joe heard Bob and Charlie running for all they were worth up Flower Street and away into the night. But he wasn't safe yet. Bob and Charlie might not know where Joe Rat disappeared to in Pound's Field but Billy did. If he saw the dog, Joe was done for. There were only seconds before Billy and the rest of the gang were on him.

Wedging himself more firmly in the drain, Joe eased the grating up an inch. The dog sprang back, but his eyes never left Joe.

'Boy!' hissed Joe. 'Here, Boy!'

The dog looked at him, head down, ears down, tail down. For a long moment he didn't move. Then he looked up the street where Bob and Charlie had disappeared. He looked across the road for Billy. Finally he flattened his belly into the mud and filth of the roadway, and inch by inch, crawling on his stomach, he edged towards Joe.

When the dog was less than a yard away, Joe shot a look across the road. Billy and two of his boys were silhouetted against a streetlamp no more than a dozen paces away, looking up and down the street, trying to decide which way to go.

Joe snaked out an arm, grasping Boy firmly around his middle, pulling him down through the grating.

Then he disappeared once more beneath the streets of Pound's Field.